That Which Can't Be Washed Away

XU HUAIZHONG

Translated by
Haiwang Yuan and **Will Spence**

SINOIST

ACA Publishing Ltd
University House
11-13 Lower Grosvenor Place,
London SW1W 0EX, UK
Tel: +44 20 3289 3885
E-mail: info@alaincharlesasia.com
www.alaincharlesasia.com
www.sinoistbooks.com

Beijing Office
Tel: +86(0)10 8472 1250

Author: Xu Huaizhong
Translators: Haiwang Yuan and Will Spence

Published by Sinoist Books (an imprint of ACA Publishing Ltd) in
arrangement with People's Literature Publishing House Co., Ltd.

Original Chinese Text © 牵风记 (Qian Feng Ji) 2019, People's Literature
Publishing House Co., Ltd.

English Translation text © 2023 ACA Publishing Ltd, London, UK

Paperback ISBN: 978-1-83890-562-0
eBook ISBN: 978-1-83890-563-7

A catalogue record for *That Which Can't Be Washed Away* is available from the
National Bibliographic Service of the British Library.

THAT WHICH CAN'T BE WASHED AWAY

XU HUAIZHONG

TRANSLATED BY
HAIWANG YUAN AND WILL SPENCE

SINOIST BOOKS

Overture After the Performance

In a time of war, soldiers in the same army unit enjoy a closer relationship with each other than they have even with their own relatives. After retirement, many establish a tradition of getting together once a year. And each time, they will feast. However, eating comes behind drinking and toasting, which in turn comes behind reminiscing about the past. What topics do they talk about except for the embers of history they try to fan with their ever-indistinguishable flames of fervour?

The old political commissar, the "Number Two" chief officer of the 9th Independent Brigade of the Jin-Ji-Lu-Yu[1] Field Army, initiated get-togethers involving the brigade's high- and middle-ranking officers. When everyone is present, the party starts with the familiar practice of passing around an enlarged, framed group photo. The people cramming the picture are wearing the same grey uniform. Men stand in rows behind the women sitting on the ground in the front, beaming with joy.

Everyone has a copy of the photo hanging in their living room. But copies don't count. Only the original is worth viewing. Carried over the Yangtze River amid the boom and smoke of gunfire by the photographer himself, the photo is of historical significance. The veteran commanders pass it around with great care from one hand to another as if it were a piece of blue-and-white porcelain from the official kiln of the Ming dynasty. Then, the conversation turns to Xiao Wang, the ninth female comrade from the right in the front row.

A caption at the bottom of the picture reads, "Taken on the eve of speedily crossing the Yellow River on 30 June 1947". This group portrait was the last time she appeared in any photograph, and it freeze-framed her at the age of nineteen.

She was a literacy instructor. Since starting work in the brigade's headquarters, she was called a staff officer like all the other staffers. Staff Officer Wang, a title imbued with the flavour of war and courage, evoked curiosity and friendliness when conferred to a student from Peking who happened to dress like a Westerner. Officers and soldiers all preferred calling her Staff Officer Wang or Xiao Wang (Young Wang). Seldom did they call her Wang Keyu, the official name that appeared on the muster roll.

"It's incredible!" says the former political instructor of the Publicity Team. "Quite incredible!" He can never understand why his eyes are always drawn to the beaming face of Wang Keyu each time he looks at the photo. His eyes never rest on anyone else. Never. He asks the others why.

The first explanation is that she was looking directly into the lens at the precise moment the shutter button was pressed. This effect was clear after the film's development. You're looking at the picture, and she's looking back at you as if she were trying to greet you first. "Look into the lens! Smile! Smile! Smile! One, two, three!" The photographer afforded her the same treatment as all the other subjects in that split-second exposure.

The second explanation goes that when she first came to the Anti-Japanese base in the Taihang Mountains, Xiao Wang brought with her a *guqin*, a plucked seven-string ancient Chinese musical instrument. In the photo, she's holding a wooden case containing the *guqin*. Few people were aware of the musical instrument at that time, mistaking it for some kind of odd weapon. Since it looked so exotic, they would naturally be drawn to the *guqin*-playing young woman from Peking. But this hypothesis doesn't hold water because other publicity team members are also shown carrying equally exotic musical instruments such as the *huqin*, a bowed string instrument, and the *sanxian*, a three-stringed plucked lute.

There's still another interpretation. Most of the people at the party are men, and they all had a secret crush on Xiao Wang. Whenever they recall the old days, they can't resist the temptation to look into the young woman's eyes. Nonsense! Nonsense! Women, without exception, are equally drawn to the image of Xiao Wang in the photo. So how can we interpret this phenomenon?

Someone offers another explanation. We all cherish the memory of this revolutionary martyr. Therefore, we can't help focusing our eyes on her. This assumption seems reasonable but sounds farfetched on reflection. A few comrades-in-arms in the photo also gave up their lives in the Dabie Mountains. Why single out this one in particular?

To get to the bottom of things, they experimented by calling in some people who didn't know any of the photographed individuals. They showed the strangers the photo without telling them anything about the investigation, and nor did they provide any hints beforehand. Like them, the strangers also noticed the ninth person from the right in the front row, namely Wang Keyu.

The phenomenon is perplexing, no matter how they regard it.

Petty Officer Cai, a young Eighth Route Army soldier at the time, took the group photo. His particular camera was far from impressive. Professional photographers in the Field Army and its other columns all boasted international brands such as Leica or Zeiss and accessories like tripods. Xiao Cai only had a worn-out Rolleiflex captured from enemy troops. As if that were not enough, the brigade didn't give him any film, saying he should procure it wherever he could. And where could he? Today, however, he is known as Revered Mr Cai in the circle of photographers. Hanging from his neck are fancy cameras with various lenses. His best-known photos, mostly featuring "extemporaneous battlefield scenes", are well-known in and outside the People's Liberation Army (PLA).

Revered Mr Cai stands up. Everyone knows he is going to give a speech, and they quieten down immediately.

"Each year as we get together, we begin our conversation with this photo and focus on Xiao Wang's signature smile. But I remain reticent each time. I know what I say is always ridiculous and lacks credence. My old friends from the Ninth Brigade are all scientific-minded. They give their opinions based on scientific experiments or theoretical data. All are critical of my view.

"Now I've got the authoritative answer. I read a news item from the science and technology column of a newspaper. It says that a study conducted by a psycholinguistic research institute in the Netherlands concludes that, 'Smiling and relaxed expressions are hard-wired. All other expressions of feelings are acquired.' The report is concise, taking up no more than a couple of square inches of newsprint. But it has answered all my questions.

"OK! Let's imagine without restraint that our mind is on a heavenly steed soaring across the skies. From the long river of humanity flows a brook. As it babbles along, it erupts at the end through Xiao Wang's expression. No, it's not quite right to describe it as an eruption, which would imply that Xiao Wang laughed heartily. She merely smiled, and her smile is like a crystal spring hidden in her heart. It flows slowly and gurgles in all directions without the possibility of drying up.

"I believe that everyone present had the same feeling. When we first met Xiao Wang and saw her sparkling eyes as crystal clear as those of an antelope, we felt the distance between her and us immediately erased as if we had known her for ages.

"All right! Let's come back to this photo. Please take a closer look. All the officers and soldiers are smiling happily, like flowers blooming all at once. But their smile is water without its source or a tree without its roots. All wear the same monotonous smile."

CHAPTER 1

A PIECE OF SUBLIME MUSIC
AMID THE THUNDER OF GUNS

The "Field Political Art Troupe", known fully as The Art Troupe of the Jin-Ji-Lu-Yu Field Army's Political Department, dispatched a team to the 9th Regiment to perform as a mark of appreciation. The team comprised fewer than ten people, so they could only perform a variety of shows such as male and female solos, musical instrument solos, a form of rapping known as *kuaibanju* and "living newspapers". The audience had no problem with the content as it was all based on the heroic deeds exhibited during previous battles. It was the familiar faces that came and went on the stage that bored them. They began to make things difficult for the performers by yelling, "We've had enough of this! Show us something different!"

There were only a few troublemakers initially, but their clamour proved as contagious as a highly infectious disease. Soon the entire audience was shrieking and whistling. A few wounded soldiers were especially boisterous as they wielded their crutches and kept yelling. Wave after wave of catcalls eventually led to the performers being booed off the stage.

The stage announcer squeezed himself out between the

curtains. Each time he appeared on the stage to address the audience, he would give the false impression that the art troupe had amended the show. But instead, he stubbornly stuck to the scheduled programme list and unhurriedly announced the next performance. The audience screamed, "Let an actress perform a female role! Let an actress perform a female role!"

The uproar was chaotic at first, without a clear-cut message. The art troupe initially couldn't work out what the audience was demanding. Now, it was clear: they wanted to see actresses performing female roles. How could you fool us with a show that involved hastily putting together seven or eight "male singles?"

The leader of the art troupe came out and stood in front of the curtains. With a particularly stern expression, he shouted, "Hey, hey, hey! Ours isn't a theatrical troupe of the old society. We aren't performers hired to entertain wealthy people in their homes! Our female performers are members of a revolutionary army led by the CPC. They're part of our commanders and fighters. I can tell you responsibly that we don't have any 'actresses' of the sort you might expect. None at all!"

"You have actresses!" "You have actresses!" the audience rejoindered in chorus.

There were indeed two actresses in the art troupe. But there were no female roles in the shows according to the scheduled programme. The young women had to play the parts of two Japanese soldiers, with their hair tucked under the helmets and a Hitler-type toothbrush moustache attached to each of their upper lips. They hid their figures by wearing the uniforms and boots seized from Japanese troops. They were asked not to speak a word lest their feminine voices gave them away. Did the audience have X-ray eyes? How could they see through their disguise?

The art troupe could have avoided serious confrontation if it had been a bit more open-minded. That is, it could have let the two female performers take off the uniforms of the "Great Royal Army of Japan" to perform a few variety numbers. The shows could present a mixture of male and female performers in a perfect performance. Wouldn't that make everyone happy? But, no, the troupe wouldn't allow such a thing to happen. Referring to our female comrades as actresses would be the ultimate insult to them. It was a matter of principle, and there was no room for negotiation.

After learning about the riot, Regiment Commander Qi Jing rushed over like wind.

When the curtain rose, a blue light shone from the mantle of a kerosene lamp above the downstage area. It turned the darkness of night on and off the stage into daylight. Qi Jing strode purposefully to the edge of the stage and stood as straight as a ramrod. He was both motionless and speechless. He was apparently about to make a statement to the audience. I've got ample time and patience, he said to himself. Just wait for the riot to spend itself. I won't speak until you quieten down.

Some of the audience recognised their regiment commander and reminded each other, "It's Number One!"[1]

The audience in the first few rows sat up straight. Those sitting further back found something unusual going on and didn't dare to make a stir. Qi Jing began to address his troops. "I must congratulate everyone for breaking a record," he said with a touch of sarcasm. "We've never had such a commotion like tonight since our regiment was established." Then, he suddenly roared an octave higher, "You're making a spectacle of yourselves! You're making a fool of our Eighth Route Army! You're a disgrace to the officers and fighters of our Tiger Regiment!"

The Independent 9th Regiment was famous for night combat. It performed meritorious feats repeatedly during the Hundred Regiment Campaign against the Japanese in 1940. The Eighth Route Army's front-line headquarters granted it the title "Night Tiger Regiment". It became the pride of every soldier, who would use the title whenever they referred to the regiment or its commanders.

Suppressing his anger, Qi Jing switched to a calmer tone. "I know we've suffered heavy casualties in recent battles," he continued. "Some who have suffered severe wounds are downbeat and pessimistic. But none of your feelings can justify a crowd disturbance. By booing the actors, you're telling the Field Army's headquarters who dispatched the art troupe that you don't appreciate their kindness. Let me make it clear, you can't blame me for saying that no riot leader is above punishment, no matter if they're officers or soldiers or whether they're lightly or seriously wounded. Don't tell me that your regiment commander is hard-hearted. You've invited disciplinary punishment upon yourselves!"

For a moment, the atmosphere seemed to freeze. It was so tense that the audience's heartbeats were almost audible. The Number One chief commander lowered his voice further, saying, "I couldn't imagine that things would get so out of hand. So, the political commissar and I have to make self-criticism with our superiors and ask them for disciplinary measures." As he finished, Qi Jing waved to the event director and said, "Dismiss! All commanders, lead your men back to their respective barracks!"

The director gave his order in a resonant voice, "Everybody, stand up..."

꾼꾼★ꞅꞅ

The troops rose as one and ranked themselves in line. The local civilians who occupied the other half of the square also stood up simultaneously, although the director's order didn't apply to them. "What a good show," they said, "but it's a shame it had to end like this."

"Please hold on! Please hold on!" a young woman shouted.

Qi Jing saw from a distance that the young woman was standing at the end of the ground, holding a long object in one hand. Sitting separately, the troops and the civilians seemed to leave a passage specifically for her. She trotted to the front of the stage, with a natural smile on her face. She looked confident, her carriage indicating that she was well-educated. Qi Jing recognised what the young woman was holding in front of her chest. It was a *guqin*, wrapped tightly in a brocade bag.

The young woman raised her head and started negotiating with Qi Jing who was standing high on the stage. "How do you do, Chief Commander!" she said. "I happen to have my *guqin* with me. Would you mind if I played a piece for them?"

Qi Jing simply couldn't believe his eyes when he saw a young woman suddenly appearing in front of the troops holding a *guqin*. The local cadre accompanying the young woman introduced her to Qi Jing. "She's a Peking student. She's here to register for the entrance examination set by the Taihang Number Two Middle School run by the Border Region government. We were passing by and happened to see that your Tiger Regiment was holding an evening party."

Qi Jing blushed. Now his regiment was in danger of becoming a laughing stock in the eyes of a young woman from an enemy-occupied area. The female student had come forward and asked for permission to play a *guqin* piece. And her request set the Number One chief commander to think hard. To accept her suggestion or decline it? He had given the order to dismiss the troops and announced his plan to strengthen discipline in the coming days. He recalled the words of the military strategist Sunzi, who stated that a leader would lose his authority by indulging his troops, thereby making it impossible to enforce his commands. He found it hard to accept the *guqin* player's offer while thinking of Sunzi's classic teachings.

But he had to tell himself to be aware of what a half-sensible young woman might think about his rejection. He could have stopped her from doing what she was about to do. But as the highest-ranking commander present, he must not wear a poker face and reject the offer from a lively and enthusiastic female student.

"Welcome! Welcome! Please come on stage! Please come on stage!" Qi Jing invited her formally.

Once on stage, Wang Keyu couldn't wait to open the bag and take out the *guqin*.

"Oh, my God! Isn't that a Song-dynasty *guqin*?" exclaimed Qi Jing.

How could the commander of the Night Tiger Regiment, a military leader, instantly recognise a Song-dynasty *guqin*? What particularly astonished the young Peking woman was that he seemed to like it so much that he couldn't help running his hand over the instrument. Meanwhile, he was able to recite some lines from Bai Juyi's poem *A Forsaken Guqin*: "Made of silk and tung tree wood, it produces the sound of antiquity / Simple and elegant, the music doesn't fit today's vulgar flavour."

Tapping into his mood, the female student reciprocated with a few lines from another poem by Bai Juyi. "The seven strings are its bosom friends, so are the listening ears," she recited. "Mind calm and harmonious with the simple sound, one can't distinguish antiquity from the present."

Qi Jing suddenly realised that he had neglected the troops while discussing the *guqin* and reciting poems with the female student from Peking. He hurriedly gestured for the troops to sit down. The director of the event issued his command, "Attention! Everyone, sit down!"

The civilians also returned and gathered together, waiting for the show to resume. The young woman sat cross-legged near the edge of the stage and placed the *guqin* on her lap. The Chinese have played the *guqin* on crossed legs since ancient times.

Qi Jing naturally became the announcer. Only then did he remember to ask the Peking student her name.

"My family name is Wang, and my full name is Wang Keyu. The character 'wang' is the one with three water drops as its radical, the 'ke' has the meaning of *keyi* or 'can', and *yu* is the word that means 'surpass'."[2]

"Be quiet, everybody! Be quiet! Now, let me introduce to you this student Wang Keyu, who will play her *guqin*. As you see, the *guqin* is also known as the *qixianqin* [seven-stringed lute] or *yaoqin* [fine-jade lute] or even *yuqin* [simply, jade lute]. It's the earliest Chinese plucked musical instrument that recorded historical documents can verify. It has been traced back to the Yao and Shun eras over four thousand years ago. All right, if I go on any longer I'll become a nuisance. Let's welcome the student Xiao Wang to perform for us. Is that OK?"

"OK!" The response from the audience was a little unenthusiastic because the soldiers were mostly from peasant families whose ancestors might not have known what a *guqin* was.

The young woman Wang slowly lifted her right hand and plucked a *sanyin*, an open note produced by the right hand. Her Song-dynasty *guqin* resonated as powerfully as a bronze bell. The regiment commander could tell that this student had never performed on an open-air stage like this. She didn't know she had to shout out the title of the musical piece before playing it.

"Xiao Wang," Qi Jing asked her, "what piece are you going to play first?"

"*Gaoshan Liushui*."

Qi Jing knew something about this musical piece. In the Tang dynasty, it split into two musical pieces, namely *Gaoshan* (*High Mountains*) and *Liushui* (*Flowing Waters*). Later, Zhang Kongshan, the *guqin* master of the Shu (Sichuan) School in the Qing dynasty, rearranged it using the techniques of *gunfu* (running up and down the strings with the index and middle fingers to create glissandi), *chuo* (upward slide) and *zhu* (downward slide). Known as the *"72-gunfu"*, the new techniques produced the effect of splashing water. Today, the two pieces are still always played separately, and all the *guqin* players follow the musical note of *Liushui* handed down from Zhang Kongshan. All this made Qi Jing suspicious: could this female *guqin* player be an extraordinary talent at such a tender age?

"May I ask you, Xiao Wang, if you're going to play *Gaoshan* or *Liushui*?"

"Neither *Gaoshan* nor *Liushui*," Wang Keyu answered emphatically. "I will play *Gaoshan Liushui*!"

"You mean you'll play neither *Gaoshan* nor *Liushui*?"

"No, I'll only play *Gaoshan Liushui*."

"Who instructed you to do that, your teacher or your parents?"

"Neither my instructor nor my parents tell me what to do. It's completely my own idea."

Qi Jing asked in a consultative tone, "Many people say that the 'Seventy-Two-*gunfu*' sounds like magnificent rolling waves and produces the most splendid climax. Why don't you give it a try?"

The female *guqin* player responded with calmness, "I don't play the music that has rapids frequently alternating with calm water. I allow the water to flow down and give my listeners the impression of time's constancy. Don't you think this rendering possesses more inner charm?"

Qi Jing nodded, turned around and announced the first piece: *Gaoshan Liushui*.

Standing not too far away from the stage, the audience could vaguely hear gunshots in the distance. But they were already oblivious to the din of war. A *guqin* musical piece created an illusion transcending any other sensations of sound. The music, coupled with the breeze, the bright moon and the immediate quiet surroundings, intoxicated the soldiers and civilians, making them feel calm and contented.

In those days, the worst thing that could happen during an evening entertainment show was for the gas lamps to suddenly "stage a strike". When the Taihang Theatrical Troupe put on Cao Yu's play *Sunrise*, no one could remember how many times the lamps stopped working and had to be fixed. When the play reached its finale, the audience was able to catch sight of the morning glow coating the rolling mountains behind them. Someone jeered loudly, "I see the real sunrise now!"

As soon as Xiao Wang finished *Gaoshan Liushui*, the gas lamps went out. A long time had elapsed, and they had yet to be repaired. The Number One chief commander couldn't bear to see this young performer sitting on the stage in embarrassment. He went up and chatted with her. Even without the lamplight, it was not pitch-dark. Watched by everyone off the stage, Qi Jing and the female Peking student sat talking with ease and fluency. It looked like a short interlude play between the *guqin* performances.

Qi Jing noticed that the young woman began and ended the central part of her solo recital with an "open note". "Xiao Wang," he asked, "do you always make the same special arrangement each time you play?"

"Yes," she responded proudly. "It's something I established myself. I've been fascinated with the 'free-string' technique since childhood."

Qi Jing couldn't help but ask, "This... I don't quite understand. The *guqin* has three timbres that enhance each other's beauty, namely *sanyin* [scattered sound], *fanyin* [floating sound] and *an'yin* [stopped sound] to create spectacular musical pieces. Why do you only have a penchant for the *sanyin*?"

"I'm not so naïve that I must distinguish between primary and secondary timbres. But maybe because of a personal obsession, I've been treating the *sanyin* as the essential monophonic element in *guqin* music. The entire length of the strings is in a state of suspension with neither frets nor external limitations. In this specific sense, what's between the free strings is infinity. Based on this infinite natural space, the Chinese *guqin* outshines all the other plucked musical instruments in the world."

Number One took exception to her argument and didn't even try to conceal his intention to use his age to prove his superiority and authority. "It's child's play," he said. "Child's play! You can't play the free string throughout the performance for your audience, can you?"

Still beaming, Wang Keyu responded, "Yes, I can. I think you must know musicians before the Han dynasty only played the open note in *guqin* recitals. Later, they tentatively tried to use the left hand to produce sounds by pressing the strings. In reality, not many days have passed between the Han dynasty and today!"

It's natural for a young woman to initiate an argument out of impetuosity. But now things had turned in the opposite direction: a high-ranking older man was attacking a female student. Isn't that both irregular and awkward? When this realisation dawned on Qi Jing, he burst into a laugh to mask his embarrassment.

Staring into his eyes, Wang Keyu said, "You're quite overbearing when you speak, giving others no chance to rebut you."

Qi Jing shook his head repeatedly. "No, no, no. Didn't you see I was just kidding when I engaged you in a verbal joust?"

⁂

The gas lamps now fixed, the *guqin* recital resumed. Before Wang Keyu finished a piece called *Pingsha Luoyan* (*Wild Geese Descending on a Sandbank*), the lamps went out again and had to be lowered and fixed.

The civilians in the audience didn't complain because it

worked to their advantage. Young mothers could take the opportunity of this unexpected intermission to go back home to suckle their babies left to the care of their mothers-in-law. They went out to watch the shows without bringing their babies along for fear that they might catch a cold. Then they would hurry back while buttoning up the diagonal front part of their *dajin* shirts on the way. Elderly peasants were able to go home to add some fodder to the troughs for their draft animals. After stirring the feed a bit, they could return to catch the performance without missing anything important.

Teenagers sat comfortably on the forks of trees as if they were luxuriating in the boxes of a swanky theatre. Some men used the cover of darkness to satisfy their lustful desires by grabbing the buttocks of neighbouring girls.

The girls would complain, "Mum, someone's grabbing me!"

Their mothers would respond reprovingly, "Don't show yourself up! Watch the show! Watch the show!"

The entire audience waited quietly and patiently in the dark, none wanting to destroy the perfect ambience.

Years later, a Chinese Civil War writing group from the PLA Academy of Military Science revisited the revolutionary base in the Taihang Mountains. At the onset of the War of Resistance Against Japan, many famous battles took place in this area. The Japanese Army launched its largest ever "mopping-up operations" in May 1942. This area was the epicentre of the atrocities that occurred during these operations. Locals in their seventies and eighties were all interviewed as living witnesses.

To the interviewers' disappointment, these older people's memories of the vivid and touching details of the battles fought in those years had already become fuzzy. The visitors failed to extract from them more than just a few words about the fighting. But the older folk found it difficult to forget a teenage student from Peking. She had left an indelible impression on them with the few musical pieces she played with imperfect skill. They could even recount precise details, such as how she sat on the stage cross-legged, placed the *guqin* on her lap, raised her hand slowly and plucked an open note with the nail of the middle finger of her right hand.

The military history writing group were astounded that the evening party held by the Independent 9th Brigade that evening had far superseded the meaning of entertainment.

In reality, the war situation that night was most urgent. The Japanese Army had completed its concealed encirclement and deployment. It had formed a "special advance killing detachment" in an attempt to strike Taihang District's headquarters at lightning speed. The Eighth Route Army adopted the tactics of "countering the enemy's advances with advances". At opportune moments, it launched a series of fierce assaults on the Japanese Army's communication lines and strongholds in its rear area. By forcing the enemy to retreat to reinforce its troops at the rear, the Eighth Route Army attempted to turn defence into attack. The enemy's combat command telegraph signals mixed with those of the Eighth Route Army, forming an invisible network in the air under the vast night sky. Miss Wang's vibrating *guqin* music leisurely penetrated the air filled with telecommunication waves and spread far and wide with the strong wind and flitting clouds.

Qi Jing received an urgent telegram headed with four "A's", indicating a message of the highest emergency. Having no time to say goodbye to Miss Wang and ask her to end the recital, he issued a blunt order to the troops in the audience, "Everyone, stand up! Move out!"

The stage emptied in the blink of an eye. With the curtains stowed away, there was not a trace of the stage left. Number One and his two bodyguards had mounted their horses. The director of the regiment's Mass Movement Section rushed over to report that the female student from Peking wanted to join the army and insisted on moving out with the troops.

Qi Jing became angry upon hearing the request. "Can't you think straight? She's going to study at the Taihang Number Two Middle School with a letter of introduction from the Border Region government. What could I possibly tell the government if you decided to abduct her?" Then, he saw Xiao Wang in the distance staggering on the uneven ground towards him. Pointing at the Mass Movement Section director's nose, he demanded, "Throw her out! Do you hear me? Throw her out!"

Qi Jing yanked on the reins and galloped away, with the two bodyguards closely following him into the darkness.

CHAPTER 2

LET SPRING FOLLOW SOON

Wang Keyu had followed her second big brother to Yan'an. The underground CPC organisation in Peking had planned a route for them. Following it, they were supposed to be on their way to Xi'an via Luoyang, Lingbao, Tongguan and Huayin. From there, they could have taken a military vehicle to Yan'an from the Eighth Route Army's Xi'an office. The intensifying warfare blocked the flow of traffic between Tongguan and Huayin, so they had to walk to their destination, which they didn't initially see as a problem. But a difficulty presented itself in the form of having to cross a small tributary of the Yellow River. This meant forgoing the most direct route in favour of a more roundabout one and necessitated traversing the entire Central Plains to avoid the checkpoint at the Fenglingdu Ferry. But now they encountered another ferry crossing, involving more rigorous inspections. It was soul-destroying!

The liaison hired a sampan, and they agreed to stay far away from the ferry and sneak across the river at a relatively concealed location. However, the current was so rapid that the boat couldn't reach the far bank despite it being only a dozen yards away from it. Luckily, there was an exposed rock in the water, and her brother managed to jump onto it before leaping into the boat. He then went back to pick up his sister.

His sister intended to step onto the rock and cast her smaller items of luggage into the boat one by one. Then she would climb onto the sampan while holding her *guqin*. But she reckoned the task was beyond her ability. Her *guqin* would be damaged if she dropped it into the river. The instrument, wrapped in a cotton-padded bag, would be smashed to pieces if she should throw it into the boat and follow it empty-handed. What should I do? she wondered. The young woman hesitated.

Her brother decided to jump back to the rock to take the *guqin* from his sister so that she could hop onto the boat empty-handed. The boatman grasped hold of him, warning that his actions might accidentally knock his sister into the water along with her *guqin*. While holding on to the brother, the boatman neglected to anchor the boat with his punt pole. The sampan was suddenly rushed downstream and soon became a little dot in Wang Keyu's view.

Her brother's hoarse cry drifted from the boat, "Go home! Go home!"

It was impossible to get in touch with the CPC's underground organisation in Peking, and it was also impractical to return to the city. Wang Keyu had to change route and took the Dezhou-Shijiazhuang train westward. She got off at a small station in Hengshui and came to the seat of the Fifth Prefectural Commissioner's office of the Anti-Japanese South Hebei District government. She contacted the CPC's underground organisation in Peking, which decided that she should study at the Taihang Number Two Middle School in the county of She in Henan Province.

In life, mistakes that result from a combination of circumstances are sometimes unavoidable. A completely different, inevitable historical opportunity can flow from an accidental change in the smallest chain of events.

If she hadn't missed the boat because of her *guqin* and arrived in Yan'an as scheduled, her life would have taken a quite different, vivid and fascinating path. Instead, she happened to pass by where the Night Tiger Regiment was stationed on her way to register at the Taihang Number Two Middle School. And as luck would have it, she arrived in time to witness a disturbance made by some of the regiment's soldiers at the evening party. All these chance events led to her acquaintance with Qi Jing, commander of the Independent 9th Regiment of the Jin-Ji-Lu-Yu Military Zone.

It's no exaggeration to say that this female student's acquaintance with Qi Jing transformed her life trajectory.

⁘☆⁘

Moving around to escape Japanese mopping-up operations, the Taihang Number Two Middle School didn't hold its graduation ceremony for Wang Keyu and her fellow students until the fourth year.

Meanwhile, the Independent 9th Brigade was officially formed based on the 9th Regiment which had already expanded to a nominal brigade. Ancient Chinese regarded "nine" as the largest number, and the word is also auspicious because it is homophonic with the character that means "a long time". Therefore, the number "nine", now having the derived meaning of "invincibility during years of fighting", was mostly conferred to newly established independent army units. The same number was also branded on the buttocks of Qi Jing's mount Tanzao, meaning "Yellow River Beach Jujube".

Someone from the Military Affairs Office reported to Qi Jing that the female student who had played the *guqin* at the evening party a few years before had graduated from the Taihang Number Two Middle School. After joining the PLA, she asked to be assigned to the "acquainted" unit and had her request granted. Today, she had arrived at the 9th Brigade headquarters to report for duty. In line with army regulations, all officers above platoon level who came to assume their positions were required to see the brigade's "Number Five" commander, Chief of Staff Qi Jing.

Giving a military salute, Wang Keyu said, "Number One, do you still remember me?"

The head of the Military Affairs Department corrected her. "Don't call him that any more. He's now the Number Five chief commander of our Independent Ninth Brigade."

Qi Jing rushed forward and took the *guqin* off Wang Keyu's shoulder, saying, "Glad to see you again, Comrade Xiao Wang! You could report to the Military Region Art Troupe without a letter of introduction. They'd be only too glad to have you and would even slaughter a pig for your welcome dinner. But you've happened to meet up with our Ninth Brigade. All our officers and soldiers are proud of you."

Squinting her eyes, Xiao Wang asked Qi Jing, "May I ask Number Five why you ordered the head of the Mass Movement Department to throw me out after I asked him to keep me in the Ninth Regiment after the evening party that year? Was I that repellent?"

Five years on from their last meeting, Qi Jing would have never expected the young woman to hold him accountable for that order. He said in haste, "You misunderstood me. How could I so rudely prevent a woman comrade from voluntarily joining the army? But at the time, the Border Region government sent you to the Taihang Number Two Middle School. I would've gone against organisation rules to 'abduct' you on your way to the school."

The explanation sounded reasonable, even acceptable. But Number Five suddenly realised that smooth talking would only be interpreted by this young woman as hypocritical. He immediately corrected himself by saying, "Xiao Wang, I won't beat about the bush. Frankly, the gas lamps above the stage went out several times that evening, and I realised that you were night blind, and I also noticed that you were flat-footed. The troops' task that night was a forced march of seventy kilometres to press on to the Baikuizhen-Jincheng Highway front line in Shanxi. It would have been impractical to bring you with us. Please pardon me."

It's surely reasonable for the army to exclude from its ranks those suffering from nyctalopia. You couldn't expect others to support her during a night march. But what about someone with flat feet? An individual's foot is connected by several small bones that form the medial longitudinal arch curving above the ground when they are walking. Without the curve, their heel hits the ground first and flattens out with a slap, thus lacking elasticity and straining the muscles and tendons, which causes fatigue. If one can't walk, who in the army will tolerate you? But since she was already wearing her uniform, she could get by without anyone making a fuss. That was why Number Five started blurting out without thinking. But when he saw Wang Keyu draw a long face, he realised that he had put his foot in his mouth.

Xiao Wang suddenly felt worried. She had been night blind since childhood, and now she also had flat feet. Her parents had had no idea that, with these conditions, their daughter shouldn't have gone to Yan'an. Now, she was fully aware of her unsuitability as a soldier, especially a combatant. She feared that she would eventually face the embarrassment of being thrown out.

Seeing her expression of concern, Number Five tried his best to soothe her. "We've left the Taihang Mountains," he said. "Next, we'll participate in the Peking-Hankou Campaign on the Heibei-Shandong Plain. When we march at night, you can just follow the person in front of you. The worst thing that could happen would be for you to trip over the spreading stems of a sweet potato plant. You wouldn't fall too hard anyway."

The decision was taken for Wang Keyu to work in the brigade's headquarters as a literacy instructor. Her primary responsibility was to teach the office staffers how to read and write. Since there was no such manning quota for "secretary" or "instructor", she adopted a military staff officer's title.

✷

According to an Indian scholar of culture, gender awareness among the public is always prominent. He gave an example. What's the first thought that comes to your mind when you see a corpse after a plane crash? You're never anxious to know whether it's an Indian, a Chinese or a Malay; nor do you rush to figure out the person's age, name, social status or education. The first thing you are eager to learn is if this is a man or a woman.

Qi Jing wondered if his gender awareness was in play. Why am I so nervous? he asked himself. Why am I afraid of Wang Keyu's transfer from the 9th Brigade?

The 9th Brigade was a combat force and had little need for a *guqin* artist. As long as the Military Region issued a "letter of consultative transfer", the brigade had no reason not to let her go.

Almost five years had passed. Everything about Wang Keyu had changed except the signature smile set to win the favour of all beholders. She was no longer the skinny, tanned student. She was now a seventeen-year-old Eighth Route Army soldier who seemed fuller-figured with a fair complexion and shapely body. Compared with other young women, her breasts sat a little higher. As she walked, she would throw her chest out a bit, a carriage that added to her grace and beauty.

Qi Jing had scrutinised her hands when they first met. The thumb and index finger of her left hand had a shallow depression caused by their constant pressure on the strings, but they were not conspicuous from a distance. "It's not because I don't cherish my jade-like hands / But because a *guqin* expert requires three layers of callus." While this was a popular saying among *guqin* players, the instrument's effect on the hands wasn't that dramatic in real life.

Throughout the headquarters, the female comrades were envious of Wang Keyu's hands, which became a talking point. They argued that short women had hands with stubby, fleshy fingers, whereas tall women revealed unsightly wizened fingers when they opened their hands. But Wang Keyu's hands had pointed fingertips and distinct joints. If tied tightly with a thin thread, the fleshy tips of her fingers would appear perfectly round without being pudgy. Together with the palm, they looked impeccably harmonious.

It's said that among all the plucked instruments, the *guqin* is the most visually pleasing and aesthetic when played. Why is that? If you had seen Xiao Wang play her *guqin*, the answer would be self-explanatory. She used more than fifty fingering techniques between the wide range of four octaves, gently indexing in and out. How could her hands fail to be alluring?

Qi Jing would never confide to anyone that his ideal "better half" would be tall, healthy and graceful but not that well-built. The more delicate-looking woman was his type. In reality, he couldn't give a reason for his preference for a tall and curvy woman who still retained her feminine delicateness. That was because such an image came from the mould of Xiao Wang.

He became cautious and made sure not to disclose, even to his closest friends, the parts of a woman's body that captivated him the most. In short, he seemed to have been hit by a bullet when he saw Wang Keyu this time. Luckily, he didn't collapse to the ground with the impact.

He wrote the following in his journal that day:

Five years on, how could I have expected her to come to the headquarters to report for duty with her *guqin*? In one of his poems, Han Yu wrote, "The rain over the Chang'an streets falls like silk / The remotely dense grass is sparse when viewed up close." The 9th Brigade headquarters has long been blanketed with lush grass, whether viewed remotely or up close. Let spring rush over afterwards. I must be on guard against myself, starting today.

✻★✻

Besides Wang Keyu, some of the other new arrivals in Taihang District were also from big cities such as Peking, Chongqing or Shanghai. They modelled themselves after the veteran staffers in every aspect. Before long, they became out-and-out "veterans" themselves. Wang Keyu, however, differed in this regard. She didn't change herself one bit. She insisted on living differently from them. She remained Xiao (Young) Wang and could never become Lao (Old) Wang.

An example of her idiosyncrasy was how she opened or closed a door. She regarded part of the lock stile of a door to be unsanitary since it was frequently touched by people. So, she would always reach her hand up to push the door close by its top rail. Then she would use her heel to click it shut with a soft bang behind her. Many wondered if anyone else in the world would open a door in such a peculiar manner.

Someone said sarcastically that her bed was like a "forbidden royal area" because she allowed no one to sit on the sheet regardless of age or gender. The statement proved to be accurate, but she avoided the embarrassing situation of having to drive away people for transgressing this rule by spreading a piece of white cloth over the bed's edge for people to sit on and laundering it every few days. She never complained about the unsanitary habits of others. Nor did her own hygienic habits intrude on anyone else. Like the water in a well and a river, each minded his or her own business.

When paying the monthly dues to the Communist Youth League (CYL), Xiao Wang would always place the cash in a small woollen handkerchief and hand it in. She would get the handkerchief back and use it again after laundering.

The CYL group leader would fly into a rage. "Comrade Wang Keyu," he said, "now that you've gone through your probation period, surely you should know by now that it's the sacred duty of a Youth League member to pay membership dues. The money is the authentic currency issued by the Taihang Border Region government. Why can't you touch it? Have you ever thought of the nature of your behaviour?"

The CYL group leader was even younger than Xiao Wang. In Xiao Wang's eyes, his haughty manner made her laugh.

"So what? What's the problem with receiving the money in a handkerchief?"

Wang Keyu had another strange habit. Even when she was snuggled in bed, she would force herself to rise and line up her shoes in the correct position before she could relax and go to sleep. She could never bear to see them the wrong way around.

The host put up an antithetical couplet on the jambs of his house door. It read, "In spring with early rain, blossoms bloom early. / In autumn, with no frost, leaves fall late." The couplet lines were not flush at the top. What's worse, they were in reverse order. She could have made a detour around the house to avoid seeing the couplets, but that was not possible since she had to go in and out of the house every day. It was killing her.

Xiao Wang wrote another couplet with the same content using a borrowed pen brush. She wanted to substitute it for the existing one, but the elderly host wouldn't let her. Xiao Wang explained patiently, "We can't change the order of sowing spring, growing summer, harvesting autumn and storing winter. It's unacceptable for the couplet lines to be in the wrong order."

The elderly host chuckled, "I haven't seen any household mess up the four seasons when it comes to putting up couplets. That has never happened since Pan Gu separated heaven and earth and the Three Sage Kings and Five Virtuous Emperors ruled the world."

Xiao Wang and the elderly host were still arguing by the time the troops set out. There was no use talking Xiao Wang into giving up. She wouldn't relent until the four seasons were in the right order. The staff officer of Military Affairs tried to persuade the elderly host. "It's up to you to decide which couplet to place on your door," she said, "but the wrong order has turned it into a curse. But as I say, it's up to you."

The elderly host wholeheartedly embraced her argument. "Let's switch the order! Let's switch the order!"

Director Jiang of the brigade's Political Department's Publicity Section was known as "Marx Jiang". [1] He had given a lecture to all commanders in the brigade on Ai Siqi's philosophical work *Philosophy for the Masses*. According to a theory of this academic authority, Staff Officer Wang's "strange habit" might be interpreted as "the sense of balance", which could also be called "aesthetic intuition". Section Director Marx Jiang said, "Let me tell you seriously that this is an innate awareness. It's a common fault shared by all humanity. Not only is Xiao Wang subject to it, but I am, too. So are illiterate people who know nothing about aesthetics. There's nothing to be surprised at."

The telegraph operator from the Cipher Office ran into Wang Keyu for the first time. Xiao Wang smiled at him from a distance and said softly, "How do you do?"

It would have been easy for him to reciprocate with the same greeting and go his own way. But to this telegraph operator, the chance meeting plunged him into a dilemma. Thrown into an uncomfortable situation, he was agape and tongue-tied, not knowing how to respond.

Rural people customarily greeted each other with the question, "Have you eaten?" But in the army, where troops ate together simultaneously, it would be absurd for them to ask the question. Instead, they would omit the formality and just call at each other loudly, pat each other on the shoulder or give a respectful punch in the chest, which conveyed their friendship and brotherhood. But whether one could withstand that punch would be a different matter.

One particular soldier was quite a character, well known for being talkative and bitterly sarcastic. He poked fun at Staff Officer Wang when he ran into her. When Xiao Wang greeted him politely with "How are you?" he immediately asked back, "Which part of me do you mean?"

Xiao Wang was stunned because no one had ever responded to her like that. She had to reply, "Every aspect."

Pretending to be embarrassed, the soldier replied, "Gosh, that's complicated. The question I asked may seem personal, but it's really about foreign and domestic affairs. It's hard to explain in a few words, I'm afraid."

All the female staffers in the various offices of the headquarters shared the same experience: a female voice came in the dark of the night, "How are you!" Since it was too dark to see her face, they sensed her smiling warmth coming from the bottom of her heart because her friendly tone told them she would show her signature smile even when she was asleep.

Staff Officer Wang was so persistent that she seemed to be bent on promoting her type of folk custom. Someone once asked her, "You always greet people with 'How are you?' Has anyone reciprocated you with the same?" Xiao Wang shook her head. Feeling embarrassed to tell the truth and disinclined to give a negative answer, she hemmed and hawed before replying, "There may be some, I think."

Unfortunately, she had never enjoyed a "How are you" greeting from any of her 9th Brigade comrades-in-arm until her death.

CHAPTER 3

A TREMBLING CREPE-MYRTLE

Since the Marco Polo Bridge Incident, Big Sister Cao had worked as director of a village's Women's National Salvation Association (WNSA), or to give it its full name, the Women's Anti-Japanese National Salvation Association. Like cutting Chinese chives that would grow back again and again, she had talked one batch after another of the village's youngsters into joining the PLA and sent them away decorated with red ribbons and flowers. For her contribution, she became a "Model for Army Expansion". She had also attended the Conference to Celebrate the Achievements of Heroic Fighters and Model Workers in the Taihang Anti-Japanese Border Region. And from it, she had received an award certificate endorsed by the Border Region government with its big seal on it.

Almost without knowing it, she was already in her late twenties. She couldn't wait any longer. Big Sister Cao began to think of marriage. She turned around, and her eyes fell on the Chinese chives in the plot and found them too young to be cut. Well, the age of the candidate for a life partner was no longer a concern. Director Cao had no alternative but to adopt a "little brother approach", that is, find a man younger than she was.

Her first target was Cao Shui'er. Though too young to join the army, he was already tall enough for her to have to tilt her head back to look at him. What other presentable candidates could she possibly find? She set her mind on him!

A procession of village youngsters joined the army, and before their departure, they would all get married in haste lest their fiancees change their minds. Encouraged by other early teens, Cao Shui'er had participated in teasing a pair of newly-weds at the end of their wedding ceremony. As he was young and inexperienced, he mistook Big Sister Cao, the director of the village's WNSA, as the bride and fumbled all over her. The director had scratched him, leaving a faint scar on his face. But she hadn't expected that she would choose Cao Shui'er to be her young bridegroom.

Other women had managed to find younger husbands, but Big Sister Cao faced a hurdle: Cao Shui'er was her distant relation, a member of her clan, which posed an unbreachable barrier. Merely cherishing the idea of marrying him would offend public decency and insult her ancestors. But the WNSA director found a loophole, that is, Cao Shui'er was an adopted son from somewhere else, so he was not consanguineously related to the family. She managed to get their marriage licence.

On the night of consummation, the bride finally realised the truth of what others had told her: she had been clever all her life but stupid on this single occasion. She made the mistake of picking an unripe melon as her chosen one. Now, she was having the taste of it. This melon was so unripe that no matter how she tried to arouse and teach him, he couldn't do what she desired of him. Pounding him on the chest repeatedly, the bride wailed nonstop.

The bridegroom, however, was unaware of the great event unfolding before him. He was at a loss what to do. He tentatively addressed her as "Big Sister!" Unexpectedly, the bride shot back, "Who's your sister?" Cao Shui'er immediately corrected himself, "Sorry, but Director Cao!" It enraged her even more. She kicked him off the *kang* bed-stove.

His nominal age made him qualified for both marriage and army enlistment. She had no problem with that. She had talked others into joining the army in her capacity as the village's WNSA director, saying, "As quality iron must be turned into nails, so competent men must be made soldiers." So, how could she keep a man to her bed? She waited for the roosters to croak cock-a-doodle-doo at dawn so that she could send the newly enlisted soldiers away amid drumming and gonging.

At this point, the bride woke up her husband. "Cao Shui'er, it's OK if you don't want me," she said. "But couldn't you at least kiss me? We're husband and wife after all."

"Where should I plant my kiss?" asked Cao Shui'er timidly.

"I don't care. You may start from my hair to my toes. I've washed them clean." Cao Shui'er thought he'd better obey the order instead of standing on ceremony. He began to act like a quiet, hard-working veteran peasant in the Taihang Mountains. A pickaxe in hand, he cut down cluster after cluster of silvery wormwood and dug open a compacted layer of earth. He finally opened up a barren slope without neglecting the slightest bit of soil in the crack of the rock.

The War of Resistance Against Japanese Aggression was about to end when Cao Shui'er joined the army. Therefore, he had worn the arm badge with "18ᵗʰ GA" printed on it, in reference to the 18th Group Army of the National Revolutionary Army. As soon as Japan surrendered, it changed to "Eighth Route" printed in a white oval space on a blue background. By March 1947, the badge became the "Chinese People's Liberation Army" armlet.

On the armlet's rear side were spaces where the wearer would fill in their name, age, gender, ethnicity, place of birth and blood type. The last item was more important than the others because of the sheer number of severely wounded in battle and the need to transfuse blood according to the correct type. Otherwise, it would be fatal. However, it was impossible to test all the troops as it was way too expensive. As a result, everyone, from the top Commander-in-Chief Zhu De down to rank-and-file soldiers, left the blood-type space blank.

A rumour went that Cao Shui'er died gloriously in battle in the Dabieshan Mountains in 1948. His wife Big Sister Cao was composed and emotionless upon hearing the news. When the army entered the mountains, it fought without the support of the rear area. The battles were fierce and ruthless. Therefore, soldiers' wives were all mentally prepared for the worst. Big Sister Cao laughed at herself and thought, He hasn't shown up for several years after the liberation. If he hadn't died in glory, could he have become a son-in-law of a foreign kingdom?

The rumour that Cao Shui'er had died gloriously in the Dabieshan Mountains later gave way to gossip that he had been executed, trussed up for the crime of sexual assault. His wife could only laugh at the idea. "I'd believe it if they accused him of a hundred other crimes. To say he was a rapist is way off-beam. That criminal must be my hubby's namesake."

The gossip was not verified by Cao Shui'er's superiors, so the plaque "Glorious Armyman's Relatives" remained on the lintel of her door.

Those who saw Big Sister Cao, the first-generation director of the village's Women's National Salvation Association, would often comment on her beauty when she was young. Years later, many young women came to ask her about the secret of maintaining her looks: "What foundation powder do you use?" "What brand of face cream are you applying?" They told this granny what they genuinely thought: "We'd love to look like you do when we're your age."

It wasn't easy for the young women to remain as miraculously young as the elderly Big Sister Cao. First of all, they had to be willing to accept a wedding night that didn't involve a true consummation of the marriage. They had to be nominal wives, living all by themselves year in and year out. Otherwise, how could they have such black hair, such a supple complexion and such ample breasts when they were in their sixties or seventies?

Several of Cao Shui'er's comrades-in-arms who had left the village with him were demobilised and returned one after another. Big Sister Cao visited them at their homes. Instead of learning about anything useful in terms of locating Cao Shui'er, she got something from them that would upset her down the road. These veterans of questionable character lavished cheap solaces upon her in her presence but, behind her back, spread many falsehoods about Cao Shui'er, accusing him of being a womaniser. This information would later circulate in embroidered fashion in the surrounding villages.

Her sisters and sisters-in-law tried to talk her into remarriage. They said she was excellent in every aspect, being an outstanding woman in the region and the entire country. Why did she have to make herself suffer? Let this unfaithful, ungrateful Cao Shui'er go to hell! Big Sister Cao asked them in a suppressed voice, "Do you believe that an 'unripe melon' like Cao Shui'er could suddenly become a womaniser as soon as he grew up a bit?"

People laughed at her. "Having grown up in the countryside, you should know that different cereal crops ripen at different times. Some grow wild and tall ahead of the season. But in fact, they have long been growing and maturing without anyone noticing. As the saying goes, 'Rice ripens in a day, wheat ripens in an afternoon.' You can't harvest it too early. But if you leave it too long, the wheat kernels will pop out and fall to the ground. As they're hard to pick up, you must leave them alone."

Big Sister responded in all sincerity, "I'm not that narrow-minded. If the stories you're telling about him are true, I'll resign myself to the fact. Since I voluntarily sent my husband to the battleground, why can't I loan him to other women with the same voluntary spirit? Who knows how I gave him up to others? 'Bow to sky and earth first, bow to mutual parents next, then bow to each other and be sent to the boudoir.' After the wedding ritual, time was up. He had just lifted the red bridal veil off my head when I sent the kid on his way."

That was what had been weighing on the mind of the elderly Big Sister. She had condensed all her life into the wedding ritual. Time flew by, and she was no longer young. But she still felt the wedding night ended too abruptly. She had been expecting to complete it with her "little brother" day and night with tender affection.

Though its trunk was already dry and hollow, this old crepe-myrtle tree still had sensitive nerve fibres. A few gentle scratches on its bark with the tip of a man's finger would send an irresistible shock to its crown, causing its leaves, flowers and branch tips to tremble in intoxication.

After finishing his training in the cavalry company, Cao Shui'er became a horse messenger in the same unit.

The company commander asked him to send a message to the regiment headquarters and advised him, "When you arrive at the door, say 'Sir, Messenger Cao reporting!' Don't enter unless they ask you. If you're told not to enter, just wait outside for a while."

When he came to the regiment headquarters, Cao Shui'er repeated the company commander's words to the letter, "Sir, Messenger Cao reporting! I won't enter unless you ask me. If I'm told not to enter, I'll wait outside for a while!"

The people in the room bent over with laughter. But when the messenger gave them a neat military salute, they were awed.

The commander of the Officer-Training Corps walked around Cao Shui'er in silence. As he surveyed him, he made comments about his appearance from head to toe. Cao Shui'er hadn't expected this senior commander to like him so much the first time he carried out a mission. The Officer-Training Corps commander immediately told a staff officer, "Tell the recruiting company that I'll keep Cao Shui'er here to work as my bodyguard. I just want the person, however, and will return the horse and rifle to them. They can find someone else to fill their vacancy."

In those years, a high-ranking officer needed to have "four biggies". They were referring to an excellent horse, if possible a "heavenly horse"; a quality watch, better an artillery watch; a pocket handgun, such as a revolver, an FN Browning M1900, a Colt Model 1903 or preferably a Belgium-made FN Browning 1910; and, finally, an outstanding bodyguard. The lack of any one of these essentials would, in their eyes, disgrace them in public.

The top attribute of a bodyguard was his spirit of self-sacrifice. In critical situations, he had to shield the senior officer with his body like a bastion of iron to guarantee his safety. When taking care of the senior officer in daily life, he was supposed to be thoughtful and meticulous, and to be on guard for any careless omission. During fierce battles, a bodyguard could be asked to take hot meals to the senior officer anytime and anywhere. As for where to get them, the senior officer couldn't care in the heat of battle. He would only gobble up a few bites of the meal and cast the chopsticks aside.

Some of the officers didn't embrace the idea of appointing Cao Shui'er as the regiment commander's bodyguard. They objected that this stuttering, tall soldier could hardly speak a complete sentence, not to mention his many other disqualifications.

"So what if he's a mute?" the commander rebutted. "He's not working as my interpreter."

Cao Shui'er had to catch up with other bodyguards in terms of his clothing and appearance. From the headquarters to the grassroots units, bodyguards at all levels were fully standardised as if they were all cast from the same mould.

Ordinary soldiers wore caps with the size of their brims preset in the factories. The bodyguards' cap brims were all extended, it was claimed, to provide better shade from the dazzling sun. In reality, they wanted the shade above their eyebrows to give them a high-and-mighty look. But Cao Shui'er had great difficulty extending the brim a few centimetres, and this made him exceedingly anxious. Eventually, he managed to get a used, modified cap.

Soldiers usually carried weapons in their wide waist belts. They couldn't decorate them with any objects. But bodyguards were the exception. They used a 10-to-13-centimetre-wide red cloth band to wrap around the belt beside the brass buckle. The band had no useful function except to add some style. It was said to have originated when a bodyguard found his belt broken, and he connected it with an iron wire and covered his embarrassment with a piece of red cloth. But now, in Cao Shui'er's time, he had to cut a new belt into two, connect the broken parts with an iron wire and cover it with a red band like all the others.

Since ancient days, soldiers have worn puttees to develop the strength of their calf muscles. Otherwise, they would find it hard to endure long marches. Ordinary soldiers wore a set of puttees and would be fine. But bodyguards had two, with one worn around the lower calf above the ankles and the other over the entire calf. This way, the calves seemed to have the same thickness from top to bottom and made the wearers look smarter and more robust.

Some went to the extreme of wearing three sets of puttees.

Cao Shui'er was one of them. With three sets, the lower part of his calves appeared thicker. This leg shape helped exaggerate his already tall and erect stature. Most others folded each of the puttees into a series of stacked inverted "V" shapes. Cao Shui'er's had two series of inverted "V", a pattern he named "Double Inverted V's", which became an object of envy in everybody's eyes.

Typically, a senior officer's bodyguard had both a long and short gun, namely an M1 Garand rifle and a Mauser C96. However, Cao Shui'er had two Mauser C96s besides the rifle, which he carried on his back with the sling straps across his chest and over his shoulders. On his hips, he carried the two German-made Mausers, popularly known as "Twenty Pops". He strung them with a silk twine thread with each end fastened to the grip's lanyard ring. He would hang the handguns over his neck during battle to prevent them from slipping out of his hands. In peacetime, the strings served as decorative tassels. As he walked, they would sway to and fro to make him look "stylish".

Cao Shui'er excelled in riding, shooting, swordsmanship and first aid in the cavalry training team. He was particularly good at shooting with the handgun. He got ten bullets as his reward after each successful assessment. He saved all of them as his "buddies". With his M1 Garand rifle and two Mauser C96s, he could repel an intensified assault launched by enemy troops.

Of course, the personal image of a bodyguard had to exceed that of the average person. It had to be presentable so that the bodyguard would neither taint the senior officer's image of superiority nor make him look stereotypical and old-fashioned. No matter where they went, the bodyguard had to reflect positively on the senior officer at first glance by being impressively eye-catching. So much so that he had to make his senior officer look as if he were "a red flower among a million green leaves".

During a break in the Independent 9th Brigade's year-end combat appraisal meeting, the brigade and regiment commanders took out their pocket pistols to show each other. After careful comparisons, they found the most stunning piece to be the Browning M1906 owned by Qi Jing, the brigade's chief of staff, and it was the latest model. Reaching the acme of perfection, it eclipsed all the other handguns of various makes.

The Browning M1906 pistol was only slightly bigger than a cigarette packet, easy to be stowed away without notice. It could "greet" an adversary while its owner kept it in his pocket. Therefore, it had the nickname "Smile Across". Those anonymous heroes and heroines who devoted their lives to the secret service often depended on the "sneers" of such an M1906 when in imminent peril.

The improved version of the M1906, plated with precious metal, glistened with a bluish brilliance on a jet-black background. The main body had exquisite carvings of geometrical patterns. The grip was made of ivory instead of bakelite. Not so much an automatic pocket handgun as a luxurious piece of handicraft, it was the favourite among upper-class ladies in the old days. The tragedy of this Browning pistol lay in the fact that it would become as useless as a pet kitten, unable to pee or poo once fallen in the hands of these women.

The training corps commander grabbed the Browning M1906 from Qi Jing's hands and hid it behind him, saying, "Number Five, how about you loan it to me for a few days? I can write you an IOU if you're at all worried."

Qi Jing burst into laughter. "We're buddies, aren't we? Please take it and return it when you're tired of it."

After the meeting, the attendees shook hands to say goodbye to each other. Number Five told the training corps commander, "Comrade Cao Shui'er's transfer to the Brigade headquarters is a done deal. He works as a bodyguard. I merely want the person, so I'll return his horse and rifle to you. You have the autonomy to find someone to fill his vacancy."

Only then did the commander of the training corps realise what had happened. Typically, Qi Jing was reluctant to show his Browning M1906. No wonder he became so generous that day! Since he had asked to borrow his pistol, the training corps commander found it hard to say no any more. Qi Jing could have kept Cao Sui'er with a notice of approval from the Military Affairs Office in a business-like manner instead of a fair exchange as a token of friendship.

Qi Jing had used up his quota of two bodyguards. With the upper-level officer's approval, he had a horse messenger added to his staffing quota. He was explicitly frank when he proclaimed, "No one else could do justice to this kid's talent if he hadn't been assigned to me."

CHAPTER 4

THE CREEPING GRASS AFIELD

B efore long, the director of the brigade's Political Department reported to Qi Jing on Cao Shui'er. "We weren't prudent when we assigned this lanky soldier to you," he said. "Our department made a mistake and chose the wrong person. He's nothing but a thick-headed young peasant. He also has dubious relationships with women."

Qi Jing's first reaction was that it was a slander against not only someone working with him but also himself. He had the impression that Cao Shui'er had never left his sight all day long and wouldn't have had time to go out. Qi Jing said that he had decided to transfer this bodyguard here, and he, not the Political Department, should make a self-criticism. "Take your time," he said. "Tell me what you've found out first."

The Political Department director told Qi Jing a lot about Cao Shui'er's alleged illicit relations with women. He especially mentioned a song popular with the soldiers. Such lewd songs would naturally only circulate "underground". "Not only do we have a negative example like Cao Shui'er," he added, "but we also face the problem of seeing the public morality of our troops corrupted. When in a bad mood, someone would sing at the top of his lungs:

> *Fighting the Japanese aggressors for eight years,*
> *We've no time to heed girls pretty or unpretentious.*
> *Becoming a soldier, I've got nothing but tears.*
> *My sensual enjoyment suppressed, I shed tears."*

The Political Department director continued, "Along with this *Single's Song*, a string of obscene remarks started circulating. One of them went, 'Each of us ordinary soldiers has a Chinese made-Type 79 rifle, complete with all the necessary parts like front and rear sights, bolt and firing pin. Even though we've got everything, we're still idling. Who can we blame? Look at Cao Shui'er! Whether he fights in battle or marches on the road, he never stops sowing his seeds and never misses the farming season...'"

Qi Jing chuckled. "It sounds pretty exciting. But the complaints don't count without responsible accusations buttressed with solid evidence."

Feeling a surge of embarrassment, the Political Department director explained, "I heard that most of the accusations relate to the hostess of the house in which he's staying. He's said to fool around with her in 'guerrilla-war' fashion during the breaks in our marches. That means he fires a shot in one location and moves to the next when he's finished. It's hard to investigate."

"Since you haven't investigated it," Qi Jing responded, "why are you in such a hurry? Even if you've decided to take disciplinary action against him, how would you proceed? The only option is to demote him to the mess. When we set out on a long march, he could always help the cooks carry their field cauldrons, chatting and laughing. Therefore, this established disciplinary method may work for others, but not necessarily for Cao Shui'er. No one would know he was being punished.

"The worst disciplinary action would be to place him in confinement. It'd be easy to implement, but we must let him out to march with the troops anyway when we move out. If the vanguard of our tactical formation engages itself with the enemy, what are we to do? Are we going to reduce our fighting capacity by having someone guard him? In that case, you'd have to lift the confinement and let him join the battle. Then, we'd compromise the severity and austerity of the punishment, wouldn't we?"

✻★✻

A rumour circulated that Cao Shui'er might be able to have a romantic encounter by taking advantage of the short respites between marches. Each meeting was swift. It also said that he would knock on the door and go away if he saw a man in the house and move on to the next household. Men usually hid far away from their homes lest they might be drafted as stretcher-bearers on the battlefront, leaving their wives behind. Cao Shui'er would approach a woman with a gunny sack in hand, trying to strike up a conversation with her. "Sister-in-Law, here's a bag of wheat flour. I want to trade it for some oats. Either maize or sorghum will do. I hope Sister-in-Law will help me, won't you?"

Believe it or not. Cao Shui'er could tell whether a woman would surrender just by glancing at her. His experience guaranteed a perfect rate of success. Young wives were always nervous and at a loss. But their eyes shot out scorching flames of lust. They firmed the deal as soon as their eyes met, leaving no regret to haunt them afterwards.

It was so strange! How could he fare so well without any difficulties? But one had to understand that Cao Shui'er's tall stature not only made him ideal for the job of horse messenger but also the essential standard by which women courted the opposite sex despite his rough and slightly tanned complexion. Besides, women don't like baby-faced men. Such a gargantuan buck with its magnificent antlers was never short of does, and they would form a long queue, submissively expecting his inspection.

Flames of war and concomitant chaos and turbulence proved disastrous for the people but broke the solitude and isolation that the peasants had endured for several thousand years. Why couldn't rural women yearn for emancipation from their cooking duties and for exploring an endlessly fascinating world outside their kitchens? Why couldn't they weave their beautiful dreams of romantic adventure?

In the old days, rural women often broke through family barriers to elope with someone. It could be an actor playing a martial character's role in an amateur theatrical troupe, a trumpeter or drummer of a band performing at weddings and funerals, or a young itinerant merchant peddling floral cloth fabric in the alleys and streets. Now, who could be a better "prince on a white horse" than a young Eighth Route Army man? Many married and unmarried young women would like to go with Cao Shui'er, but he categorically rejected them. Otherwise, he could have raised a female detachment of considerable size.

꙳★꙳

The troops marched through an area full of coal mines. As the local men were working in the shafts and pits, it was a God-given opportunity for Cao Shui'er. He had just untied his puttees when, alas, the bugle call for fall-in sounded. To avoid disciplinary action, Cao Shui'er had to leave his woman and return to the unit. He was like the fox spirit or the ghost incarnate described in Pu Songling's *Strange Stories from a Chinese*

Studio that must forsake his lover and vanish in the dark of the foggy night at the sound of roosters before dawn and change back to his original form.

He quickly tied his puttees again, not one but three sets, and in the pattern of stacked-up vertical "V's". He was so anxious that sweat kept dripping to the floor from his forehead. This horse messenger met his defeat in the "first battle", and he didn't have the time to take a good look at the miner's wife before evacuating the "battleground".

His action confused the miner's wife. What is he doing? she asked herself. He had untied his puttees but unexpectedly re-tied them and went away, leaving her stunned and disappointed. Later, the next-door auntie tried to explain things to the woman. "A soldier may always get hit by a stray bullet in battle," she said. "His 'miner's lamp' may have been knocked off so he can't work in the shaft. He can only find some odd jobs to do in the nooks and crannies of a brick kiln on a mountain slope."

Since then, the gossip had an extra spice: Cao Shui'er would fool around with women without untying his puttees, something that appalled the women. They were puzzled, wondering what kind of a joke this stalwart "Eighth Route Army soldier" was poking at them by adamantly refusing to unfasten his puttees. Then, they had to copulate with him in weird positions that only animals, birds or insects would adopt. Only after he finished did the women realise that their sex lives with their husbands were merely perfunctory. In a word, they had wasted their womanhood!

There was also a rumour with something of a literary flavour. It went that an ancestor of no one knows which genera-tion in the Cao family had read the oldest collection of Chinese poetry, the *Classic of Poetry*. When the line of descendants came down to Cao Shui'er's times, things became different. He might be illiterate and unaware of the monetary value of the "classic poems", but he was well versed in the folk customs permeating the odes in the *Classic of Poetry*. He was living a colourful life based on the ancient poems, using them as his blueprint.

During the Zhou dynasty (1046-256 BCE), wars were frequent. The monarch allowed men and women to enjoy free love to multiply the population during *zhongchun* (the second month of spring). He tolerated extramarital cohabitation and elopement. In the *guofeng* (airs or customs of states) category of the *Classic of Poetry*, many collected odes related to festivals. Reading them, it is clear that the ancestral Chinese lived simple, happy and unrestrained lives.

In the poem entitled "Afield the Creeping Grass", there's a description of such a lifestyle:

> *Afield the creeping grass,*
> *With round dewdrops overspread,*
> *There's a beautiful lass,*
> *With clear eyes and a fine forehead.*
> *When I meet the clear-eyed*
> *Amid the grass, let's hide.*

How frank and vivid that description is! According to Zhu Xi's interpretation in his *Collected Commentaries to the Odes*, the words "let's hide" in the final line mean "each gets what he or she desires". This affection and scene vividly portray Cao Shui'er's multiple "chance encounters" with rural women. What this horse messenger excelled in was refusing to passively wait for peacetime to come. On the contrary, he adopted for himself an amorous life as romantic as "afield the creeping grass" during the flames of war that were raging everywhere — a life he couldn't stop even if he wanted to.

※

Here was a more detailed and vivid line of gossip:

Instead of changing tactics, Cao Shui'er played the same old trick. Carrying a gunny sack, he went up and said, "Sister-in-Law, here's a bag of wheat flour. I want to trade it for some oats. Either maize or sorghum will do. I do hope Sister-in-Law will help me, won't you?"

The woman didn't respond. Covering her face with her hands, she remained quiet, smiling expectantly. She was waiting to see what this man was going to do next. Only then did Cao Shui'er realise that she was pregnant and that her belly was already showing. Without saying another word, he turned to step out. He had walked a few paces when he suddenly remembered seeing this "sister-in-law" somewhere before. He turned around, only to find the woman leaning on the doorframe miserably disappointed, with tears streaming down her cheeks.

It could be expected that a woman who had contributed to her husband's lineage by producing a male heir to carry on his family line would see her status rising significantly in the clan. At the very least, her parents-in-law might stop hating her and greet her with broad smiles. She might also receive the little care and affection that her husband had long begrudged her. In the past, having a baby son was the only opportunity for a rural woman to change her fate.

Nevertheless, this woman had flagrantly chosen to go against this tradition. Now that she couldn't hide her increasingly apparent pregnancy, she had to confess everything to her husband.

Being beaten black and blue was the least that loose women like her deserved. The woman dropped to her knees and begged for mercy. "You may kick me in the head and bash my chest but, please, never let your foot touch my belly!" Her plea enraged her husband further. He was so angry that he gave her a good kick in the abdomen, sending her rolling about, dishevelled on the ground in the courtyard.

Cao Shui'er had never envisaged such a turn of events and

was at a loss. He didn't realise that he should have been responsible for this pregnant woman. But, at least, he knew he couldn't walk away without finding a solution to the problem. Like a naughty boy who had been caught red-handed, he stood there obediently, waiting to hear how she would deal with him.

The woman dragged her feet close to Cao Shui'er, grabbed his large hands and pressed them to her abdomen. Cao Shui'er was so frightened that he wanted to snatch his hands away. The woman gave him a hard slap on the back of his hand. He pressed his hands down and stopped moving them. The woman said tearfully, "This is your flesh and blood. As long as I'm still breathing, I'll give birth to this child and bring it up for you. No matter where you travel or how far you go, remember to come back to pick up your child!"

Cao Shui'er mumbled indistinctly and incoherently. He was calculating the due date. The bugle call for fall-in would sound at any moment, so he fidgeted in anxiety.

The woman held him from behind and pressed her face hard against his back that felt as flat as a vast plain. She said nothing about the brutal beating she had suffered. She was taking in his body temperature and masculine breath.

The bugle call sounded, and Cao Shui'er struggled out of the woman's arms. He was about to leave when the woman grabbed him by the strap of his rifle and asked, "Are you sure you have wheat flour in this gunny sack?" Her question reminded Cao Shui'er of the bag. He had meant to leave the few kilograms of wheat flour to the sister-in-law. He didn't want her to regard soldiers as cold-hearted. But he soon dismissed the idea because he knew this was the rationed feed supply for the warhorse. How could Tanzao go without fodder? Seeing Cao Shui'er hesitating, the woman yanked the bag from his hand and forced a chuckle. "Little bro!" she said. "Just consider these few kilograms of wheat flour as lost and picked up innocently by your sister-in-law."

The woman didn't mean to ask him for compensation for what he had done to her body. This debt wasn't something that Cao Shui'er could meet with the few kilograms of horse feed he was holding. An expectant mother had to find whatever she needed for childbirth and nursing. She could trade the wheat flour for some newly harvested millet. In case her breast milk was insufficient, she could feed the baby thick millet congee, which would be better than nothing.

The bugle call for fall-in was urgent so Cao Shui'er had no time to delay. He gave the sister-in-law a salute and rushed out. The woman yelled behind him, "Remember to come and pick up your child! Remember to come and pick up your child!"

The sister-in-law totally forgot that it was a scandal that should never be publicised. But this expectant mother was showing her defiance. Echoing the resonant bugle call, she was proclaiming to the world that she would have a baby and emerge triumphant!

CHAPTER 5

THE HORSE MESSENGER DISCOVERS AN UNNAMED ASTEROID

Qi Jing named his mount Tanzao, meaning "Beach Jujube", as you might expect, after the Yellow River Beach Jujube. After drying in the sun, the berries were the biggest and most delicious of all dried fruits. Everyone loved them. His foreign-bred bay horse was outstanding, a perfect match for the equally exceptional berry.

Very few of the wounded soldiers of the 9th Brigade had failed to enjoy a ride on Number Five's mount. Now, here came the physically challenged Wang Keyu. The chief commander ordered that she receive special treatment. Whenever the troops marched at night, the horse messenger Cao Shui'er would wait by the roadside with the big foreign horse and say, "Staff Officer Wang, the chief commander told me it's your turn to ride on the horse for a while."

Wang Keyu had initially been afraid of Tanzao. She would stand some distance away, not daring to approach, let alone ride him on a march. But with the kind help and encouragement of the horse messenger Cao Shui'er, Xiao Wang soon made friends with this understanding, veteran warhorse. Her horsemanship was also rapidly improving.

Tanzao had repeatedly served with distinction in previous battles. He carried his head high, and his legs were long and slender. There was a white stripe like that on a Beijing opera mask, running from its forehead down to its muzzle, seemingly splitting its narrow face into two. This facial marking gave people an impression of fantasy and a feeling that it was towering, sturdy, graceful and well-mannered. One of a horse's blind spots is directly in front of its nose. Therefore, Tanzao turned his head slightly sideways to size up this strange army woman with his big, sparkling eyes.

Xiao Wang inched towards the horse's neck as it turned to look at her. She slowly reached out to touch its head and kept calling its name gently: "Tanzao! Tanzao!" The bay horse sniffed Xiao Wang's body, trying to gauge if she was a danger.

Sensing that the horse's appearance was still affable, Xiao Wang felt encouraged. She touched his face and scratched his withers. Swivelling his ears casually, Tanzao didn't regard her as a threat and acquiesced to Xiao Wang's ingratiating scratches. He had already accepted her. Like all beginners, Xiao Wang also went through the necessary emotions of fear mixed with excitement.

Instead of hands-on tutorship, Cao Shui'er just gave her some quick tips and reminders. Xiao Wang, however, managed to master every skill straight away and made Tanzao extremely happy. Cao Shui'er complimented this female rider on her skills. "You have a real feeling for horses, Staff Officer Wang. You're not only talented but innately talented!"

A natural connection between horse and rider is a mutual bond. It can only arise when there are no barriers to communication between rider and horse. Without using voice commands, the two can understand and anticipate each other's every move. They can act in coordination without either party giving a hint beforehand. Such harmony in horsemanship cannot be achieved through hard training alone. The feeling has to be inborn. Equestrians call it "the unity of horse and rider". That is, the two have become one so that one doesn't feel the existence of the other.

Many riders were unable to find compatibility with their mounts. Some naughty horses often took sudden turns to shake the riders off their backs. Others even enjoyed teasing their riders. They would trot in such a way that the jolting made the rider feel that their insides might fly out of their mouth.

"It's not that I have the touch of a horse rider," Staff Officer Wang said. "It's just that Tanzao is so tolerant and takes care of me. I know it."

⁕

Xiao Wang wanted to thank Tanzao, but how? She racked her brain and finally decided to play him a musical piece on her *guqin*. She knew the idea was a little silly. It would seem odd and somewhat affected to make such a gesture even to a good friend, let alone a horse. People might think she had too much time on her hands!

Xiao Wang decided on *Moon Over Mountain Pass*, one of the well-known tunes of the Mei'an Guqin School of the 20th century. Vigorous and yet unsophisticated, it reflects the homesickness of a soldier sent on an expedition to fight for his country. It's also an ode to the majestic, unstoppable warhorses and chariots in the heat of battle.

Indeed, Tang of the Shang dynasty overthrew Jie of the Xia dynasty with merely seventy excellent chariots. The most important battle tactics in ancient China involved chariots, each drawn by four horses. Therefore, just seventy excellent chariots pulled by 280 warhorses were deployed by Tang to storm the capital of Xia and topple the dynasty. In the famous Battle of Chengpu during the Spring and Autumn period, the Jin State Army's main force comprised only 700 chariots, putting the state in a disadvantageous position. The Duke of Wen of Jin worked hard to strengthen the state by increasing the number of chariots to 4,000, and they eventually proved invincible in battle.

The musical piece lasts less than three minutes, but it's not easy to master. The difficulty lies in pulling off the so-called "snake's shape and crane's gait", which is the *guoxian* technique involving uninterrupted string shifting that is unique to the *guqin*. Wang Keyu intensified her practice. As her fingertips struck the strings gently yet forcefully, she painted a musical scene of cavalrymen galloping over from a distance, drumming and singing in the dusty wind. Simultaneously, a horse neighed and snorted, galloping over from afar, the sound of its clip-clopping becoming increasingly distinct.

With a rattle, the rear window of the small rural house was bumped open from the outside. A bay horse appeared at the window. Wang Keyu seemed to be hallucinating. She wondered whether it might be possible for a sturdy, ancient warhorse to rush over upon hearing the music. She looked closely, only to see Tanzao, the personal mount of Number Five. He pushed the window open with his head, mist-like white foam still spraying from his nostrils.

The astonished Cao Shui'er followed hurriedly behind and stuttered, "Ma'am, Horse Messenger Cao Shui'er reporting! I was about to wash the horse when he bolted and left me for the village. I guessed he must have heard something. He must be imagining things! But what can a horse hear? So, I followed it here in haste. Now, it turns out you're playing the *guqin*."

"Yes, I'm practising a *guqin* piece," said Wang Keyu.

"But this horse has never heard you play. How come he ran directly to you here?"

"Cao Shui'er, I don't know how to explain this phenomenon to make you understand it. Tanzao may have never heard me playing the *guqin*. However, since ancient times, as chariots rolled and warhorses galloped, one *guqin* military musical piece after another has been circulating the battlegrounds. I'm certain that Tanzao must be very familiar with this piece *Moon Over Mountain Pass* I'm playing."

Cao Shui'er seemed to have realised something. "No wonder he ran so fast and left me far behind. He acted as if the *guqin* piece was being played for no one else. He must have felt that if he didn't come, he would let the player down!"

Staff Officer Wang broke into laughter. "You're perfectly right. *Moon Over Mountain Pass* is my present for Tanzao. I haven't played it for a long time and was merely practising. Though my performance was far from perfect, luckily the horse wasn't fussy and came anyway."

This *guqin* player had many fans when she was young. They told her in person which specific musical piece fascinated them and what particular techniques they most appreciated. But how could she have dreamed that a horse in the People's Liberation Army would become a mute connoisseur of her music and a bosom friend of hers?

Wang Keyu pressed her glossy, supple and rosy face to the horse with affection. The horse stuck out his tongue and gave this army woman a gentle lick on her hands and cheek. The horse messenger grinned. "He-he, I've looked after this horse for several years, but he has always given me the cold shoulder. He has never granted me such a reward!"

☆

A slew of unfounded rumours and malicious slanders began to circulate since the female literacy instructor came to the head-quarters. Some, for instance, said, "The one with seven bullet holes in his body can only be qualified for the job of horse boy, while someone with a single hole never worries about having a chance of riding a horse."

Some middle- and lower-level officers didn't have the luck to find a spouse. Therefore, they uttered such lewd words to vent their pent-up frustration and anger. Under the "25-8-Regiment" regulation of the PLA, only regiment-level officers of at least twenty-five years of age and eight years of CPC membership had permission to get married. Both requirements were considered essential. There were as many reasons for embracing the regulations as there were reasons for dismissing them as unfair. But only heaven knew whether it was fair or not.

Not only did the rumours and slanders spread in the Taihang Border Region, but they also flew around in North Shaanxi and the Jin-Sui and Jin-Cha-Ji border areas. No one openly owned up to spreading such malicious gossip. But it was a different case in the 9th Brigade headquarters, where there were many names and specific details. Some people even embroidered the gossip and added juicy details, turning it into a boisterous farce as if they wanted to see the headquarters plunged into chaos.

The troops were in the middle of strategic manoeuvres dubbed "advancing and withdrawing at fast speed". They marched day and night. Cao Shui'er would always wait by the roadside with Tanzao. "Staff Officer Wang," he called out, "the chief commander asked me to let you ride him for a while!" At first, Wang Keyu declined. But she changed her mind after getting badly hurt after repeated falls when marching on foot. Tanzao naturally became her personal mount unless there were seriously wounded soldiers who were more deserving.

Wang Keyu suffered from acute night blindness and flat feet, but the gossipers never cared. They all had a tacit understanding that their real target was none other than Chief of Staff Qi Jing.

Apart from Qi Jing, all the chief officers with code numbers were married. Qi Jing himself amply qualified the requirements for the 25-8-Regiment. But he always made known that he wasn't interested in women. Holding fast to his status as a bachelor, he couldn't keep himself from being the subject of repeated gossip, be it trivial or significant. In the past, Number Five would launch a fierce counterattack against those "slick liberals" and never let the slanderers escape without being held accountable. But he was holding off taking any action this time.

"So be it. I'll wait to see how low the slanderers can go!"

꘎꙰★꙰꘎

When she found Cao Shui'er, Wang Keyu asked him, "I heard some people say someone with seven or eight holes can only be a horse boy, while those with only one will always have a horse to ride. What does it mean?"

Cao Shui'er's face changed colour instantly. He panicked and involuntarily clicked his heels to stand to attention. He was ready for a dressing down.

All this gossip seemed to blame Xiao Wang on behalf of the horse messenger Cao Shui'er. It was the biggest irony in the world because Cao Shui'er found nothing in the gossip to complain about. He even laughed at himself in private conversations, grinning cheekily, "I'm only too eager to lead the horse and hold the stirrups for our literacy instructor. It'd be better if I could trade my role with Tanzao so he can lead me while the instructor rides on my back."

He was only enjoying himself by talking because he never had any physical contact with this female soldier from the Eighth Route Army. He feared that Wang Keyu might think that he had fabricated this gossip of "seven or eight holes" and would reckon with him at any time. Sure enough, she stormed in. Well, it was a good opportunity to clear the air. How could he tell her everything about this enigmatic gossip without her initiating a conversation on the topic herself?

"Please don't get angry. If you... you... want to say something, take it easy," stuttered Cao Shui'er, suddenly losing his fluency.

Wang Keyu was perplexed. "Why are you so nervous? I just came to ask you a simple question."

Cao Shui'er's tone became bolder. "Why choose me?"

"Some comrades told me that I shouldn't ask anyone else. I'd better ask you."

"They mean no good. They're just making fun of you." Just then, it began to rain. Cao Shui'er wanted to take the opportunity to sneak away. "Well, it's raining, Staff Officer Wang. I've got to go. Talk to you later."

Wang Keyu blocked his way. "Don't worry. It'll stop soon. Xiao Cao, let's talk about something other than holes. Let me ask you this. Have you ever been wounded?"

"Yes, I have. The Japanese devil's artillery once greeted me."

"Where were you hurt? Could you show me?"

Cao Shui'er pulled up his sleeves and then his trouser legs to show Xiao Wang his scars. He explained that entry wounds tend to be small and leave scars that barely protrude from the skin. But exit wounds are more extensive and leave scars that rise above the skin and spread conspicuously beyond.

It was the first time Xiao Wang had ever seen gunshot wounds. Though a little scared, she ran her hand gently over Xiao Cao's wounds. She asked caringly, "Do they hurt?"

"Some of the shrapnel could be removed while others couldn't. They only hurt on overcast or rainy days when I feel a dull pain and itch. They come every time the weather turns."

"How many wounds do you have in total?"

"The entry and exit wounds put together have left me a total of eight holes."

As soon as the word "hole" escaped his mouth, Xiao Cao realised that his tongue had slipped. His eight wounds corresponded to the number of holes mentioned in the gossip. He tried to hastily correct himself but couldn't find the right words. He froze.

Patting herself on the forehead repeatedly, Wang Keyu blurted out, "I see! I see! You've got seven or eight holes and can only be a horse boy for someone. Well then, who's the one who can always find a horse to ride?"

Cao Shui'er was cornered. No one else in the world could face such an embarrassing, pointed and unbearable situation. If there had been a cliff before him, he would have thrown himself off it immediately to escape Xiao Wang's detailed questioning. Feeling trapped, he paced around on the spot like a spinning top. "Gosh, you're killing me. I wouldn't know how to answer even if you cut me down with your gun!"

"Comrade Xiao Cao, what the devil is the meaning of this gossip that I alone seem to be sheltered from?"

Cao Shui'er knew there was no way out. He adjusted his cap and stated categorically, "Staff Officer Wang, who else can it be? It's you, of course!"

"You're talking nonsense! I've never had the chance to take part in a battle and get wounded. That's why I've been feeling sorry that I've got no hole in my body."

As she spoke, it dawned upon Wang Keyu what the word "hole" in the gossip meant. She immediately doubled over in uncontrollable guffaws. She then realised that it was too much for a female comrade to laugh without scruples and hurriedly covered her mouth with her hands. Heavy rain was imminent. She ran to her dwelling, leaving behind her a trail of giggles.

✦

Cao Shui'er would have accepted it if Staff Officer Wang had flown into a rage and spat on him. I deserve it, he thought. I can't blame her for overreacting, no matter how berserk she might get. How can a woman suffer such a personal insult?

During the march that night, the horse messenger paid particular attention to Staff Officer Wang to anticipate her reaction. He stood on the roadside to wait for her as usual. "Staff Officer Wang!" he said when she came. "The chief commander said it's your turn to ride on the horse for a while." Xiao Wang didn't decline, and she went to catch up with the troops on Tanzao's back as usual. Any other female comrade would rather stumble and fall to the ground while marching than have the privilege of riding on Number Five's bay red horse.

Such rumours were so unacceptably vulgar that they could even make gossipers blush. They were no less filthy than excrement being poured over one's head. But Staff Officer Wang responded merely with a burst of laughter. Good heavens, they thought. How can she laugh and still ride on the chief officer's horse even when she's conscious of the rumour? She acted as if she were an outsider who had nothing to do with the gossip that was so offensive to the ear.

The impact of her reaction on Cao Shui'er was profound, equivalent to the two atomic bombs dropped on Hiroshima and Nagasaki by a Boeing B-29 Superfortress. Only something on the scale of a nuclear-fission shock wave could awaken and civilise Cao Shui'er.

Never one to feel deprived of sexual desire, he had always felt his blood boiling. Other than that, he had nothing else to be proud of. Today, this strong horse boy did a lot of thinking and became highly enlightened. Suddenly, he had a new understanding of Staff Officer Wang, with whom he had been already very familiar.

He analysed Wang Keyu like a psychiatrist. He said to himself that, apart from her flat feet and night blindness, she turned out to have another innate "defect": lack of sophistication. She never seemed to be on alert to guard against anyone, nor against the intricate politics of human society. One can't attack and capture a completely unfortified city. To her, rumours and slanders were as harmless as a punch on a pile of cotton. She would only brush them aside and laugh!

Admiration and awe for this Eighth Route Army soldier welled up in his heart. His reverence for her was like that of a pilgrim prostrating himself before the statue of a goddess. Cao Shui'er began to look at her by raising his head at a forty-five-degree angle. He looked up into the night sky thousands of kilometres away, only to spot a bright, twinkling asteroid that was orbiting the sun. According to the unified numbering of the 1940 edition of a certain international authority, Cao Shui'er had apparently discovered a hitherto unnamed free-flying celestial body, thus adding to the 1,564 asteroids that had already been discovered.

Cao Shui'er felt his idolised Wang Keyu too distant to approach. Though ashamed of his inferiority, he had infinite sympathy and pity for the object of his worship. She appeared so lonely, fragile and helpless in the rough and collectivised military structure. The situation would only get more perilous now they were about to cross the Yellow River. Heaven knows if she could adapt to the new environment.

In everyone else's eyes, this female literacy instructor would have been easy prey for a notorious philanderer like Cao Shui'er. Now, there was a total reversal of the roles. That is, the horse messenger set his mind on protecting this Peking student from any unbearably vulgar comments that would tarnish her reputation. He would do everything possible to give her practical help. Every time he thought of this, he would feel a hundred times more spirited and brim with pride and solemnity. A special obligation fell on this horse messenger's shoulders.

Cao Shui'er warned himself: I must always maintain a

normal relationship with Staff Officer Wang that is appropriate between "a horse boy" and "a horse rider". Never maltreat her, you shameless, nasty scoundrel! Never even lay a finger on her!

Wang Keyu was so feeble that she barely had the strength to truss up a chicken. Therefore, she found it challenging to mount a horse. Every time she tried to get up on Tanzao, she would unwittingly thrust her round bottom into Cao Shui'er's view. He could have easily pushed it to help her up. But Cao Shui'er never once reached out his hands. He preferred watching Staff Officer Wang fail time after time. Now, Xiao Cao would proactively crouch down to assume a "horse stance" so that Xiao Wang could step on his lap and mount the horse.

Staff Officer Wang on horseback would look back with a smile and say, "Thank you, Xiao Cao!"

Back in the 1920s during the warlord era, it was easy for young, handsome private horse boys to prey on their officers' wives or daughters. While the rumours circulating in the 9th Brigade headquarters finally ran out of steam, some nosy parkers began to spread new gossip. They would say, "Let's wait and see. The best part of the show is yet to come."

CHAPTER 6

A BRILLIANT BATTLEFIELD SCENE

A literacy instructor's job in the headquarters was to teach the officers and soldiers how to read and write. But now Wang Keyu went through one campaign after another with no respite. Literacy classes had long become sidelined. Feeling ill at ease because of her underemployment, she went to ask Number Five for things to do. But Qi Jing didn't think of it as a big deal.

"You can use the time to play the *guqin*, can't you?" he suggested.

It was all very well to spend her days practising the *guqin* in an art troupe because she would be admired as someone aspiring to improve her skills, and both the officers and soldiers would commend her for it. But now she was working in the headquarters, Wang Keyu was worried about spending too much time on her instrument since that might trigger adverse reactions, some of which could be unpleasant to hear. But no one would bother if she practised her *guqin* after her literacy classes. Xiao Wang's concern conformed to the actual situation.

Number Five sent for Director Jiang of the Political Department's Publicity Section and recommended the literacy instructor Wang Keyu to him. He asked the director to arrange for Xiao Wang to work in the Publicity Section's Slogan and Poster Group. Director Jiang knew that Xiao Wang came from a well-known family of calligraphers in Peking and that the Slogan and Poster Group couldn't find a better candidate. Beyond himself with secret joy, he pretended to be apprehensive, saying, "Chief Commander! How could I recruit Staff Officer Wang, such a talented woman? Our group members would pass out from fear. Who would dare to write slogans any more?"

"Don't be sarcastic, Director Jiang! My assignment is to paint slogans on walls. It's a challenging task. I must apprentice myself to your group members and learn from them," said Staff Officer Wang with great respect. "I learned the small regular script from my father for a few days when I was a child. But lacking the gifts of a calligrapher, I always made my father anxious. I may not live up to your expectations in helping your team add to the bright and splendid battlefield scene."

"Don't be modest, Xiao Wang," Qi Jing chimed in. "You wrote for others and advertised your services when you were young. I heard that you even worked out a price list, didn't you?"

Wang Keyu broke into laughter. "You're right!" she replied. "I charged four yuan for a one-metre-long antithetical couplet; eight yuan if it was 1.5 metres long; and twelve yuan if it was 2.5 metres. As for scrolls and albums, I charged four yuan for those with an area of between twenty-five and fifty square centimetres. The price doubled if a scroll or album was more than thirty-three square centimetres. I asked for four yuan for the calligraphy between fan ribs and eight yuan across them for round and folding fans. The price for birthday scrolls was negotiable. The calligraphy cost on white paper was also negotiable and followed the tradition of paying extra for wetting the brush before writing."

"You see! How can we afford to hire her!" joked Director Jiang.

"I'm really not that good. Father always took me with him when he was invited out to write for others. He was easygoing and lived a carefree life. Each time I finished writing, he would take it over and sign it for me, putting down my infant name Wang Crumpled Paper Ball." Staff Officer Wang broke into another burst of laughter.

Most people are shy to mention their childhood names, treating them as something private. But Xiao Wang didn't care at all. She had already told the female comrades in the head-quarters how her father had given her the name.

Xiao Wang had five elder brothers because the goddess of fertility allegedly loathed giving out girls. Her calligrapher father had sized the rice paper with a paper knife and was about to write something in a cursive script when the telephone rang. The hospital's obstetrics and gynaecology department said, "Congratulations! Your wife has given birth to a daughter!" Her father crumpled the paper he had just cut into a ball and meant to throw it into the wastebasket. Overjoyed, he didn't know what to do and absent-mindedly cast it into a glass of water.

As the calligrapher guffawed, his daughter's name popped into his mind. Fine, we'll call her "Crumpled Paper Ball".

"Xiao Wang," Number Five asked, "did your father tell you that this name he gave you has a particular connotation?"

"He just came up with it on a whim. It was nothing but an infant's name, with no special connotation."

Qi Jing clapped his hands in delight. "This name is certainly unique and intriguing. It's full of family warmth and the down-to-earth flavour of daily life. Unfortunately, we have regulations in the army. Otherwise, it would be nice for us to call you 'Wang Crumpled Paper Ball'!"

"No, no, no! We'd better keep things above board!" said Xiao Wang in all seriousness.

Marx Jiang accepted a significant task that he couldn't ignore. He decided to take it upon himself to teach Wang Keyu to write big-character posters.

First, Xiao Wang had to learn how to dig soil, which needed to be high-quality pottery clay for kilning porcelain. It was so sticky that it wouldn't peel off easily and was orange-red when written as characters. "If you add a little bit of soot to it," said the director, "you'll get another colour, namely umber. You must pick out the clumps and sift them a couple of times using a fine-mesh basket so you can make the characters look delicate and glossy. You write white characters with limestone powder. As soon as you pour it into a bucket, make sure to cover the container to avoid hurting your eyes."

It was more challenging to get the black colour. The group members had to go door to door with a bucket to ask the villagers to allow them to scrub the soot off their pots, stoves and chimneys, an act the villagers deemed taboo. Of course, Xiao Wang made a big difference. The aunties would beam as they greeted her. "We know you need the soot to write slogans," they would say. "Help yourself. But please be gentle. We can't afford to compensate you if your fair face gets smeared with soot."

Initially, the paint that Wang Keyu mixed was too thin for the characters to show on the walls. She didn't know why. When Director Jiang checked, he found that she had mishandled the process of adding water to the soot. The stir had to be forceful and the water added little by little. The paint had to be pasty. Diluting it with too much water would render it useless.

Since the black colour was hard to come by, the Slogan and Poster Group members used it sparingly for outlining red or white characters. Xiao Wang quickly mastered the tracing technique as it was not difficult. There were two ways of tracing the characters. One was to outline each of them. The other was to trace each character with positive and negative perspectives. The group members only needed to blacken each horizontal stroke's bottom and right-side edges and each vertical stroke's right side. And the strokes of throw and press required a little dab on the left bottom. These tricks would turn the two-dimensional characters into three dimensions. The added shading made the slogans appear more eye-catching.

The brush used to write slogans, also known as "row brush" in Chinese, was easily worn. The group members had to mass-produce it themselves. Director Jiang had told Xiao Wang that the group would provide her with her row brushes so she didn't have to learn how to make them. But after a few cuts on her fingers with tinplate, she eventually mastered the craft.

Hog bristles, wool and jute were hard to procure. Xiao Wang experimented with cloth strips instead. She tied them into the brush bristle prototype, reinforced with a few thin bamboo slips to keep the toe from collapsing. The characters written with this type of brush looked so neat and regular because the edges weren't ragged.

Staff Officer Wang had worked as an assistant before becoming the backbone of the Slogan and Poster Group. Director Jiang assigned two soldiers to her. They did odd jobs like making sure she wouldn't fall from a ladder.

Now that Xiao Wang worked independently, she replaced her artistic calligraphy style with Liu Gongquan's regular script, thus bringing her childhood talent into full play. She might find it harder to show the style's real beauty on the walls than on paper, but it was more acceptable to the viewers. They commented, "This Eighth Route Army soldier writes differently from the others. We can easily read what she writes without having to guess."

She fared pretty well in spring and autumn, but it required some mettle to brush slogans on the walls in the scorching days of July and August. Overexposure to intense sunlight led to severe sunburn, with peeling skin on the shoulders and arms being the first symptoms. In winter, Xiao Wang would shiver on top of the wooden ladder while reaching her arm above her head to brush the slogans. The cold lime solution dripped down her arm and along her armpit, groin, thigh and calf right to the sole of her foot. Especially for a woman like her, the irritation in her crotch area caused a pain that she couldn't reveal to anybody.

As soon as the troops stopped for a lunch break on their march, the Slogan and Poster Group members dispersed. No walls in the village would be bare for long. The only thing the group members feared was that they would still be brushing the slogans when the brigade suddenly moved out upon hearing the bugle call for fall-in. They would panic and have to clear up their mess and rush to catch up with the troops. Xiao Wang had experienced this situation on a number of occasions. Like cats on hot bricks, the two young soldiers kept yelling, "Staff Officer Wang, hurry! Come down! Come down! The troops are far away!"

Wang Keyu acted as if she hadn't heard them. She kept on brushing the slogan as she stood on the ladder. She couldn't bear to see it half-finished on the wall if they were to stop abruptly and run after the troops. That would never be acceptable to her. She completed her work by finishing the last character and tracing its edges black.

By now, the troops were already a few kilometres away. They ran desperately until Wang Keyu was panting and couldn't move any more. The two soldiers had to abandon their paint buckets and sprint, carrying her between them.

Marx Jiang came to inspect the slogan-brushing site as director of the Political Publicity Section. He would brush one or two slogans with Wang Keyu. Seeing her swaying on the wooden ladder, he rushed to stabilise it lest she might fall. "Director Jiang!" Wang Keyu said, feeling a little uneasy. "You don't have to do that. I've already got two young comrades to help here."

"Let them take a break. I'll assist you."

After finishing a slogan, Wang Keyu handed the paste bucket to the director down below and stepped down slowly from the ladder facing out. As she reached the last two or three rungs, Director Jiang reached out his hands to receive her. In the past, she would reach out to grasp a man's hands while climbing down steadily. But Wang Keyu was now long accustomed to climbing ladders. She shunned the enthusiastic hands and hopped to the ground with a light thump to show she didn't need any assistance. But she still said, "Thank you very much!"

Director Jiang felt extremely frustrated. Shaking hands with Xiao Wang was the least of what he had aspired to do. He had missed many opportunities of being more intimate with her. Today, he had anticipated the best chance of achieving his goal because Xiao Wang would have needed his help while clambering down the ladder. But she gave this Marx Jiang the cold shoulder.

Wang Keyu had the best attendance record of all members of the Poster and Slogan Group. As the troops marched on the vast Ji-Lu Plains, her regular-script handwriting was visible on many walls. The slogans of her calligraphy presented themselves as splendid battlefield scenery. The brigade's Political Department held a meeting at the slogan-brushing site to commend her for outstanding work on the publicity front. The head of the Political Department presided over the meeting while the Publicity Section director read out the citation dispatch.

The presentation of the certificate of merit came next. It was just a piece of cardboard, following the army's tradition. The prize was a white towel, purchased with Director Jiang's own money as prizes were not in the section's budget. The transaction wasn't to be announced.

The master of ceremonies announced with a clear and loud voice, "Comrade Wang Keyu, please come to the podium to receive the award!" The announcement prompted a burst of applause from the audience. But the recipient Xiao Wang continued to sit on a long stool in the back row with a smile on her face. She adamantly declined the certificate and prize despite repeated urging and her dire need for a towel. Tied around the wrist of her right hand, it could have prevented the lime solution from dripping down her sleeve.

It was not because she disliked the ceremony but because she felt disturbed, regarding the whole business as childish. As if I need this for me to continue to work hard!

Worried that if the stalemate continued, no one could get out of this embarrassing situation unscathed, the Political Department head gave Publicity Section Jiang a signal, who announced, "Today's meeting has concluded successfully. Let's call it a day."

Marx Jiang hadn't expected things to end up like this. He stumbled and fell in front of Wang Keyu. It pushed him further into a mood of despair. His friend, the Political Department head, teased him. "What are you afraid of? With the Twenty-Four-Eight-Regiment condition, why can't you take the initiative to go after her? If you find it embarrassing to talk to her face to face, you can instead write her a letter to test the waters."

How could Director Jiang be so audacious? He was fully aware that Number Five and Xiao Wang enjoyed a special relationship beyond comradeship. Number Five stood erect and proud, like a stately lion, an expert predator. Compared with him, a director was merely a wolf. He had to be discreet in word and deed instead of acting recklessly to invite humiliation on himself.

The head of the Political Department tried to encourage his friend. "Only time will tell," he said. "I believe Xiao Wang will one day become your Jenny!"[1]

CHAPTER 7

THE ART OF MILITARY COMMAND IS THE CRYSTALLISATION OF THE UNYIELDING SPIRIT OF SOLDIERS

The 9th Brigade held occasional public lectures on current events. They called them "Big Reports". The keynote speaker of today's Big Report was Qi Jing, the brigade's chief of staff. He gave a talk entitled "A Close Analysis of the Situation of the Enemy and Us". His speech was well received. The troops compared it to a thirst-quenching downpour.

When he spoke, Qi Jing never used a script. He calmly and objectively analysed the war situation with a little military theorisation. He also brought into full play his talent for passionate and subjective oration, packing his talk with humour and energy and turning his speech into a war proclamation.

The talks of other high-ranking commanders were poorly received. But they didn't mind because of the ready explanation that Qi Jing had studied in Japan where he had learned oration and forensics, knowing how to use various gestures as he spoke. They said they were no match for him being as rustic as they were.

Four officers in the Field Army had studied in Japan, with one heading the army's publicity department and two leading their columns' publicity departments. And the fourth was Qi

Jing. His father had paid his tuition fees by selling one of the family's old houses. He studied in the Arts Department of one of Japan's imperial universities majoring in Shakespeare, with oil painting and fine-art photography as his minors. The League of Left-Wing Writers of China's Tokyo Chapter started a literature and art magazine known as *East Current*, publicising fiction and essays written by progressive-leaning authors. Qj Jing was a frequent contributor.

Angry at Japan's role in the Marco Polo Bridge Incident, he returned to China and managed to locate the Eighth Route Army's front headquarters in Taihang District. He was supposed to be the art director of the headquarters' Experimental Art Troupe, but he categorically rejected the offer. Then he repeatedly declined a position in the Enemy Troop Work Department, part of the army's psychological warfare effort. He set his mind on getting involved in military affairs. He wanted to meet force with force and take a commander's responsibility despite his lack of relevant competency.

He differed from the other officers who joined the army in 1938 in that he was not from a peasant or worker family background. Besides, he was too old to get a promotion. He had to blaze a trail to get where he wanted. The art of military command is the crystallisation of iron and blood. He had to fight real battles to gain as much experience of commanding as possible. He had to draw on his strong points to offset his weaknesses. Otherwise, he could never expect to squeeze into the cohort of elite military commanders.

Before each fierce battle, a meeting would be held to decide who would go to the front or remain in the rear. They had to prevent the possibility of all their commanders and deputies being wiped out simultaneously at the front line, which would leave the troops leaderless. Qi Jing could always find a convincing reason for his participation at the front line. Day after day and year after year, he gained more practical combat experience than other commanders. A student of fine art graduating from Japan was far more impressive than the other commanders. Qi Jing had never been wounded in action up to now, not even slightly. Who wouldn't admire him?

Wang Keyu sat in the front row, listening attentively to Number Five giving his Big Report, jotting down some crucial phrases in a notebook. Gazing steadily at the young commander, she had no intention of concealing her admiration for him. Her intense look was as good as an inadvertent betrayal of her inner feelings.

At the end of the lecture, Ji Qing had meant to ask Wang Keyu to come to his dwelling to discuss a matter, but he stopped short. It was inappropriate for a chief officer to ask someone to go to his place in person. He should have had his messenger send her a note to make the invitation formal and above board. Back at his place, he asked Cao Shui'er to tell Staff Officer Wang to come.

Number Five was exaggerating the importance of the matter because the discussion involved nothing but getting Xiao Wang's feedback on his keynote speech "A Close Observation of the Situation of the Enemy and Us". He wanted to see how it shocked and moved her. He also wanted to know if some particular paragraphs or phrases had caught her attention and if Xiao Wang appreciated his tone and gestures.

Wang Keyu was out brushing slogans. She didn't come until Qi Jing had been waiting for a long time. "I'm sorry I'm late! Sir, Chief Officer, what can I do for you?"

Qi Jing blew the dust off a stool and said, "Please be seated, Xiao Wang. What did you intuitively feel about my speech? I hope it wasn't too boring, but I can't be sure."

Staff Officer Wang didn't respond to the question. Instead,

she repeated a few paragraphs of his talk from memory: "This is no longer a secret. The Field Army is about to fight its way across the Yellow River with three columns. They'll penetrate thousands of kilometres into the Dabie Mountains. I'm not bragging, but our Field Army will lead the country from strategic defence to strategic offence. Comrades, brothers, it's incredible!

"I know you may think it's impossible since Yan'an is still in the hands of the enemy, and they outnumber us in both forces and weaponry. However, it would take too long to wait for our forces to exceed theirs before launching an attack. We must have the determination to leave the rear alone and attack our foes where they are. The sudden appearance of tens of thousands of PLA troops between Wuhan and Nanjing will be like planting the burning wick of a war of attrition in the enemy's belly button. Let's see if Generalissimo Chiang Kai-shek can still peacefully enjoy his chicken soup with all the meat discarded.

"Comrades, brothers! Keep your ears to the ground and listen carefully. As the Chinese People's Liberation Army is leaping forward, you can hear the world's historical footsteps rising and falling! Everybody, including me, must sincerely ask the same question: by attacking the enemy where they are, like removing firewood from a stove, are we afraid of burning our hands? Are we fearful of tempering ourselves in this struggle with its heat reaching two thousand degrees?"

Qi Jing applauded. "Thank you, Xiao Wang, for memorising those long paragraphs!"

"Not only can she recite them," Cao Shui'er said, "but she also posted them on the wall."

"Really? That's quick! You've telegraphed, not brushed them!"

"You may inspect them if you want, Chief Officer," Xiao Wang responded enthusiastically. "See if I copied them correctly."

Staff Officer Wang planned to move on from brushing clumsy big-character slogans. Instead, she would post smaller-sized text to increase the number of characters and have room to write more about what was going on. The posts would be somewhat more educational and livelier in style. So much so that they would be captivating enough to make the villagers stop in their tracks to finish reading the content sentence by sentence.

The difficulty of changing to a smaller font lay in the unavailability of pen brushes and ink. Staff Officer Wang learned from her father that some artists used home-made charcoal pencils to make sketches. Xiao Wang followed the same method. She peeled willow twigs as thick as a chopstick and broke them into sections as long as a piece of chalk. Placing them in a tin can, Xiao Wang shut it tight with a mud lid, in which she bored a small hole. After covering the top with another layer of mud, Xiao Wang baked the can over a fire. The manufacture of the charcoal pencils would be deemed a success when no smoke came out of the holes. She took a couple of pencils and bashed them at each other so that they rattled with metallic clicks. They were ready to use and as good as commercial high-grade charcoal pencils.

It was hard to write on rough brick walls with charcoal pencils, so Staff Officer Wang and the two young soldiers went to the riverbank to dig sand. They mixed the sand well with lime before plastering the wall to create a smooth surface on which the charcoal pencils would write even better, especially when painted white with a lime solution.

Since then, Wang Keyu said goodbye to the banner-like slogans with grand characters. Now, she adhered to the traditional way of writing Chinese from right to left. Her original small-character "slogans" were eye-openers to the villagers.

In those places where villagers gathered to chat when they

were not working, Wang Keyu created three surfaces on the nearby walls by plastering them into square, rectangular and oval shapes. What would she write on them? It happened that Number Five had just given a speech on current events. On impulse, she selected three paragraphs of about a hundred characters each and wrote each paragraph on one of the surfaces. She then inscribed "Political Publicity" and the brigade's army formation sequence "793216".

Before Staff Officer Wang finished the last character, a large crowd of villagers, men and women, old and young, had gathered beneath her ladder. They asked her a lot of questions. Xiao Wang knew that she couldn't answer them in terms of "strategy" and "having the military initiative". Those notions might confuse them. Therefore, she offered a general explanation in popular vernacular, to which everyone nodded to show their complete comprehension.

Their nodding approval encouraged Wang Keyu. A tedious job now transformed itself into a lively platform where the writer and readers could interact with questions and answers with mutual affinity. It was no longer a situation in which she brushed indifferently while the villagers were walking by paying no heed to her.

When he walked up to the walls, Qi Jing found his understanding of publicity change fundamentally. What he beheld was a hard-tipped-pen calligraphy show rather than slogans brushed by the Slogan and Poster Group of the 9th Brigade's Publicity Department.

Ordinary calligraphers might be good at writing individual characters. But any scroll they attempted, with all the characters organised together, would look like an eyesore. Since she had been trained by a famous calligrapher, Wang Keyu knew how to lay out the characters and lines in an aesthetic way. Spaced appropriately, the entire text looked lively and as artistic as a landscape painting scroll viewed from a distance. Meanwhile, she paid meticulous attention to each character's strokes and how they coordinated with the characters above and below. Xiao Wang's three long scrolls were impeccable. There was neither a single faulty stroke nor an ugly character.

What Number Five liked most was the coherence of the entire text written so smoothly in one go. He could find an easy explanation: as she understood the content of what she was writing, she could write freely and unaffectedly, with her wrist intuitively leading the way and keeping her momentum consistent. Luckily, the hard-tipped charcoal pencil was perfectly suited to her Liu Gongquan style of calligraphy, which required that the strokes be well-balanced, thin but powerful, brisk and neat, and robust and vigorous. One poem read, "Writing with smoothness results in beautiful characters; thin and vigorous strokes lead to marvellous calligraphy." Xiao Wang's artwork fully embodied the beauty of the lines in Chinese characters.

The Number Five chief officer enjoyed viewing the three lime-plastered walls. He attributed the success of the calligraphy on show to teamwork, a tremendous undertaking he and Wang Keyu had accomplished. He provided the original text while she committed it to the walls. The thought that they worked like a pair of swans made him feel extremely contented. But Qi Jing had the wisdom to appreciate his limitations. He knew he was not yet eligible enough to propose to her in public. Therefore, he could only say, "Xiao Wang! Since you're a professional calligrapher, I'm not in a position to critique your work. But if you insist, I do have something to say. I focus more on your effort to turn slogan-brushing into an aesthetic appreciation of Chinese characters. You've greatly expanded the scope of the educational function of publicity. You're no longer writing slogans devoid of content but what's heard and seen on the battleground, the source of which can be inexhaustible. It's simply wonderful!"

"Come on! Come on! Commanders at all levels have a habit of disguising their criticism with compliments. I really need to bathe now!"

꙰☆꙰

Wang Keyu had an extravagant habit. She could do without eating or drinking, but not without showering.

While the flames of war were raging every day and everywhere, who would have been so resourceful to accommodate a female comrade's bathing needs? No one would have openly condoned the habit. On the contrary, it might invite showers of abuse and ridicule. But Xiao Wang was lucky enough to be in the 9th Brigade headquarters, where she didn't have to worry about such things.

The Number Five chief officer took cold showers throughout the year, even in the chilly winter months. Each time he would scrub his skin red and pour a bucket of cold water over his head to conclude the soak. Whenever the troops stayed somewhere, his bodyguards would form a semi-circle in the corner of a courtyard with reed mats to create a "shower room". They placed a few stone slabs on the "floor" so that he could stand on them without smearing his feet with mud while changing and bathing.

The female comrades working in the headquarters often came in threes or fives to use the Number Five's mat area to bathe. One group came with their water buckets while another went on watch. Then they would switch.

If things went wrong, the chief officer's kindness might give rise to negative public opinion. So Qi Jing took a drastic measure: when the female comrades came to bathe, he would stay far away with his bodyguards and didn't return until the young women had left, singing.

Today, only Staff Officer Wang came because she couldn't find any female companions. But she insisted on taking a shower alone. Qi Jing went out to give her privacy. He asked his horse messenger Cao Shui'er to prevent visitors from coming into the courtyard.

Wang Keyu took off her clothes and poured one gourd ladle of cold water after another over her head and body. Then, she suddenly realised that she had left her towel outside the enclosure. She called the horse messenger from a distance, "Cao Shui'er, would you please hand me the towel?"

Cao Shui'er was tall enough to see everything in the enclosure. As he approached the mat bathroom, he arched his back as if he were in a trench dodging enemy bullets. Then, he reached his hand up to hang the towel over the mat fence and returned to where he had been. "Staff Officer Wang, your towel," he said in a raised voice. "Can you see it?"

After the shower, Wang Keyu came out. She asked, "Cao Shui'er, where's the chief officer?"

Cao Shui'er could tell that Staff Officer Wang was a bit anxious. Not knowing what was on her mind, he volunteered to find the chief officer for her.

The Number Five chief officer came in no time. He caught sight of Wang Keyu standing sideways, crouching a little over, with her hair flowing down dripping with water. She was flicking her hair loose to dry it, with her hands held together by intertwined fingers. Qi Jing felt the scent of a woman emerging from a shower assailing his nostrils. He stopped and stepped back a reasonable distance.

Wang Keyu asked bluntly, "Chief Officer, am I on the list of people to return to Handan?"

The headquarters had received the notification. The troops would soon fight on exterior lines. It had to draw up a list to include all the severely wounded soldiers, and new and expectant mothers, and report to the upper-level commanders. These people wouldn't have to cross the Yellow River. According to gossip, Staff Officer Wang's name was on the long list of those to be sent to the rear because of her physical limitations.

Qi Jing immediately looked grave. "Who told you that?"

"No one. It's just came to my mind," Staff Officer Wang replied, keeping the source secret.

Number Five categorically denied what he deemed "hearsay". "It's absurd. I should know who's on the list or not. There're no rigid regulations regarding physical handicaps. We treat each specific case individually. You've gone through the four-year training at Taihang Number Two Middle School as well as the brutal 'May Mopping Up'. So your departure from the Ninth Brigade is out of the question, unless you apply for it."

"Is this your view, or the chief officer's, or was a decision made at the CPC Committee meeting?"

"Staff Officer Wang, do you want me to cross my heart?"

Xiao Wang broke into a smile, tears welling in her eyes.

CHAPTER 8

HEARING THE RECURRENT
FOOTSTEPS OF HISTORY

No one knew the identity of the person who witnessed Qi Jing snapping a "battlefield scene" and then reported it to the Number Two chief commander, the brigade's political commissar. The veteran political commissar didn't make any comments. Instead, he drew a long face and warned the whistle-blower: "Let this stay between you and me. Never tell anyone else. If you should gossip, don't blame me for punishing you in my unconventional manner!"

The brigade commander of the Independent 9th Brigade had just received a transfer order and left. This naturally meant that the political commissar was the one responsible for handling the Qi Jing incident. The Field Army was about to fight its way across the Yellow River and forge thousands of kilometres into the Dabie Mountains when suddenly an order came and transferred the commander elsewhere. Though remaining quiet, everyone was secretly guessing why.

No, they weren't guessing. They were quite certain about the reason: the vacation of the 9th Brigade commander's position on the eve of a great campaign was reserved for Chief of Staff Qi Jing. But unfortunately, he made a huge blunder at this critical juncture. It might have seemed trivial, but it was grave enough to ruin the bright future of an excellent military commander.

After hearing the whistleblower's report, Number Two was so incensed at Qi Jing that his face warped. Having been told the complete story, however, his attitude changed. Patting Qi Jing on the shoulder, he said, "Oh, Qi Jing! Haven't we been sharing food from the same field cauldron for all these years? Who'd clear up the mess for you if I didn't?"

The Number Two chief officer asked all the CPC Committee members of the brigade for opinions so that they could establish a common view and claim responsibility collectively. If he could win a majority, he wouldn't have to report Qi Jing to the higher-level leadership, and the case would be like "a fart blown away by the wind".

The political commissar lost no time talking to the deputy commissar, the Political Department head and the Logistics Section director. Now he had only one person to consult, Number Three, namely the deputy head of the brigade. But he was the toughest nut to crack. Number Three started with a barrage of compliments. "We've worked for so many years," he said. "Do you think I have no feelings for him when he's made such a mistake? This military officer's intellect far surpasses that of any other commander. He's worked his way up from battalion commander to chief of staff, bypassing all the deputy positions. He forges ahead with flying colours."

From this lavish flattery, the political commissar heard the underlying message: You've been arrogant all the time, haven't you? You're always talking in philosophical terms and have a talent for public speaking, don't you? You walk on air and disdain being a deputy, don't you? See what's happened to you now! Thoroughly disgraced and demoted, you're finished!

The political commissar reminded him, "We've got the reputation as the Night Tiger Regiment. Of course, we commanders and fighters have fought hard to earn that reputation, but everyone knows that Qi Jing has been instrumental in that fight."

The deputy brigade commander couldn't help but rebuke the political commissar. "Sir, Political Commissar, no matter how you defend him with your glib tongue, this is undeniably a pernicious incident. The best option is to report it to the senior leadership, and the sooner, the better. We can't escape the consequence of any delay."

The political commissar smiled to appease the deputy brigade commander, before replying, "The Field Army Front-Line Command Post has issued the order to cross the Yellow River. Our brigade will fight its way across before the thirtieth of June at the latest. Then we'll head into the Dabie Mountains. This is the time when we need all our military talent. The Ninth Brigade can't do without Qi Jing."

"That's not true! Since we're going to fight big battles, we can't afford to have someone who has made such a grave mistake on the front line. Where will our CPC discipline and martial law be when we laud an immoral person to the sky, saying that he's unique and irreplaceable?"

"We must be objective. Qi Jing only needs a little more moral cultivation. No big deal."

"No big deal? It could blow up if we don't handle it properly."

The political commissar flew into a rage. "How dare you attack a comrade-in-arms at such an important time, and use such vulgar and vicious language? You're not doing this to uphold disciplinary principles but to vent your grievances. You're out of line!"

"That's absurd! You talk as if this is about me, not Qi Jing. Please tell me what line I've crossed!"

"None of the other CPC Committee members are as extreme as you are. You've bottled up too many personal grievances," responded the political commissar, who was trying hard to suppress his anger.

"Do you think I'm jealous of him?"

"You think no one else can see through your ambition?"

The deputy brigade commander slapped his hand on the desk and roared, "What you're saying is as good as cursing me, 'A good dog won't block the way of others'!"

"Don't put words into my mouth! If I wanted to say something critical, it would be more ear-jarring!"

The deputy brigade commander said with a sullen smirk, "Political Commissar, I'm not joking. I can get you dismissed from your position over this. Do you believe me?"

"Yes, I do. Submit a disclosure letter, and you can wait for the good news."

"It's up to you. Don't make me."

"Go ahead. My conscience is clear."

"It's me who should feel that way because I'm trying to stop you from making a mistake."

"But you'll become infamous, and your ill fame will stink!"

The seething deputy brigade commander turned around and fell silent.

"OK, you can express your reservations, and I won't force you to change your mind. But you must put up with me when I request that you promise not to tell anyone about this incident."

"OK, I promise if it'll make you happy," the deputy brigade commander mumbled.

Staring into his eyes, the political commissar demanded, "Please repeat your promise."

"I promise! I promise!" the deputy brigade commander bellowed.

⁂

It was a common occurrence at the start of a meeting for the veteran political commissar to burst out in his authentic Shaanxi accent. "Please hold! I'm going to pee for us."

Here the Shaanxi vernacular "for us" was both unique and meaningful. This peacemaker had attained such a degree of perfection in mediating differences at the sacrifice of principles that he even turned his personal need for urinating into a common cause.

His handling of the Qi Jing photography incident completely subverted his subordinates' set view of him. They all used to speak of him as having an innocent face and playing the role of Kitchen God who "speaks well of the family that worships him to the celestial palace and brings good luck when returning". Now, they found they were wrong! He wasn't the person they thought he had been. This nice guy turned out to be an iron-handed strongman. He had accomplished a mission impossible with sweeping decisiveness.

That evening, the 9th Brigade CPC Committee's enlarged meeting convened in the small courtyard of a peasant family. No one had leaked anything before the meeting, but all the attendees tried to guess. Sure enough, Number Two announced Qi Jing's appointment as commander of the 9th Brigade. According to the released order, he was to take up the position immediately.

"To take up the position immediately" meant that both the brigade's internal documents and the Field Army's public news reports could refer to the 9th Brigade as the Qi Brigade, a Chinese military convention handed down from antiquity. Back in the days of the Three Kingdoms, the famous general Zhao Zilong had his name "Zhao" embroidered on his army's banners.

The atmosphere in the meeting was solemn and so quiet that the attendees could hear the beating of their hearts. The rumour had finally become reality. The attendees went up to shake hands with Qi Jing. But for some reason, he was feeling limp. He couldn't stand up even after trying several times. It would appear arrogant to accept the congratulations sitting down, so he felt obliged to apologise. "I'm so sorry, but I've no idea what's wrong with my legs."

In fact, there was nothing wrong with his legs. All that had happened was his knees went into spasm, and he temporarily lost control. The newly appointed chief commander of the 9th Brigade was enduring a strange sensation. It was like a fish, gutted, salted and sealed in a jar in order to be preserved. Then, out of the blue, someone released the fish back into the sea, and it wagged its tail a bit and swam to the depth of the azure ocean.

⁂

Simultaneously, the brigade's CPC Committee decided to transfer the headquarters' literacy instructor Wang Keyu to a teaching position in a school for the children of officials in Handan. Her transfer went into effect right away.

Opinions differed among the headquarters' staff members. Some defended the committee's decision but most thought that Wang Keyu should go ahead and demand justice. The photo-taking incident involved two people, and the CPC Committee should have made it clear who was more responsible and there-fore deserving of punishment. Since the investigation concluded that there was no evidence of wrongdoing, why did the committee think it necessary to transfer a lower-ranking staff officer?

The Personnel Section director talked with Staff Officer Wang Keyu without mentioning the incident. He only said that the troops were about to travel a thousand kilometres into the Dabie Mountains and fight on exterior lines. Her physical condition would severely impair her mobility, meaning she couldn't keep pace with the troops' movements. The CPC

Committee had to consider this reality and make necessary arrangements. He hoped that she could bring her talents into full play in her new position.

Wang Keyu repeated her claim that she had no problem marching with the troops. But the Personnel Section director reiterated that political fervour was one thing but causing trouble to the forces was another, something that would benefit no one. As the director became increasingly impervious to the feelings of Staff Officer Wang, she felt impelled to bring up her previous conversation with Qi Jing. "I've discussed my job with Number Five and got his approval."

"You meant Number One, right?" the Personnel Section director corrected her.

Qi Jing was no longer the 9th Brigade's chief of staff. He had become the Number One chief officer, bypassing the Numbers Two, Three and Four commanders. A temporarily confused Wang Keyu was failing to keep abreast of developments. She smiled apologetically. "Yes, of course. I haven't congratulated Number One on his promotion yet!"

The Personnel Section director intended to tell her frankly that the brigade's CPC Committee members' decision to transfer her was unanimous, and that Number One was at the meeting. If she had heard those words, Wang Keyu would have given up any hope and decided not to hassle Number One. But the director stopped short of this disclosure since it would violate the CPC's disciplinary principles. Retracting what was on the tip of his tongue, he only said, "Staff Officer Wang, you don't have to go to Number One to put him in an embarrassing position. He must comply with the CPC Committee's decision even if he had a dissenting opinion. He can't override it with his opinion."

Wang Keyu found it hard to understand. "Why's that? When I first came to the brigade, I had worries about my handicap. But the chief officer told me that I no longer had a problem after working for a few years at Taihang Number Two Middle School and going through the May Anti-Mop-up Campaign. Everything's been fine until now. Why did the committee suddenly raise this issue?"

"I'm not asking for your opinion here. You must comply with the committee's decision."

Wang Keyu finally gave up her attempt to change his mind. "Of course, I'll comply. But I want to see the chief officer one last time before my departure. I'll say nothing but goodbye to him."

"The chief officer went to inspect the troops. He won't be around when you visit him."

≫≫☆≪≪

All those going to Handan had gathered and set out. Two horse-drawn carts took the wounded soldiers and the pregnant women to a specified place to assemble as they couldn't keep pace with the others.

Carrying the *guqin* on her back, Wang Keyu tagged along. She looked back from time to time though she was aware that everyone had a tight schedule and couldn't come to see her off. Suddenly, the big foreign horse Tanzao galloped towards her. The column quickly parted to make way for it. Tanzao came to an abrupt stop and turned around, effectively blocking the entire column's path.

The people looked at each other, wondering what was going on. Only Wang Keyu knew that this veteran warhorse had come for her. Tanzao meekly lowered his head in front of Staff Officer Wang, who pressed her face to its neck teary-eyed. She was about to leave after picking up her *guqin* when Tanzao craned his neck. It tried desperately to prevent her from moving forwards even though she tried to shift left and then right. Deeply touched, Xiao Wang couldn't suppress the outpouring of her emotions. Covering her face with her hands, she burst into tears in the crowd's presence.

Just then, the horse messenger Cao Shui'er rushed over. It was clear that he was the director of this drama.

Wiping away her tears, Wang Keyu said, "You've come just in time. Please take Tanzao with you now. He's blocking our path and forcing everyone else to wait."

Cao Shui'er laughed. "He may not be able to speak, but this veteran warhorse knows everything. He's aware of your reluctance to go to Handan. Why don't you stay?"

"No, I can't," Staff Officer Wang proclaimed in haste. "I've promised the Personnel Section director. I can't change now."

"Let me talk with Number One on your behalf. Then, you can talk with anyone you like. Since you've already reached the northern bank of the Yellow River, you'll regret not crossing it for the rest of your life."

Xiao Wang's fierce internal conflict was evident because she was quiet for a long time, finding it hard to make up her mind. Cao Shui'er didn't waste time saying anything more. He put Staff Officer Wang's luggage on the horse's saddle, held her *guqin* in his arm and strode away alone, leading the horse by the reins. Wang Keyu faltered momentarily before running to catch up with him.

Like a new broom sweeping a room, Qi Jing went to inspect the troops as soon as he got his assignment. He would visit each of the four regiments. But he would never divulge his private plan for a quick departure from the headquarters: he could shun Xiao Wang whom he had expected to come to say goodbye. It would also save him from seeing her off. Although he was the cause of the "severe incident" in the doorway, Xiao Wang had to bear the consequences and leave the 9th Brigade in the end. He considered himself mean. Therefore, how could he have the brass face to see her?

The horse messenger Cao Shui'er took Xao Wang to see Number One, hoping that the chief officer would put in a good word for her. It was an opportunity to which Qi Jing had been looking forward so that he could save himself the embarrassment. He rushed out of the room to greet her, holding her hands tight in his. He trembled uncontrollably as he said, "You're back, Xiao Wang! Wonderful! That's wonderful!"

Staff Officer Wang managed to break free from his plier-like grip. Qi Jing mistakenly thought that she was revulsed by his sweaty hands. A sense of unworthiness crept upon him, and he repeatedly apologised. "Sorry! I'm sorry! I've got some paper. Would you like to wipe your hands?"

Xiao Wang beamed. "No, it was just that I felt my hands being crushed. I had to pull away!"

Then she burst into a laugh with Cao Shui'er who was standing by.

Sensing his opportunity, Cao Shui'er said, "Sir, Chief Officer! Staff Officer Wang doesn't want to go to the rear. Please keep her with our Ninth Brigade."

"I'm hearing the world's historical footsteps rising and falling," Wang Keyu said. "No matter what, I'd rather keep pace with those steps than wait to read somebody's memoir in years to come. Would that be possible? I don't want to put Sir Chief Officer in a difficult position."

From the look of innocence, earnestness and anticipation in Xiao Wang's eyes, Qi Jing saw neither complaint nor grievance against him. Number One immediately perked up. "It's no big deal," he said. "I'll try my best. I don't think there'll be any problem."

"I appreciate it," said Staff Officer Wang.

Her face flushing in the hot weather, Xiao Wang unfastened the collar hook of her uniform and used a handkerchief to fan cool air into her shirt. Taking the opportunity to talk to his subordinate, Qi Jing boldly stared at her neckline. The scorching look was as clear as Morse code. Xiao Wang got the message. Despite having lived a life of innocence, this Peking student didn't panic. She just didn't know how to meet the challenge. Hesitating, she tried to find an excuse to escape this small peasant courtyard. She stepped back a little but somehow baulked at retreating further.

Walking her to the door leading out to the street, the Number One chief commander of the 9th Brigade openly held up the dainty face of the literacy instructor and kissed her forcefully and passionately.

Wang Keyu slowly opened her eyes and asked impatiently, "What took you so long?"

CHAPTER 9

CHOOSING THE WRONG YEAR TO BE BORN

The Field Army was ready to cross the Yellow River. The Rear Political Department of the Jin-Ji-Lu-Yu Military District sent a delegation to the 9th Brigade to convey its appreciation. The intention was clear: to bid farewell to the brigade before it went on the expedition.

The show that the Appreciation Delegation put on was *Deep-Seated Hatred*. It was a Qinqiang opera from Shaanxi, now adapted into Hebei *bangzi* to cater to an audience speaking their local dialect. The most popular show of those years was a musical called *The White-Haired Girl*, created by the Yan'an Lu Xun Academy of Fine Arts. *Deep-Seated Hatred* was nearly as famous.

The plot of the opera concerned a poor peasant named Wang Renhou. Along with his family, he had to escape his native, Kuomintang-ruled province of Henan. There, he suffered from oppression and persecution by the reactionary regime and the local despotic landowners. On their way, his son became press-ganged into the Kuomintang Army and his daughter-in-law was raped by the same gang. The humiliation drove her to kill herself with a pair of scissors. The protagonist

Wang Renhou finally arrived in the old liberated area in northern Shaanxi with his daughter and young grandson, Gouwa, literally meaning "Puppy". He and his family regained freedom and started a happy life with honest labour.

Named Liu Chunhu, the young actor who played Puppy was only eleven. He was a peasant boy who had received no school education. But he was a talented actor who understood the part well and played his character without a hint of pretentiousness. When his emotion broke out, he could move the merciless heaven and earth. Puppy looked up to the sky and screamed "Mum ..." with inconsolable grief at the sight of his mother committing suicide. During a rehearsal, his performance brought tears from the old director, then from the actors on stage, who wailed and covered their faces with their hands. The rehearsal had to pause before resuming.

The opera troupe's director claimed without exaggeration, "A leading actor of immense talent like this boy is only seen every fifty or sixty years. If it weren't for the years of continuous warfare, Liu Chunhu, this bed-wetting boy, would dominate the Chinese opera stage in the next sixty years without the worry of being superseded by anyone else." The director sighed with deep emotion when he said to this young actor, "It's a shame you selected the wrong year to come into this world!"

The boy wetted his bed 365 days a year without respite and would always hide his dampened bedding during the day and use it again at night. His habit naturally gave rise to his nickname "Little Pisspot". People gave him that name with the best of intentions, and he always responded with a smile. The nickname became his brand.

The actresses took turns to attend to young Chunhu during his sleep by waking him up to pee. One night, Staff Officer Wang from the brigade's headquarters volunteered to take care of him. The actresses felt her sincerity and were only too glad to entrust the boy to her care. Xiao Wang felt that someone had to lend a compassionate and loving hand to this lone and helpless lad. Wang Keyu had never allowed others to touch her bedsheets, but she now had to open up her "forbidden royal area". Little Chunhu slept on the side of the *kang* bed-stove against the wall while she slept close to the edge. Wang Keyu was careful to take necessary measures by spreading a piece of military oilcloth beneath the bedsheets under Chunhu.

During the night, Staff Officer Wang tried to wake the boy, but no matter how much she tried, he wouldn't open his eyes. She dragged him up, but he laid down again. Xiao Wang shone her torch on him, only to find a scary sight. The manhood of this eleven-year-old was as erect as a flagpole. It was as though he was crouched and ready to receive the relay baton from the previous runner and determined to pass it to the next. But the scene caught Xiao Wang off guard. Pacing up and down by the *kang*, she was at a loss as to how to respond.

"He's holding his pee!" concluded an actress who came and took a close look.

☆

The opera troupe reduced its members to the minimum to perform for the troops on the front. It now comprised only the leading actors and actresses along with the musicians. They had to find the many extras from the locals.

The extras who got selected might not play their roles very well, but their performances were tolerable. However, some who played only the walk-on parts without any lines made a monkey of themselves, resulting in an awkward end to the show. The horse messenger Cao Shui'er, for instance, played the part of a press-ganged conscript. He should have shown submission when a policeman whipped him, but instead, he roared, "How dare you hit me for real?"

And then there was Lao Wang, the brigade's Political

Department mess officer. Though illiterate, he had an impressive air. People good-humouredly called him "Mess Head Wang". Therefore, the troupe selected him to play a county magistrate of the people's government in the revolutionary base. As soon as the protagonist Wang Renhou, his daughter and Puppy arrived in the liberated area, the county magistrate came to see them. The elderly man Wang Renhou dropped to his knees, saying, "You don't have to do this, Lord Magistrate!"

According to the opera's script, the county magistrate should help the elderly refugee up to his feet and say, "Please don't do this, Grandpa. We're all equal here in the revolutionary base. My surname is Li, so you can call me Lao Li in the future."

Nevertheless, the mess officer got confused when he came on the stage. Helping the elderly man up, he said, "Please don't do this, Grandpa. We're all equal here in the revolutionary base. My surname is Li, so you can call me Mess Head Wang in the future!"

He gave the opera's role his real surname. But he was right when he referred to himself as "head" because he was a mess officer anyway.

All the performers on the stage bent over with laughter. However, the audience didn't seem either surprised or perturbed, watching as attentively and quietly as usual, which was perplexing to the troupe. Actually, this was the benefit of performing on a stage in the open air, where the acoustics were not as good as indoors. It was more so when it was windy, as not all the monologues and dialogues could be heard clearly by the audience.

The many flaws in the show didn't seem to affect the publicity efforts. The People's Liberation Army comprised both peasants and "liberated fighters" who had left the forces of the Kuomintang. Both had suffered bitterly from the same oppression and brutality by the reactionary regime and despotic landowners. They had deep empathy for the miseries suffered by the protagonists in the opera *Deep-Seated Hatred*. Accidents, in which someone tried to hurt the actor playing the main villain, occurred often. In one case, a member of the audience levelled his gun and fired a bullet of vengeance at a "local Kuomintang *baojia* head".[1]

The head of the *baojia* narrowly escaped the shot and rushed to the front of the stage and yelled, "Which rascal did it? How can you use a real weapon? Who would dare play a villain in the future?" After the accident, troops had to hand in their bullets and hand grenades before watching *Deep-Seated Hatred*. At the army chief officer's repeated requests, company commanders and platoon leaders had to keep a close eye on their troops. If they found someone unable to restrain his impulse, they would have him carried out by his armpits.

Many Kuomintang POWs who replaced fallen PLA troops without even having the time to change their Kuomintang caps went to the battlefield after watching *The White-Haired Girl* or *Deep-Seated Hatred*. During the short time that elapsed from the start of the show to curtain call, these POWs found their ideological awareness significantly improved. When the others met them the next day, they were already combating heroes.

⁂

The Field Army's Political Department in the Rear telegraphed the Appreciation Delegation, telling it to "end its performing tour and return to Handan as soon as possible".

The short telegraph message upset the delegation leader. He was facing a sensitive and thorny dilemma.

The young actor Liu Chunhu came from a landowning family. The Poor Peasant Association of his home village had submitted a petition to the army for his return. The Political Department had responded that he was a child actor, and it was challenging to find a replacement at short notice. It promised to contact the association after the troupe finished its performing tour. Today's telegraph neither mentioned Liu Chunhu's name nor demanded his return to his native village. But why did it explicitly emphasise the return of every member? Was the department afraid of the boy's escape?

According to documented policies, no family's class status was supposed to be attached to a person's name in their profile if the person was under legal age. Therefore, no one could apply the label "son of a landowning bitch" to young Chunhu. Emboldened by the policy, the delegation leader tried to reassure the boy's parents by saying, "Rest assured. I'll see to it that we return your son to you after this tour."

The veteran delegation leader acted the protagonist Wang Renhou in the opera. But he found it hard to concentrate. So much so that he could barely sing antiphonally with Puppy. Always on his mind was the boy's inevitable return home, and no one had the guts to stand up to the political decision and refuse to let him go. But what could he do to protect him from this "doom"?

The veteran delegation leader mulled over the boy's deliverance. He thought that the Appreciation Delegation's activity had just begun. If it could stay and continue the tour, it would be on the other side of the Yellow River when it finished performing for the entire brigade's troops. Once on the southern side, all the remaining issues between the army and the local authorities would vaporise. Since neither party could get in touch with the other, Little Pisspot would win his freedom.

Someone told the Appreciation Delegation leader in private that Staff Officer Wang had some influence over Number One. He suggested that he ask her to talk the chief officer into telegraphing the Political Department in the Rear to request a delay for the delegation's return to Handan until it completed the entire performing tour in the 9th Brigade. If the department replied with no objection, then there'd be nothing to worry about any more.

The veteran delegation leader thought that Wang Keyu, a literacy instructor, had no direct connection with Qi Jing in terms of their military positions. Furthermore, he considered it impertinent to ask an unmarried young female comrade to do something like this. He was afraid that doing so would be tantamount to insulting her integrity, putting her in an embarrassing position. She might ask him, "Why do you think it appropriate for me to pass on the message to the Number One chief officer?"

To his surprise, Staff Officer Wang readily complied with his request. The young female comrade didn't show the slightest hint of displeasure.

✼

Xiao Wang relayed the delegation leader's request. Number One enthusiastically signalled his agreement. He even complimented the Appreciation Delegation for its genuine commitment to the front-line troops. He added that the opera *Deep-Seated Hatred* was a living textbook for mobilisation before battle and an inspiration that could directly be translated into fighting capability.

Following his train of thought, Wang Keyu said, "You're right! Excuse me, may I trouble you to request the Political Department in the Rear postpone the delegation's return so we can guarantee that everyone in our brigade will get the opportunity to enjoy this opera?"

"It might not be a violation of the army's disciplinary principles if I sent a telegraph in my name asking for a deferment of their return. But–"

"What I'm afraid of is the Chief Officer's 'but'. I couldn't imagine you questioning such a trivial matter!"

"Xiao Wang! We've got two issues to address. The troops would have crossed the Yellow River even if the delegation were to follow their original schedule. The Front Command Post requires that we put rigid restrictions on the number of people crossing the river that would exceed the prescribed manning quota."

"What difference does it make if we cross the Yellow River?" Staff Officer Wang retorted forcefully. "Do we no longer need literary and artistic publicity work? Do our troops no longer need ideological mobilisation?"

"The other issue is the young actor who plays Puppy. His hometown persists in asking for him back. If the delegation put off their return to Handan, we would have to embroil the boy in a tug-of-war, wouldn't we? Xiao Wang, one of your finest qualities is your eagerness to help others. But sometimes things are not as simple or straightforward as you imagine."

Staff Officer Wang chuckled. "Yes, frankly, someone is taking advantage of me. But I have nothing to lose, and indeed it's my pleasure to be used. I like the boy. Otherwise, how could I be so cooperative with them for no reason at all? The veteran delegation leader had some reservations. He would rather hold back his real intent than tell the whole story. I think it's better to have a tacit mutual understanding."

Qi Jing said he followed what she meant. "They know the political fallout, so they must compromise to protect themselves."

"Sir, Chief Officer, don't you think that's a little unfair? They're thinking of my interests rather than protecting themselves. They're trying to prevent me from getting involved too deeply."

It was evident that Xiao Wang's spontaneous remark touched Qi Jing, who took her words as a rebuke as if to say, How selfish you are as a chief officer with a code number!

Sizing up Staff Officer Wang, Number One remained reticent for a long while. He needed to clarify his thinking.

Staff Officer Wang pressed him for an answer. "Can I tell them that the chief officer has agreed to send a telegraph and let them wait for the good news?"

Number One forced a smile. "Xiao Wang, give me some time, please."

"When will you give me the answer then, Chief Officer?"

"You know how swamped I am."

"This matter demands immediate attention. Can't you put other things off?"

"I must at least consult the political commissar."

"And when will that be?"

Xiao Wang's impertinence astonished Qi Jing, who burst into a laugh. "Xiao Wang, oh, Xiao Wang! When a staff officer is talking to her immediate superior, she can't wilfully yell at him as if he were a POW!"

"Oh, my gosh! You mean I've got a communication problem? Please forgive me, sir, Chief Officer!"

"No, no, no! I didn't mean to reprove you. Not at all! Your communication method is like your *guqin*'s open note, which is your distinctive character. It's wonderful! Quite wonderful!"

⁂

The Qi Brigade received the order to cross the Yellow River in secret three days before the Field Army's main force fought their way across it. Its objective was to help the Independent 1st and 2nd Brigades from the local Ji-Lu-Yu Military District on the other side.

It now dawned upon Staff Officer Wang that the Number One chief officer had already made his calculations and arrangements, but had found it inconvenient to disclose them to her. He cleverly took advantage of the time difference created by the 9th Brigade's river-crossing operation ahead of schedule. It turned out that he didn't send the telegraph until the brigade was about to reach the other side. It would be ideal if the Rear Political Department consented to the request, but it would be too late to change things if they rejected it. By then, the Appreciation Delegation had been south of the Yellow River with the 9th Brigade for three days.

The troops on the north bank had been waiting patiently for the order to set sail. The young actor Liu Chunhu had already fallen asleep. He was slumbering when, all of a sudden, he screamed, "Mum!" His voice pierced the silent night and sounded both jarring and terrifying. Staff Officer Wang put her hand over his mouth, lest he might shout again.

Everyone smiled understandingly. The young Chunhu had reached the climax of the opera *Deep-Seated Hatred* in his dream. The mother killed herself with a pair of scissors as she couldn't bear the humiliation of being violated. Only the veteran delegation leader detected the terror and heart-wrenching undertone in his scream, an emotion he had never expressed before during his performances. It wasn't hard to imagine that he was missing his real mother rather than re-enacting the opera's episode. He must have been dreaming of her.

"What did you see in your dream? What did you see in your dream?" asked the opera troupe members one after another.

Young Chunhu sobbed but refused to respond while the troupe members insisted on asking him. The veteran delegation leader stopped them angrily. "You pig-heads! Why do you have to persist in pestering him when you all know the boy's family circumstances?"

It was Young Chunhu, however, who volunteered an answer. "I dreamed of my mum hanging from a common prickly ash tree. But I didn't think she would die because the branch was too thin to bear her weight."

Silence reigned in the dark of night. Only the troupe

members' suppressed sobs were vaguely audible.

"Get ready to embark!" the order came. "Get ready to embark!"

The troops had anticipated fierce fighting while crossing the river and even repeatedly practised plugging leaks from bullet punctures in the boats. But the crossing turned out to be peaceful. They reached the other bank in less than twenty minutes. As soon as they disembarked, the veteran opera troupe leader and members congratulated young Chunhu on his freedom. Staff Officer Wang was even more excited. Reaching out her arms, she gave him a warm hug.

Liu Chunhu had rightly become a PLA soldier and wouldn't be sent back to his native village.

Two months later, a sudden enemy attack took Liu Chunhu's life. He died gloriously as a member of the District and Township Work Team. The veteran troupe leader felt profoundly guilty and perturbed. It was he who had taken the talented young actor from his parents and promised to return him to them. He found the only object young Chunhu had left behind, namely his armlet. Years had passed, and not until the early days of the People's Republic of China was the martyr's armband sent back to his old home.

Printed on the armlet were his name, gender, age, ethnicity, unit, title and birthplace. It was the most authoritative item to prove his official identity as a PLA soldier. A "Glorious Martyr's Relatives" plaque was naturally placed above the door to the house of young Chunhu's parents.

The veteran troupe leader never had the chance to meet young Chunhu's mother. He didn't have the heart to ask, but he eventually made cautious enquiries. Sure enough, what had happened coincided with what the boy had seen in his dream. But even though he didn't believe his mother would hang herself, she had made up her mind to commit suicide, and the common prickly ash tree had lent her a sturdy branch.

CHAPTER 10

AN EIGHTH ROUTE ARMY FEMALE SOLDIER, A EURASIAN COLLARED DOVE AND A CLUMP OF DANDELIONS

After completing its training and consolidation, the Field Army set out from Anyang. They force-marched for five days at a stretch and manoeuvred towards the Yellow River front line, ready to cross to the south and launch the Southeast Shandong Campaign.

The 9th Brigade finally camped at midnight. The troops had braved a rainstorm and their infantry packs were soaked, leaving them no dry clothes to change into. Therefore, they all stripped off, lit numerous corn stalks and toasted their clothes dry while lining up in circles. The licking flames illuminated the night sky, presenting a magnificent spectacle. The female comrades had to tough it out by drying their clothes with their own body temperature.

Wang Keyu had a piece of military oilcloth with which she could have wrapped her clothes. Then, she could have changed into them when the rain stopped. But she had used the tarp to cover her *guqin*, so the downpour drenched her. She was so exhausted that she didn't have the energy to dry her clothes. She set up a makeshift bed by removing a door panel and went to sleep in her underwear. Who cares, she thought. I'll get a good sleep first. There'll be time to put on my clothes when the bugle for fall-in sounds. But unfortunately, she overslept. It was broad daylight when she woke up.

"Gosh! I've unwittingly made too much of a scene!"

It was easy to imagine that the sight of a woman sleeping in a doorway in only her underwear would scare any man who had risen early and happened to pass by. His first instinct might be to tiptoe past the entrance and speed away from the scene. He might even have to pray in silence that no one else would run into him and accuse him of being a peeping Tom. In such circumstances, he would struggle to prove his innocence.

Let's assume that a man appeared, and it was none other than the Number Five chief officer.

Chief of Staff Qi Jing was always the first to get up in the brigade. He would stand in the middle of the parade ground with his hands clasped behind him. As soon as he found any section director or department head absent, he would immediately send for him. Usually, the late arrival would shout, "Sir, this head [or this director] reporting for duty!" The officer who led the morning exercises would respond, "Fall in!" But Qi Jing pretended not to hear the latecomer and ignored him until the end of morning exercises. Since then, no one dared to be late.

This morning, Number Five quite forgot it was his turn to lead morning exercises. In the distance, he caught sight of a woman's underwear and a pair of socks hanging from a pack strap stretched between two small trees. It was like looking out from a watchtower across the sea and spotting a mast sticking into the sky on the horizon. Qi Jing intuitively concluded that he would see a beautiful "ship" emerging. Since it was not far away, he recognised that the female literacy instructor was lying on a door panel in a doorway wearing nothing but a pair of pants.

Behind the chief officer, Cao Shui'er also found something wrong. So, he quickly reminded him, "Sir, Chief Officer! Please wait! Please wait!" He stopped himself abruptly but saw with alarm Number Five continue to walk ahead.

Looking back, Qi Jing also felt surprised at his behaviour at the time, wondering why he had been so impulsive as if he had been practising taking pictures of a nude model while studying photography in Tokyo. His brain went blank. In truth, he had only one thing on his mind: to take a candid photo of her straight away. He mustn't lose any time in taking the picture. He took out the shabby Rolleiflex captured from enemy troops and removed the lens cap.

The female model was lying on her back on the door panel with her arms crossed seemingly to cover her chest. It was evident that she had been soaked in the rain for a long time because her complexion had turned as snow-white as a life-size white marble statue of a human body on display in the doorway of this peasant house. From the angle where his lens pointed, her body appeared Rubenesque and glossy. He could see her bent legs opening like the famous encyclopaedic dictionary *Ci Hai* (*Sea of Words*). Each entry in the dictionary could provide the most authoritative, precise and detailed definitions.

Across the world and throughout history, men have cast their greedy eyes on the photos and paintings of nude women. This behaviour is universally human and also inescapably pernicious. Chief of Staff Qi Jing was one of the few to be absorbed only in the possibilities of photography. He kept his heart and soul as pure and innocent as Adam before tasting the forbidden fruit.

Portraiture had been an intoxicating and yet long-dashed dream in the recesses of his heart. Who would have expected that an opportunity should present itself and make Qi Jing's dream come true in the blink of an eye? He seemed so brave and decisive that he had a hunch that a masterpiece that could become the pinnacle of his artistic achievement was within reach.

There suddenly came a female voice. "How are you?"

The voice was only too familiar. As it was too late to leave, Qi Jing had to return the greeting. He subconsciously hid his camera and worked up enough courage to approach her. It turned out that Xiao Wang had muttered a friendly greeting to someone in her dream.

Feeling emboldened, Qi Jing clicked the shutter. While adjusting the focus, he saw his photographic subject open her eyes wide through the viewfinder. Number Five froze while awkwardly kneeling on one knee as he had no time to straighten up.

"Chief Officer, don't forget to give me some copies once you develop your photos."

This was a reasonable request, but Qi Jing took it as a sarcastic demand in response to an act of wrongdoing. He was at a loss for words and turned around. Facing away from Wang Keyu, he stuttered, "I must apologise, Comrade Xiao Wang. Please put your clothes on first."

Taking down the clothes from the pack strap, Wang Keyu sat on the door panel and started dressing. Her shirt was now quite dry, but not her uniform, which still felt extremely uncomfortable on her body. But how could she go to the parade ground to do morning exercises in her shirt only?

"Chief Officer, please don't forget to give me some copies once you develop them," Xiao Wang repeated.

Number Five knew it would be unwise for him to curse himself and try to explain away his actions since Xiao Wang might continue to harbour suspicion. The only option was to take out the film and hand it to Xiao Wang as it was. Only by doing so could he get her forgiveness. Responding in a matter-of-fact tone, he said, "Xiao Wang, that was an accident. I inadvertently took the photos. I can't develop them without your permission. Now, I'll give the film to you. You own it. I merely pressed the shutter."

Qi Jing opened the back cover of the camera in haste, only to find it contained no film. All his feverous snapping away had been in vain. But this blunder turned into a lifesaver. He almost exclaimed with joy. Mimicking the traditional posture of a surrendering POW, he hoisted the Rolleiflex camera above his head with both hands, showing Xiao Wang the empty compartment.

"Staff Officer Wang, it has no film. You see! You see!"

Film was in extremely short supply during war times. When feeling too embarrassed to turn down someone's request to photograph them, he would hold the Rolleiflex up, press the shutter and say, "Done! I'll give you the picture after I develop it." When the person asked later where the photo was, he would say, "Sorry, I accidentally exposed the film!"

"Ha! I see you've exposed your film again!" Xiao Wang gurgled.

Seeing Staff Officer Wang laughing, the Number Five chief officer suddenly realised that she didn't mind an audacious "poacher" approaching her in the doorway, which meant she didn't take the incident to heart at all. Qi Jing felt a load had been taken off his mind.

The eighteen-year-old female soldier offered up her posture in a purely natural way without following any set rules. One could take a perfect photo of her at any angle and from any distance. No effort to appreciate her artistic and noble human form could add to her beauty. For that matter, no attempt to peep at her with lewd eyes through the viewfinder could tarnish this glittering white marble statue of purity.

Prompted by an impulse, Qi Jing meant to show his talent

for portrait photography. But he messed it up and made an embarrassing scene. He couldn't help but feel his heart thump loudly. But to his surprise, the female literacy instructor was able to transform this excruciating situation into a pleasant conversation with her top supervisor. "I found out that army reporters often grab snapshots," she said, "taking some so-called 'battlefield scenes'. They're quietly accumulating their photographic works. Number Five, remember to keep your camera loaded next time. Then, you won't miss your subject matter."

"You're right! Just think about it, Xiao Wang. I've come up with a title for the 'photo' I've just taken, 'One of the Extempore Shots of the Battlefield Scenes after Thirty Hours of Forced March in a Rainstorm'. How do you think the photos would look in a European or American photography magazine? Frankly, the best-known portrait photographers in the world would be awed by my works, and would feel shamed into burning their own pictures."

"That's true!" Xiao Wang conceded with admiration at this portrait photographer in the army.

"Westerners claim that photographing the human body is an innocent and sacred art. They say that 'to strip women of all their clothes is to immortalise them'. But in reality, they're detaching women from their proper place in society. They even highlight the particular curves and features of the female form. It's simply not true to say that their photographic works are pale and lifeless."

"Let's see after the war ends. Number Five can undoubtedly take the best photos of the human body!"

"No, no, no! I'll never again take pictures of the human body because I've captured the best human image in the compartment of my camera, an image of a gorgeous Eighth Route Army soldier who's fast asleep. I'll keep it intact forever."

"Chief Officer always tries to make me feel happy."

The bugle call sounded for fall-in. The bugler played his

instrument melodiously to gently wake up the troops and villagers who had fallen asleep after a rainstorm.

Number Five said, "OK, it's time for morning exercises."

"I must get the door panel back on its frame. It's made from jujube wood, so it's extremely unwieldy."

"Leave it to me. I can't let you violate the Three Rules of Discipline and Eight Points for Attention."[1] Cao Shui'er took it upon himself to install the door panel for Wang Keyu. He had returned after seeing her getting dressed from a distance. After putting the door panel back in the frame, he, Number Five and Staff Officer Wang ran to the parade ground together.

Silence fell in the residence where Xiao Wang had been sleeping. A Eurasian collared dove was boldly perched by its nest beneath the eaves. It puffed up its wings and shook the residual rainwater off, trying to dry all its feathers from the afterfeathers to the tips. It was drying itself like the Eighth Route Army female soldier had done, only that it took considerably longer for Xiao Wang's outer garments to dry completely.

There was a large clump of dandelions by the door pier. It's safe to say that the dandelions were doing exactly what Xiao Wang had done to deal with the rainstorm. They slowly stood erect after the rainwater had dripped away. Their tongue-like petals spread out quietly and showed their yellow colour, waiting for the white, pompom-like blowballs to come out after a brief period of sunshine later in the day. Then, a puff of breath from a child would send the fluffy tufts of seeds floating into the sky.

A female Eight Route Army soldier, a Eurasian collared dove and a clump of dandelions shared the same space and experience. They all endured a rainstorm and ushered in a morning of fresh air on the vast Ji-Lu Plains.

CHAPTER 11

IN THE NAME OF JIN-JI-LU-YU'S
THIRTY MILLION PEOPLE

As soon as the Qi Brigade crossed the Yellow River, it got into position and participated in blocking the four reorganised Kuomintang divisions that had rushed over from the Shandong battleground to rescue other Kuomintang troops under attack.

According to the scheduled deployment, Wang Keyu led the Rear Political Department's Appreciation Delegation to the front to perform for the troops in their position as soon as possible. The brigade allocated two horse-drawn carts to the delegation to guarantee its speedy arrival. For some reason, they were so late that by the time they arrived the troops had accomplished their mission and evacuated from the position.

The delegation had come to a ferry where the water was shallow enough for its caravan to wade through. The delegation members unexpectedly found the bodies of more than a dozen Kuomintang soldiers lying on the riverbed. The carts would inevitably have to run over them. Wang Keyu immediately jumped off her cart and stopped the caravan. She decided to bypass the ferry and make the crossing upstream.

The troupe members objected that the dead soldiers in the

water were enemy troops. Previously, they might have killed some of our PLA soldiers. It was their karma if our horse-drawn carts rolled over them. We wouldn't be committing any sin.

The veteran delegation leader reminded her, "Staff Officer Wang, our carts won't get bogged down if we cross the river here. If they get mired elsewhere and delay our arrival, then we'd be in big trouble!"

Wang Keyu responded with only a smile. Regardless of the troupe members' objections, she set her mind on giving up the ferry.

Unfortunately, the veteran delegation leader's forewarning came to pass. Everyone rolled up their trousers and waded into the water and crossed with the empty horse-drawn carts. But the carts still got stuck in the silt. The troupe members had to push them, but they wouldn't budge even though they exerted every ounce of strength. They had to dig the silt beneath the wheels with their hands to make progress possible. They finally pushed them ashore with great effort and thanks to a bit of shanty singing.

Because of the miscalculation, they failed to complete the task of performing on the battlefield. As the army's literary and art workers, they considered it a blot on their record if not an act of disgrace. The actors and actresses were all teary-eyed.

Number One sent for Wang Keyu. He chastised her, "The Rear Political Department's Appreciation Delegation came to our Ninth Brigade on behalf of all the officers and fighters of the Jin-Ji-Lu-Yu Military District in the Rear as well as the thirty million people in the Jin-Ji-Lu-Yu Liberated Area. The performance in the position, a grave task of political significance, fell through because of your stubborn insistence in your own opinion." He told her bluntly that the brigade leadership had decided to give her a warning and make it public throughout the brigade. "I've proposed disciplinary action," he concluded. "If you think I've wronged you, please vent your anger on me."

"I've been expecting disciplinary action," Wang Keyu responded calmly. "As for the severity, that's up to you, the chief officer, to decide. I've no problem with that. Besides, a disciplinary warning is the least severe of all punitive measures."

"It's more important for you to learn a lesson from this incident. You're not a *guqin*-playing girl any more. You're a staff officer at the rank of company leader in the Ninth Brigade headquarters. Everything you say and do must be in keeping with the moral character required of a revolutionary army man or woman."

"Yes sir! Chief Commander, I know you reprimand me in the name of the thirty million people in the Jin-Ji-Lu-Yu Liberated Area. That is a heavy burden to carry, and I'll take the lesson to heart. But I won't hide my real thoughts. It may take time for me to apply the lesson in practice."

Qi Jing was seething. "I am empathetic. I know how it feels to walk barefoot on dead bodies. But why not sit on a cart so that you didn't have to be so horrified?"

"It wasn't about horror, which is something I can endure. I don't see the difference between walking barefoot on corpses or running over them on a horse-drawn cart. Faced with a similar situation in future, I'm likely to repeat my mistake."

"You mean you'll look for another place to cross the river next time you encounter the same situation, don't you?"

"I don't think such a situation will arise again," Wang Keyu replied. They both felt embarrassed.

"Sir Chief Officer, will you continue to give me assignments in the future?" asked Xiao Wang tentatively.

"It depends," responded Qi Jing with a long face.

It was evident that Number One was only trying to scare Xiao Wang. The next morning, he assigned her a new task. He made her director of the Prisoners of War Collecting Post of the Front Command Post and told her to assume her responsibilities right away.

On the night of 30 June 1947, the 1st, 2nd and 3rd Columns of the Field Army formed the first echelon and, under cover of a heavy artillery barrage, fought their way across the Yellow River using eight ferries between Zhangqiu Town and the village of Linfuji in Fu County, Shandong Province. In one swoop, they broke through the Kuomintang Army's Yellow River defence line extending 150 kilometres. It took the columns less than fifteen minutes to quietly get to the south bank where the river was at its widest and only five minutes at its narrowest.

As the prelude to the shift from strategic defence to strategic attack, the Southwest Shandong Campaign began.

In only a week, large numbers of prisoners streamed to the POW Collecting Post under escort from PLA soldiers. Meanwhile, the Front Command Post transferred many non-combatants to the collecting post as guards. The members of the Rear Political Department's Appreciation Delegation became the mainstay of the Fourth Collecting Post. As able male members worked as stretcher-bearers elsewhere, those who remained in post were females and young comrades. Fortunately, they had the bodyguard squad with them.

Many of the captured Kuomintang officers and soldiers had concealed precious metal jewellery. Having risked life and endured despair in wartime, these valuables were the only items to buttress their belief in survival. But they also became a cause of dispute among the POWs. In the worst scenario, they would blame the managerial staff for stealing them, thus throwing the collecting post into turmoil.

Wang Keyu decided to take the initiative to restore equilibrium. She wanted the valuables registered in order to know how much each individual possessed and thereby prevent any problems from occurring. The captured Kuomintang troops fell in on the threshing ground, each standing three metres from the next person. That way, they could bear witness to each other without knowing their treasures. Registration took place in the open while each individual's secret remained confidential. As long as they registered their property, they could entrust them to the collecting post for keeping, or they could keep them themselves. Each individual was supposed to be responsible for their belongings.

Even though Staff Officer Wang was clearly acting with sincerity, the POWs could not shake off their doubts and misgivings. To their mind, registration was tantamount to confiscation, and they wouldn't take it lying down. Before Staff Officer Wang finished, they began to act. They secretly dropped their gold and silver jewellery to the ground and pressed them into the dirt by twisting their heels. After burying their small pieces of jewellery, they gently stamped the spot level. Then, they looked up and around, pretending that nothing had happened.

A woman's voice is not always well suited to shouting orders. Besides, Xiao Wang had never practised doing so in front of a crowd. That majestic, high-pitched and somewhat eccentric tone of voice was not something anyone could grasp. Like a Peking girl playing house, the staff officer gave the ranks her orders. "Listen, the first three rows. Attention! Move forward ten steps! At ease!"

"Listen, the three rows in the rear! Attention! About turn! Move forward ten steps. About turn! At ease!"

"Liberated Fighter Brothers! I moved you around like this because I want to show you my good intentions. If I harboured bad intentions, I might have insisted on observers being sent for and having things dug up from the ground like harvesting potatoes. We'd certainly have an excellent yield. You could only watch on helplessly. Nothing excavated would have anything to do with you because they had grown from this soil. What do you think, everyone?"

There was quite a boisterous commotion in the panicked crowd. Staff Officer Wang shouted as sternly as she could, "Quiet! Quiet! Quiet!"

Her "ten-steps-forward" order was so abrupt that the POWs didn't have time to retrieve what they had hidden under their feet. Only ten steps forward wiped out everything they had painstakingly accumulated and thought they could trade for money. Then, they heard the director of the collecting post shout her orders again. "Listen, those in the first three rows! Attention! About turn! Move forward ten steps! At ease!"

"Listen, those in the back three rows! Attention! Move forward ten steps! At ease!"

"Please listen! You've now returned to where you were. You've got three minutes to look for what you think you've lost under your feet."

Most of them hurriedly bent down and dug their precious jewellery out of the soil with their fingers and expressed delight after regaining what they thought they had lost.

"Now, the registration of valuables begins," Staff Officer Wang declared in a raised voice.

⁕★⁕

Some of the POWs had "been liberated" twice or even three times in their military career and had become extremely cunning. Seeing that Wang Keyu was young, they tried to tease her, although showing her outward respect by starting each conversation with a "Ma'am".

"Ma'am," one said, "this bowl must be a relic from the Qing [which also means "clean"], so it barely holds any food. Please give me some more!"

Others complained about the food. "Ma'am, you've mixed too many sweet potatoes into the millet congee. It fills us up too quickly. Please add some more!"

As soon as she added more food, they gulped it down and beat their containers with their chopsticks. A wave of clanking protests broke out. Their rations soon ran out, leaving only two basins of food covered with white kitchen cloths. They were meant for the staff and guards. A staff member intended to inform the POWs, but Staff Officer Wang stopped her. She lifted the white cloths and shouted, "Come in squads in an orderly fashion to get seconds!"

As might be expected, the staff members and guards of the Fourth POW Collecting Post had to go hungry at lunch because it was impossible to rekindle the fire and cook another meal for them.

When suppertime came, the farce repeated itself. The same group of POWs demanded more food by clanking their utensils. Some post-staffers suggested they conceal the food meant for themselves and the guards from the POWs, but Staff Officer Wang disagreed. "All come up in squads to get your extra food!" she called loudly.

One particular "liberated fighter" cast an inconspicuous but authoritative look at the other POWs. They immediately stopped beating their utensils and quit clamouring. He came to be known later as a major, a vice regiment commander of the Kuomintang troops. At present, he passed as a soldier first class among the POWs. He reprimanded his subordinates by saying, "A pretty female Communist sacrifices her meal for you and goes hungry herself. In which collecting post could you find a merciful director like her? Now you're pushing a woman around for fun. But when they switch her out and send a bunch of old-hand political workers in her place, you'll have 'better' days to enjoy!"

After that, there were no more demands for extra food.

The Front Command Post dispatched a war correspondent to interview Wang Keyu. He asked her how she had managed to solve the knotty and intractable problems. He said their interview would soon appear in the *Newsletter on Political Work* published by the Field Army Political Department to share her valuable experience with others.

Not knowing whether to cry or laugh, Wang Keyu said, "To share my valuable experience, you'd better tell me what it is first!"

The *Newsletter on Political Work* article carrying the interview reached all front-line troops the next day with a generally positive reception. Some people were critical, however, accusing the correspondent of being a Kelikong – the transliteration of Kirkun, a journalist in the Russian play *The Front*. The character was good at gaining fame by fabricating news.

This dissenting opinion argued that giving food to POWs at the expense of post-staffers was an act of capitulation. Can you really go to the front on an empty stomach when you receive the order to fight?

CHAPTER 12

SPRING FLOODS ON THE YELLOW RIVER

The Qi Brigade suddenly received an order to cross the Yellow River and return north. They were responsible for escorting the non-combatants – comprising wounded soldiers, POWs and civilian stretcher teams – across the river while the troops brought up the rear.

People whispered because they couldn't understand the U-turn. In less than a month after fighting their way across the Yellow River, the Field Army prevailed in the Southwest Shandong Campaign by wiping out nine and a half Kuomintang brigades of more than 60,000 troops, thus opening up a broad path for the army's foray into the Dabie Mountains. The CPC Central Committee had issued an order of commendation of the Field Army to the entire PLA. So why, they asked, do we have to cross the river and return north in such a favourable situation?

This seemingly irrational decision naturally led people to think that the overall situation had turned for the worse. Panic seized the troops and civilians at the Yellow River Ferry. There were only five boats, each with a capacity of under a hundred people. It would take the brigade forever to cross the river.

Some local government workers began to fight for the boats regardless of military control, wielding their punt poles to hit people at random. One strike would sweep several into the water. Without intervention, the ferry would soon become a place of anarchy.

Number One chief officer took the carbine rifle from a bodyguard and fired three shots into the sky.

A group of military policemen hopped onto the ferries and drove all the people off. The front-supporting militiamen, who had been pushing and shoving with the soldiers as they were reluctant to give in, had to leave the boats after hearing the warning gunshots. Some defiant militiamen refused to let go of the sides of the boats they were holding tight. The soldiers rushed over and curtly pounded their hands with the butts of their rifles. One after another, the militiamen fell overboard, floundering in the water. The boats soon became empty.

Battalion and company commanders were too junior in rank to have access to the details of the order. They didn't have a clear understanding of the retreat to the north side of the river. Crowding around the brigade commanders, they demanded an explanation. They were so frustrated that some spoke sharply. Qi Jing, however, didn't get angry. He repeated, "Everyone knows as much as I do. And what I, the Number One officer, don't know, you don't either."

One of the more glib-tongued men said, "I presume that there's only one reasonable explanation. Our Ninth Brigade received the order to launch a diversionary attack against the enemy. So, we're supposed to put on an act for the enemy troops. Of course, we must act seriously and make the enemy believe we mean it. But we can never be too careful."

Upon hearing these words, Qi Jing couldn't help laughing, which betrayed the order's secret message. The officers were surprised at first but soon realised the unwitting disclosure. They also laughed in his wake.

"We must keep our confidentiality agreements," Qi Jing warned. "Whoever dares defy them will come to no good."

⚝

Brigade Headquarters' Staff Officer Wang Keyu was also ranked too low to hear the briefings. She thought the situation was grave. She could visualise the horrible sight of the ferry being bombarded by waves of enemy bombers. She suggested assembling all the front-supporting female civilian stretcher team members on the first boat to cross the river. The Ferry Command Post gave her its consent.

The female stretcher-bearers saw an army woman jump onto the boat, raise both her hands and declare loudly, "I'm Staff Officer Wang from the Brigade headquarters. The Ferry Command Post has decided to send the female civilian stretcher team members across the river first. Let's get on this boat, sisters! Everyone, no matter which district you're from!"

The civilian women, numbering about a hundred, vied with one another to embark. They packed the boat like matches in a box, with no space for a single extra stick.

"I'm the captain," Staff Officer Wang called out. "Everyone must obey my command. I don't want to scare you, but we can't guarantee plain sailing as the water is so choppy. As you're all wearing long-sleeved shirts and trousers, you'd get pulled under the water by their weight very quickly if the boat capsizes. So, I request that you take off your clothes now!"

She had hardly finished speaking when a commotion broke out. All the women yelled angrily in unison, "No, we won't! We won't! We won't!"

"What wrong have we done to deserve such punishment?"

"You may just as well push us into the river!"

"Just shoot and kill us all!"

Staff Officer Wang explained anxiously, "It's not that I'm

being dogmatic. Rescuers wouldn't be able to drag you out of the water dressed like that. Take them off if you want to stand a chance of survival!"

"Comrade Wang," someone asked tentatively, "will you be escorting us across the river?"

"That goes without saying. Of course!"

"You'll see us off as you stand by the river waving goodbye to us, right?"

"No, no, no! I'm going on this boat, too. I'll return when I get you all to the other side."

"Staff Officer Wang, you want to give yourself a ray of hope, don't you?"

This question reminded her that, as captain, she hadn't thought of leading by example. If I don't take the lead in taking off my clothes, she said to herself, how can I expect to persuade these women? She fell silent and started unbuttoning her clothes. She took off her uniform, starting with her outer garment and then moving on to her trousers and shirt, leaving only her underwear on her body. She then folded each piece as stipulated in the PLA's Routine Service Regulations and placed them on the deck.

An unimaginable scene presented itself to the view of the flabbergasted female civilian stretcher-bearers on the boat. At this moment, a composed-looking Wang Keyu stood on the bow in only her underwear.

Wang Keyu's unusually bold act not only shocked the female civilian stretcher-bearers but also profoundly moved them. As a staff officer from the Brigade headquarters and a female soldier of a regular army, she gave no regard to her reputation as a virgin and was even ready to sacrifice her young life. All the other women on the boat couldn't help asking themselves silently, What's she doing this for?

Initially, only one or two resolved to take off their clothes. Then a few more followed suit. Those women in the middle of the group could still be shielded from public view. However, following Staff Officer Wang's entreaty, the number of women getting undressed gradually increased, their semi-naked bodies now in the full public glare. No one knows how many eyes of the troops and civilians at the Yellow River Ferry were focused on this boat.

Only in the chaos of a major war could a hundred women decide to display themselves on a boat dressed just in their underwear. How could anyone in peacetime have the opportunity to witness such a sight? Its backdrop was not a meandering stream, not a gurgling mountain spring, but a vast, misty river with its surface connecting the horizon.

The troops of the 9th Brigade lined up in several square formations and sat by the river to wait to board the other boats. Suddenly, someone screamed, "Look there!" The troops stood up at once and, craning their necks, peered in the direction of the women's boat. Commanders of various levels came out to keep the troops in order. "Be quiet, everyone!" they said. "Sit down. We must maintain discipline!" Silence finally befell the ferry. A few persistent individuals stole some greedy glances at the women's boat while squirming their necks as if their collars were giving them discomfort.

Many civilians from poorly managed local government units left their ranks and crowded around the big boat from both sides. Some even waded into the water with their trousers rolled up. They tiptoed and threw their eyes at the bow. The civilian women tried to dodge the men but found nowhere to hide. Where could they go anyway?

In the African savannah, zebras stand in a circle with their buttocks facing outwards when confronted with a pride of lions. They kick their hind legs so that the lions can't get to them. The women on the boat adopted a similar stratagem of defence. They had to adopt the somewhat less effective tactic of turning around and offering their backs to their ogling "spectators".

The first boat suddenly became a "matriarchal community". No one else could any longer find an adequate reason to board it. Wang Keyu had to shout out to communicate with those on the bank so that the Ferry Command Post's liaison could relay her requests. When everything was ready, she should have got off the boat to report to the Command Post. But if she had put on her clothes and disembarked, the other women would have become suspicious and panicky. They might even have scattered and refused to come back. Therefore, she stood to the starboard and shouted to the liaison, "Hey! Please report to the Command Post that the leading boat is ready. And then let us know if we can set sail."

A full hour had passed, and there was still no order for the boat's departure.

The prolonged delay dissipated the initial panic and fear. In its place was joyous chitchat and laughter.

A female civilian stretcher-bearer shouted, "Look, Comrade Wang! The scoundrels are all gone!"

Only then did everyone notice that the crowd around the ferryboat was retreating as their excitement quickly gave way to boredom.

The women onboard laughed playfully. "Thinking about it, how many men or women haven't seen a naked body of the opposite sex? Only that they're lucky this time to see a hundred of us barely dressed and crammed here together. Who's so blessed to have seen such a spectacle before? But it won't take long for them to get bored."

"Well put, aunties!" Wang Keyu responded. "A long time ago, humans lived by hunting collectively. They never knew what clothes were. They were accustomed to seeing each other naked. They would never have thought to gawp like them."

"I heard that the only difference between humans and animals is that animals don't wear clothes because they have no sense of shame. The way we behave, are we going to become animals?" objected someone.

"Humans began to wear clothes to keep themselves warm instead of covering up their embarrassment," Wang Keyu explained. "It's wrong to claim that the sense of shame is derived from nudity. On the contrary, humans only began to feel shy when they started wearing clothes. Since we started to wrap ourselves up, we've felt bashful when we undress."

When they first embarked, the women had already noticed Staff Officer Wang's beauty. Now that they had more time, they discovered something beyond her pretty face. It was her curvy body. A few bold ones stood by Staff Office Wang's side, wanting to show off their figures like birds in the forest flaunting their gorgeous plumes to their peers.

"The breasts are gold on a virgin and silver on a married woman, while a mother's breasts resemble those of a female dog."

Early marriage was prevalent in the region. Most of the female stretcher-bearers had one or two children. They knew they were no match for Staff Officer Wang's impeccable bosom. They thought it was right and proper for their breasts to shrink as the years went by. They would never try to keep them in "shapes as precious as gold" by feeding their babies with millet congee instead of breast milk.

Rural women in northern China didn't have to work too hard in the open fields, thus avoiding extra ultraviolet rays. Yet, they could still catch men's attention with their slightly dusky and rosy complexion. But the difference was stark when they stood next to Staff Officer Wang: they would look coarse and dull compared with her delicate skin.

Staff Officer Wang said with modesty, "I envy you for your light coffee-toned skin, which is associated worldwide with the colour of good health. Wealthy families' young women and college students in big cities wear sunglasses and get tanned by basking in the sun for a few hours. It's the colour you have that they yearn for."

One young woman became incredibly excited. Clasping Wang Keyu by the shoulders, she said, "Comrade Wang, I feel I'm dreaming. I felt rather shy when so many men were watching us just now. Well, I'm now as bold as brass! So much so that I can stand on the bow in their full view. It's pretty scary to think of it, but how come I've become so audacious?"

Another young woman came up to Wang Keyu and said, "Sister Wang, I feel the same. When you ordered us to undress, I cried and screamed the loudest. I even threatened suicide. But in the blink of an eye, everything was turned upside down. Now I wish I could be naked forever!"

Wang Keyu was pleasantly surprised. When they first got on the boat, she found it hard to communicate with these female stretcher-bearers, let alone enjoy a close relationship with them. She was aware that there was nothing different between her and them except for their sagging breasts brought about by mother-hood. She enthusiastically explained to them, "Humans wore animal hides about a hundred and seventy thousand years ago, but it has been at least four million years since the evolution of Homo erectus. In comparison, humans have been wearing clothes for only a few days, or in the blink of an eye, as you put it. It's not surprising that we modern people can easily recollect the unwrapped and unrestrained primitive past."

CHAPTER 13

THE SPRING FLOODS RETURN IN SUMMER

Qi Jing stood at the Command Post's tent entrance, following the leading boat's passage through a pair of binoculars. Suddenly, a large assembly of scantily clad female bodies appeared in sight. Number One immediately lowered his powerful Japanese binoculars because he found it inappropriate to keep looking.

The sight of a large assembly of women dressed only in underwear intensified the visual impact and accelerated Qi Jing's heartbeat. He could sense that a disaster was imminent as they were in the middle of the Yellow River's summer flood season. Qi Jing had meant to allow the boat to set sail but now he faltered. He ordered the liaison to tell Staff Officer Wang not to leave without the Command Post's order.

The POW Collecting Corps leader came to tell Number One that Counsellor Guo requested an interview with him once again. Counsellor Guo had worked in the Nationalist government's Bureau of Investigation and Statistics in Nanjing. Before his dispatch to the Ji-Lu-Yu front line to supervise Kuomintang military operations, he had retired due to old age with the rank of colonel. His capture made him the most senior and information-valuable POW. He had repeatedly requested an interview, and with great earnestness. Qi Jing finally gave his consent.

Qi Jing met the counsellor in the shade of a small grove. They sat face to face, each on a small folding stool, with a publicity officer taking minutes to one side. Scattered in the woods were bodyguards. The appearance of so much female flesh shocked everyone at the Yellow River Ferry, including the POW Collecting Post's Kuomintang officers and soldiers. Counsellor Guo brought up the subject before the interview with the commander of the 9th Brigade.

Pointing at the ferryboat in the distance, Counsellor Guo commented, "I fully understand why they strip the women of their clothes to get them across the river. It might save many lives in case of a disaster." Seeing Qi Jing nodding, he added, "The idea is very considerate. It's very kind-hearted of you, Brigade Commander!"

"A staff officer suggested this idea, and I gave my approval."

"This scene reminds me of a section of the Yellow River in Ningxia Province. The annual floods in the third lunar month coincide with the Plum Blossom Flood Season. I fear there may be a Blossom Season Flood at the ferry even though we are in the seventh month. What do you think?"

Although not a fan of Counsellor Guo's pedantic tone, Qi Jing still responded politely, "I don't think so. But I will make sure that there are no mistakes in our preparation."

The counsellor chuckled enigmatically. "I hope so, too! But as I observed humbly, I discovered something. I'm not sure if I could confide it to you."

"Since we're meeting here, we can speak frankly about anything."

"Then, I'll show off my knowledge in front of you, the brigade commander. The Nanjing side has concluded that the Communist Army is not in a position to fight on at present. It was about to flee across the Yellow River to have a strategic respite. The Kuomintang Air Force has detected the Communist Army's concentration at several ferry crossing points along the Yellow River, which confirms the accuracy of Nanjing's judgment."

Qi Jing responded in the same unhurried tone, "Now that you're at the Yellow River Ferry, Sir Counsellor is seeing with your own eyes my brigade crossing over to the far bank in the north. I must say, your observation further confirms Nanjing's brilliant judgment."

A sneer flitting over his face, Counsellor Gao said arrogantly, "Brigade Commander, your little trick is enough to fool the Defence Department in Nanjing. Unfortunately, you have me, an old dog, as your opponent. I can say with certainty that you've received the order to feign military activity. You give a panicky appearance to create the false impression that you're retreating to the north. Your real purpose is to guarantee the swiftness of the strategic move into the Dabie Mountains. Brigade Commander, please answer with either a yes or no, would you?"

Qi Jing felt as if a martial arts master had probed his vital point with his finger. He nearly fainted. To mask his panic and confusion, he broke into an exaggerated laugh and responded, "Could you please specify what's made you see through my move?"

"Common sense teaches us that it's imperative to preserve an army's principal force. But you put all the female civilian stretcher-bearers on the first boat. OK, that'd be fine if you ordered them to leave. But you made them wait ten minutes without setting sail! Then, a further thirty minutes passed without any movement! Now, nearly two hours have elapsed, and you've still taken no action! What tricks are you up to by such procrastination, Brigade Commander? I think you know the real reason."

"I'll go crazy if we don't set sail."

Qi Jing received a note from Wang Keyu with neither title nor signature on it. He thought, how could a staff officer be so rude to her superior? Xiao Wang must be crazy! Sitting opposite Counsellor Guo, Qi Jing had to be careful not to lose his temper. He forced a smile at the counsellor and put the note away.

"So, shall we call it a day?" Counsellor Guo asked.

"No! Since Mr Guo exposed my disguised stratagem, I'd like to learn more."

"I'm flattered! Your excellency even used the word 'stratagem'. As I understand it, the term 'strategy' first appeared in a military treatise attributed to Byzantine Emperor Maurice in the late sixteenth century. Both 'stratagem' and 'strategy' come from the same Greek etymological root. In those days, they conveyed no derogatory meaning. Sir Brigade Commander is in charge of feinting a retreat, an essential part of the Field Army's strategic operations. I'm not in a position to make improper comments."

"It's worth discussing now. Sir, you refute Nanjing's judgment and think that our troops are unable to fight any more. But you simultaneously conclude that we're feinting a retreat to the north. Don't you think your logic is self-contradictory?"

"No! I disagree with their judgment that the Communist Army is unable to fight any longer."

"Well, the PLA has never had much combat capabilities in your assessment."

Counsellor Guo waved his hand in disapproval, saying, "I'm neither a political nor a publicity worker, so I'm not interested in arguing with you. Please listen while I crunch some numbers. In the month of your crossing the Yellow River to the south, you've suffered thirteen thousand casualties. You're having difficulty finding recruits. So you need to replace the losses of men with POWs. This requires brainwashing them first, but you don't have the time. Our information shows that you've consumed too much ammunition, and you've run out of artillery shells. There's only a billion fiat-money[1] left to finance the mighty Field Army..."

Qi Jing's heart skipped another beat. This old chap is pretty sharp, he thought. He hasn't been here long, so how did he get these vital strategic secrets from us? It shows we must have a major leak in our department in charge of confidential information.

To cover up his panic, Qi Jing cut the counsellor short. "Let me make it clear to you. In short, like a beast at bay, our troops are heading to our doom whether we march south or have to flee north. The only option for us is to raise a white flag and surrender to Chairman Chiang."

"No, no! Please pardon me, Brigade Commander! I was merely relating the facts and didn't mean the least disrespect. What I meant to highlight is your army's strategic courage and resourcefulness. You're determined to fight till your last breath by throwing the ultimate cross punch powerful enough to knock the opponent to the ground." Counsellor Guo finished with a cunning smile while staring straight into Qi Jing's eyes. "My independent observation isn't far from reality, is it?"

"Your Excellency has a rich imagination."

"The only thing that still bothers me is I can't determine where the punch of Yan'an will fall. Brigade Commander, are you going to dream the same old dream of the E-Yu-Wan Soviet?"[2]

This old intelligence buff could even pinpoint the Jin-Ji-Lu-Yu Field Army's purpose of reaching our destination, the Dabie Mountains! Qi Jing flannelled and showed his desire to end the conversation.

But Counsellor Guo took no heed and continued, "If you've got the chewing power, so to speak, and can take the Dabie

Mountains with one bite, you can threaten Nanjing in the east, grasp Wuhan in the west, check the Yangtze River in the south and control the Central Plains in the north. This strategic manoeuvre would push the Nationalist military defence line to the Yangtze from the Yellow River. But I have to give you a warning, which you may think is nonsense: have you heard of the proverb, 'Don't let others snore by the side of your couch'?"

"Let me respond with my own adage: 'There's no return for an arrow that has left the bow.'"

"Going five hundred kilometres deep in the opponent's strategic position doesn't make militaristic sense. You can't afford to bear the historical cost. If your army fails, you'll have to say goodbye to the Central Plains and return to your guerrilla warfare in the Taihang Mountains."

"It's true, not all strategic decisions that appear wise at the planning stage make sense on the battleground. It all depends on the will and cerebral abilities of the front-line commanders."

"I know the front-line commanders you've mentioned. In fact, I genuinely admire that one-eyed general, the commander-in-chief of the Jin-Ji-Lu-Yu Field Army. He adamantly refused to use anaesthesia during the operation to remove his necrotic eyeball for fear that it might affect his cranial nerve. He implored the doctors, 'As a soldier, I need not only immense willpower but also sound and sharp mental reasoning.'"

Following the thread of the counsellor's monologue, Qi Jing added, "The operation was a success, and he didn't cry out in pain. He told the doctors how he endured the experience, that is, counting the precise number of incisions, altogether seventy-two, which impressed the German doctor. He commented, 'You're no ordinary Chinese officer. You're a talking steel plate.'"

The old counsellor abruptly changed topic. "Sir, Chief Officer! Modern warfare requires the coordination of large troop formations and the consumption and attrition of materials. It isn't easy to win a war with willpower and intelligence alone."

"I believe in Carl von Clausewitz's motto, 'The material causes and effects are nothing but knife handles, whereas the spiritual causes and effects are precious metals and sharp blades.'"

The liaison staff officer went up to Qi Jing and said, "Sir, Chief Officer, look! They're setting sail!"

Sure enough, the leading boat was slowly leaving the shore. Qi Jing was seething: this Wang Keyu had taken personal command in defiance of all disciplines and regulations! He meant to send Cao Shui'er to stop her but suppressed the urge. Hanging his head, he fell silent, asking himself, What reason do I have not to allow her to leave? There's no reason at all. According to the original plan, all non-combatants were to be transported first to the north bank. We can't delay any longer.

Counsellor Guo rose to say goodbye. "Sir Brigade Commander, I've got a suggestion. Would you mind my–?"

"Please go ahead," said Qi Jing, who wanted to see him leave as soon as possible.

"This boat is severely overloaded. I'm afraid it may capsize. There're some well-trained frogmen among the Nationalist POWs. Their unique skills are at your disposal should the need arise."

Number One chief commander rewarded Counsellor Guo with a friendly handshake. "It may not be appropriate for a POW like you to give a suggestion, but I must thank you. We can consider enlisting their help in case of mishap."

After seeing his guest off, Qi Jing sent for the Bodyguard Company commander and said to him in a suppressed voice, "You are authorised to take drastic measures, that is, shoot to kill him as soon as you find him trying to flee!"

Trotting back to the POW Collecting Post, the Bodyguard

Company commander pondered the failure of the chief officer to say anything about what measures should be deployed to prevent him from running away. What does he mean? He intuitively felt that the commander wanted the counsellor to run so that he could have an excuse to shoot him.

Old Counsellor Guo called in around him all the imprisoned Kuomintang officials of the rank of major or colonel. "From now on," he warned them, "you must be extremely cautious about what you do and say. Raise your hands to get permission even when you need to pee. One careless move would invite the 'smiling' greetings of their submachine guns. Each bullet could be fatal."

Despite being under close watch, this retired counsellor from the Bureau of Investigation and Statistics of the Nationalist Department of Defence had escaped the POW Collecting Post.

Not until the conclusion of the Jinan Campaign in September the following year did the PLA learn from secret documents seized from the enemy that Counsellor Guo had committed suicide the same night of his flight.

After he fled the Yellow River Ferry, this aged professional army man arrived at a Kuomintang Army garrison. There, he sent an urgent telegram directly to Nanjing. He soon received a return telegram to the effect that the Commie Army was fleeing south in disorder after failing to cross over to the north bank of the Yellow River. Various intelligence sources had confirmed the information. Therefore, Sir Counsellor didn't have to bother to brief us on what he knew. Holding the telegram in his quivering hands, this old counsellor read it, "The Communist army has fled south in disorder after failing to cross over to the north." He chuckled, "This is your intelligence? How ridiculous!"

The garrison division commander offered a few comforting words to Counsellor Guo, said goodbye and stepped out. He had just walked into the yard when he heard a thump coming from the office. He sensed that something was amiss and turned around, only to see blood streaming from the gap under the door. It flowed over the smooth bluestone and seeped into the lawn. The dead counsellor was lying on the tiled floor. His corpse, when turned over, had a dagger planted into the chest. It was an American military dagger used for peeling fruit. It had a dull spine and a sharp, double-edged tip, which made it easy to pierce flesh. The hilt had an anti-slip groove, which showed how the old intelligence officer must have used every ounce of his strength when pushing the knife into his heart.

It was the first time Staff Officer Wang had carried out a mission by herself. She was highly energised and went all out, seeing to it that the boat crossed the Yellow River at maximum speed. To her, getting the civilian women across was the sole priority, no matter whether it was a decoy run or a real mission. She took it upon herself to ensure that the women reached the other side safe and sound without accident.

With a vigorous wave of her hand, she ordered the old boatman, "No more waiting! No more waiting! Let's go!"

Her order startled the dozing boatman, who sprang up and shouted as he usually did, "Every man, old and young, we're setting sail." It didn't even cross his mind that he was the only man on the boat.

The colossal boat left the shore with a slow creaking sound. When permission to head out was granted after a long delay, everyone aboard was beside herself with joy. They waved goodbye to those on land. As they watched the boatful of women with astonishment, the army's militia stretcher team members felt an ominous chill creep down their spines. "Oh my God!" they said. "Our poor 'Women's Salvation Association'!"

People didn't know how to describe these women. Terms such as "Oh, our sisters", "Oh, our relatives" and "Oh, our women compatriots" were all strange to them. "Women's Salvation Association" was a well-known term during the War of Resistance Against Japanese Aggression. Though outdated, it was the only practical appellation they thought fit to address this group.

A gust of wind blew in and swept the bow up high. Panicked, the old boatman put all his weight on the tiller and shouted to the women, "Kneel! Kneel! Pray to heaven for mercy! Pray to heaven for mercy!"

The waves kept tossing the boat up and down. The women crowded to the port side one moment and to the starboard side the next. They might have been expected to shout and cry with fear. But not now! Accustomed to being undressed, they were in a dreamlike state, oblivious to the peril they were facing. Mixed with the flashing surges were their unnatural and uncontrollable bursts of joyous laughter.

It was precisely like an auntie winnowing a huge pan of soybeans. Usually, she would try to separate the pods and stalks from the heavier beans with the help of the wind. Today, however, she used too much strength and threw the entire contents out. The boatful of women was tossed into the sky. One after another female body drifted down under the sun like a flock of swallows flitting freely beneath the clouds in the advent of imminent rain...

CHAPTER 14

A Horse with the Navigational Value of a Battlefield Map

Qi Jing couldn't eat or sleep for days. He was noticeably emaciated. His thoughts flashed back repeatedly to the brigade's CPC Committee meeting, where the majority had decided to transfer Wang Keyu to Handan instead of disciplining her. There wouldn't have been so many deaths if he had allowed the transfer to go ahead. He should never have argued so vehemently for keeping her. By taking a stand, he had almost sent her on the path to her death.

The veteran political commissar admonished Qi Jing. "As you're so emotional and sentimental, can the Qi Brigade be ready for combat?"

The horse messenger Cao Shui'er got a special mission: looking for Staff Officer Wang Keyu along the Yellow River, taking Tanzao with him. He had to find her dead or alive. Qi Jing asked him to take Staff Officer Wang's *guqin* with him so that he might plunge it into the river with a rock attached in case he failed to find her. Xiao Wang couldn't do without that Song dynasty musical instrument in the other world.

The POW Collecting Post formed a team of frogmen to help rescue the victims of the capsized boat. Someone from the Ferry

Command Post said to them at the mobilisation meeting, "We hope you will all deploy your ability and skills and try your utmost to rescue the victims. The women are mostly in their late teens. Whomever you save, you can claim as your woman!" The speaker was joking, of course. None of the POW frogmen would ever dream of the "Communist Army" keeping its promise on this particular matter. Motivated by the Buddhist belief that "saving a life was better than building a seven-storey pagoda" and equipped with the professional skill they had mastered through many hours of training, the team of a hundred or so frogmen pulled most of the floundering women to shore alive.

Wang Keyu was one of the victims fished out by a frogman. But this stubborn POW kicked up a row, yelling, "Heaven and Earth are my witness. You must be true to your word and give this woman to me!"

Cao Shui'er couldn't take it any more and gave the frogman a solid slap on both cheeks. The frogman still wanted to argue his case but he took to his heels when he saw Cao Shui'er take off one of his shoes and threaten to slap him with it.

Although it never materialised, Qi Jing's idea to plunge the *guqin* to the bottom of the river deeply touched Wang Keyu. A scene kept flashing in her mind's eye: the horse messenger Cao Shui'er letting go of the Song-dynasty *guqin* with a rock attached to it. It was about to sink into the river when she reached out her hands and grabbed it from Cao Shui'er. She couldn't wait to open the cloth cover to examine it. Then, she adjusted the strings and played an open note.

The sound drifted far away with the current of the vast Yellow River...

✸

They jumped on the last ferryboat and hurried back to the south bank. But it was too late because the brigade had moved on the previous night. Since it had disappeared without a trace, where could they look?

A female literacy instructor, a horse messenger and a veteran warhorse formed a tiny independent "iron-stream detachment". They rolled on day and night to catch up with the PLA's Field Army.

In Nanjing, the Kuomintang government predicted that the Communist Army facing the Nationalist troops would not be able to fight on. The idea might be wishful thinking on Nanjing's part, but it wasn't wholly groundless. More than a hundred thousand exhausted PLA troops were in dire need of rest, reorganisation and replenishment. Theoretically, the troops had to stay where they were. But the situation in Yan'an was critical, and the battlefields elsewhere were also hard-pressed. The Jin-Ji-Lu-Yu Field Army had no alternative but to throw a cross punch!

The Defence Department in Nanjing urgently moved eight reorganised divisions comprising 140,000 soldiers to launch a converging attack against the Jin-Ji-Lu-Yu Field Army. At the same time, it also tried to take advantage of the constant rain to find an opportunity to blow up the Yellow River dikes. The plan was to flood the PLA's field army as in the famous Battle of Fancheng fought between the Three Kingdoms' warlords Liu Bei and Cao Cao in AD 219. The Field Army Command Post dispatched hydrological experts to gauge the water level around the clock to see if it had reached the danger mark. The officers and soldiers were on tenterhooks all day long.

The Field Army Command Post finally issued a warning order on 6 August and sent an urgent telegram to the Central Military Commission the next day. That night, the Jin-Ji-Lu-Yu Field Army suddenly moved before the Nationalist Army finished its encirclement. The PLA's Field Army slipped through it between Julu and Dingtao, with the 1st Column on the right flank, the 3rd Column on the left and the Command Post leading the 2nd and 6th Columns in the middle. The Field Army brushed past the enemy troops and thrust itself into the Dabie Mountains like a dagger as it marched via the counties of Shenqiu, Xiangcheng and Xi.

In years to come, the veteran generals inevitably mentioned in their memoirs the ideal timing of the shift from strategic defence to strategic attack. Like a cicada shedding its shell, the Jin-Ji-Lu-Yu Field Army left the enemy far behind. The retired generals may have overlooked the fact that the choice of the right moment was somewhat ingenious. They may also have ignored the various uncertainties accompanying the choice and the significant risks entailed by taking the initiative in desperation.

The Central Military Commission sent two return telegrams to the Field Army Front Command Post on 9 and 10 August. The telegrams read, "Your determination is entirely correct. You can make prompt decisions in times of emergency when there is no time to ask for instructions." Apart from comfort, commendation and encouragement, the messages also conveyed a sense of heavy-heartedness, desperation and even a certain degree of sorrowful resignation to parting, with little hope of meeting again.

Alexander Suvorov, the great Russian military commander, said that the feet were the decisive factor in warfare, whereas the hands were an accessory. The PLA troops moved fast ahead on foot with nearly 200,000 motorised Nationalist forces in close pursuit. The enemy's advance guards were always hot on the heels of the PLA's rear guards.

The small iron-stream detachment comprising Cao Shui'er, Wang Keyu and Tanzao found itself sandwiched between the two armies on the move that were kicking up clouds of dust in their advance. Moving forward between the two military forces,

Cao Shui'er and Wang Keyu had two worries: the Nationalist troops behind might catch up with them, and if they caught up with the PLA's Field Army, its rear-guard might mistake them for Kuomintang Army advance guards and kill them with friendly fire.

⁂

The first hurdle to face the Field Army marching south was not an enemy defence line but a natural barrier: the "Yellow River Inundated Area".

During the War of Resistance Against Japanese Aggression, the Nationalist government ordered a breach of the Yellow River's dike at Huayuankou to halt the advance of Japanese forces. The incident caused the death of 890,000 innocent civilians and created this inundated mud area extending more than twenty kilometres wide. The mud reached the knee at its shallowest and the waist at its deepest. Trudging forward, the troops didn't dare slow down or take a break lest they get bogged down. The troops pressed on and finally emerged from the twenty-kilometre-wide marsh.

Each troop unit had a guide to lead its way through the inundated area. It turned out that the region's topography had changed considerably over the four seasons because of successive floods and droughts. Within a year, the maps that the guides had drawn were all out of date. Cao Shui'er and Wang Keyu couldn't find anyone to help with their orientation because it would be dangerous for a small contingent once exposed. But Cao Shui'er was not worried because they had Tanzao with them!

Horses are born with a well-developed sense of smell and hearing and have an extraordinary memory. A horse's eye has a light-sensitive tapetum over the retina, enabling it to see its surroundings in the dark. It can return home from a faraway place many years later thanks to its ability to detect the familiar smells and sounds of home, and remember the scenes and objects it had previously observed.

A veteran warhorse had the same navigation value as a large-scale battlefield map. Tanzao homed in on the Field Army with his unique sense and intuition, ensuring that the small "iron-stream detachment" wouldn't lose its bearings. In the endless Yellow River Inundated Area, Tanzao could hold his head high and assess where the bog was too deep to tread and where the mud was shallow enough to wade through.

Wang Keyu was on horseback the whole way except in the Yellow River Inundated Area, where too much weight would cause both the horse and rider to sink. Tanzao zigzagged his way forward, with Cao Shui'er and Staff Officer Wang following closely by tracing its hoofprints. The horse messenger gave up his job as a horse boy and, as the proverb goes, "let the horse take possession of its reins", and they followed wherever Tanzao led them.

At first, they had no idea why Tanzao decided to double back on himself, thus drawing a large circle. They then realised that the horse had led them along this twisting course in order to avoid an extensive muddy area. After travelling what seemed at the time to be an unnecessarily long way, the veteran warhorse finally took Wang Keyu and Cao Shui'er out of the maze.

⁂

Only then did Cao Shui'er see Wang Keyu's face smeared with black mud. The mud in the Yellow River Inundated Area smelt foul, but she didn't mind at all. A pair of cloth shoes were strung with hemp twine and hung around her neck. This "Westernised" Peking student had long been relaxed about her appearance.

"Oh, my God!" exclaimed Cao Shui'er, looking at the sky to celebrate their successful escape from the Yellow River Inundated Area. He hadn't expected that they would have passed so smoothly through it. He repeatedly complimented Staff Officer Wang. "Thank heavens!" he said. "What would we have done if you had put a foot wrong and got us bogged down in the mud? A fear still possesses me now, somehow!"

"No, how would I?" said Wang Keyu, equally filled with exultation. "The genus Eohippus, or 'dawn horse', used to live in the North American jungles. It then transformed into the Merychippus. This proto-horse of the family Equidae experienced ten million years of living on grassland and marshland. So, horses possess a natural navigation ability passed down from generation to generation. As long as Tanzao didn't make a misstep, I was certain to be OK."

Cao Shui'er took out a carrot and fed it to the horse as a well-deserved reward for accomplishing his mission. But Tanzao didn't heed him. He lowered his head and flipped his ears forward rhythmically before drooping them sideways. It was a way of saying to Cao Shui'er, I'm exhausted.

A horse usually holds its large and movable ears upward. They're so expressive that they have replaced the animal's vocal communication capacities. Horses express themselves by changing the position of their ears instead of making utterances. Tanzao squinted his eyes, which meant he was asleep. Typically, horses sleep standing. Wild horses in ancient times never fought back by biting when confronted by large beasts. Their only tactic was to flee as fast as possible. It would be too late to run from a lying position in times of danger.

Cao Sui'er decided to camp for forty minutes to give Tanzao some rest. He rubbed the veteran warhorse's coat with a piece of tattered uniform, combed his mane and tail, scratched him tenderly with his nails and gently lifted his calves so that Staff Officer Wang could clean his hooves.

On one knee, Xiao Wang dug out stones and other foreign objects with her hand, strictly following the sole's contour to avoid hurting the frog of each hoof. The veteran warhorse had long been accustomed to Staff Officer Wang's touch. He was sleeping soundly and comfortably at the time.

Wang Keyu cleaned the tubular tarpaulin trough and prepared straw feed. Soft, thick and a little sweet, it was Tanzao's favourite. The hard feed comprised mostly corn kernels, but they didn't contain the usual protein, calcium and minerals. Therefore, Xiao Wang mixed in some oats and added a handful of salt, considering that Tanzao had sweated so much. Sufficient watering would further balance the warhorse's nutritional intake.

Patting the veteran warhorse lightly on his neck, she woke him up and said, "Time to eat!"

The veteran warhorse had a habit of pushing the tubular tarp trough forward with its muzzle when eating. To prevent Tanzou from overturning the container, Wang Keyu scooped the straw and grain in her hands and fed them to him. Xiao Wang patiently watched the horse chewing with his upper and lower lips moving outside to inside on a slant and listened to his molars crunching the hard feed. She offered the next handful after he finished the previous one.

Tanzao ate unhurriedly while, from time to time, leaning his head against Xiao Wang or licking her hand. Horses express affinity towards humans with these gestures, but gentle as the moves were, they still almost knocked Xiao Wang off-balance.

Cao Shui'er offered some advice by saying, "Staff Officer Wang, you must tilt your shoulders a bit so he can no longer push you around."

Because the Department of Defence in Nanjing deployed its main forces to launch a concerted attack on the south bank of the Yellow River, the PLA troops found the area flanking both sides of the Longhai Railway weakly defended. They barely encountered any regular Kuomintang troops on their way. Coming out of the Yellow River Inundated Area, they successfully crossed the Wo, Sha, Ying and Hong rivers in eastern Henan. Then they reached the front line at the Ru River in Henan's Zhengyang County on 23 August.

Cao Shui'er and Wang Keyu followed the PLA troops to the north bank of the Ru.

The roar of cannons and reports of guns showed that a fierce battle was raging ahead. Balls of flames were burning on the roadsides. On closer inspection, they found battle maps, classified documents and bundles of banknotes issued by the Farmers Bank of Chung-Chou of the Liberated Areas of the Central Plains. They were all new, with currency values ranging from ten to a hundred yuan. The burning of the documents and banknotes showed how critical a situation the PLA Field Army was facing.

A major tributary of the Han River, the Ru was up to seventy metres wide and about three metres deep. Cao Shui'er's contingent couldn't cross it. Suddenly, he shouted excitedly as his eyes fell on a pontoon bridge. Needless to say, the PLA troops had built it amid artillery bombardment by connecting over a dozen boats. The bridge, paved with branches and a thick layer of dirt, measured four metres in width.

"Sit tight, Staff Officer Wang!"

With a roar, the horse messenger gave a slap on the croup of Tanzao. In no time, the horse galloped across the river over the pontoon bridge with Wang Keyu on his back and Cao Shui'er hard on his heels. Enemy mortars fired in clusters, sending up high water columns upstream and downstream.

Across the river was an open field shelled from time to time. It presented a predicament for Cao Shui'er since they were completely exposed to enemy gunfire with no topographical features or objects to provide cover. Since they had no first-aid kit, he was worried that he couldn't save Staff Officer Wang if something should happen to her.

But there was no time for hesitation as the pursuing enemy would soon arrive. They had to cross the open terrain as fast as possible to avoid capture. But riding on horseback would present an obvious and easy target on the vast open field. Cao Shui'er thought of a practical formation with Wang Keyu and him keeping a ten-metre distance as they moved forward. They would try to discern the shells' ballistic sound along the way so that they could throw themselves to the ground when the impact point sounded close.

But Cao Shui'er scrapped the idea. Repeatedly hitting the dirt would waste time and prevent them from overtaking the troops. He decided to let Staff Officer Wang ride across the open field first. He would follow soon afterwards. Wang Keyu almost burst into tears when she heard the plan. She refused to go first.

Cao Shui'er became impatient. "Staff Officer Wang! You're the chief commander all right, but you must be subordinate to me now!"

Wang Keyu suddenly came up with an idea, which she tentatively shared with Cao Shui'er. "What does the military manual say? Does it allow two people to ride the same horse?"

The horse messenger had anticipated that question. However, he said with seeming resignation, "There's no problem with the manual. It depends on Tanzao's ability in battle conditions. I suppose we can give it a try."

Holding the pommel of the saddle, he put his foot in the stirrup. At the same time, he bent over, reached out his hand, pulled Xiao Wang up and swung the other leg over so that they were both sitting on the same horse. Sitting behind the messenger, Xiao Wang reached her arms around and grabbed his military belt. With the belt buckled tight, she was secure no matter how fast the horse galloped on the bumpy ground.

The two sped across the open field, with clouds of yellow dust they kicked up trailing behind them. Mortar rounds greeted them frequently and exploded in the front and at the back, now near, now far. Shrapnel flew whistling by their ears. The dirt of the impact points sent high in the air fell rustling back to the ground.

This small iron-stream detachment kept a moderate marching pace. Thanks to the horse, it crossed Ru River at precisely the right time, neither too early nor too late, by taking advantage of the strategic opening torn by the PLA Field Army's principal forces. They had no way to know that this was the last and most dangerous pass in the thousand-kilometre journey into the Dabie Mountains.

The Nationalist 85th Reorganised Division rushed over by train along the Beiping-Hankou railway line. They had occupied the few ferries on the south bank and built defence fortresses. On its heels came three more reorganised divisions. They were only thirty kilometres from the PLA Field Army. The 1st Column on the right flank and the 3rd Column on the left had travelled far by now. Unfortunately, the Field Army headquarters, along with the 2nd and 6th Columns, remained on the north side, with their advance blocked. Now with its head and tail cut off and thrown into disarray, the entire field army was in grave danger.

After braving the bombardment by the enemy's cannons and bombers, the PLA Field Army's Number One and Number Two chief commanders suddenly came to the Ferry Command Post of the 18th Brigade of the 6th Column. The command post was a sun-dried mud-brick house. The light from a small oil lamp was so dim that no one could see each other's faces clearly. The 18th Brigade commander unfurled a map and briefly reported the movement of the enemy troops facing them. The Number One chief commander said in a raised voice, "He who is brave will win in an inevitable confrontation," as if he were reciting an ancient poem.

Then he fell silent and stared into the eyes of everyone present. His gaze meant, Do you understand what I mean by this sentence?

How could they fail to understand? These brigade and regiment commanders all knew clearly that Number One was unique among PLA generals. The military circles at home and abroad referred to him as "a scholar general". He started reading ancient Chinese military classics when young and could repeat long passages from memory. He was educated at the MV Frunze Military Academy in Moscow, where he studied the military history of the Roman Empire, the history of wars between Japan and Russia, and the military theories of Napoleon Bonaparte. At present, between marches and combat, he was translating the famous Russian martial classic *Combined Arms Tactics*.

The sentence "He who is brave will win in an inevitable confrontation" allegedly comes from one of two sources. One is *The Art of War*, an ancient Chinese military treatise attributed to the military strategist Sunzi. The other possible source is *Come Across on the Way*, a poem dating back to the Han dynasty. Its origin aside, what was important was that this brilliant Chinese ancient military wisdom, tempered in the flames of war, sounded to the 18th Brigade commanders as the call of the Field Amy's commander-in-chief.

In times of peace, people tend to regard the adage only at face value, without realising its indispensability. But now, with the Field Army's fate hanging in the balance, the call had an earth-shaking effect, and its force of inspiration increased a hundred, a thousand and ten thousand times. All the commanders and fighters became galvanised, feeling the urge to act.

A report was received stating that the enemy's advance

guards and the PLA Field Army's rear guards were exchanging fire. The atmosphere in the 18th Brigade's headquarters was so tense that it made the commanders feel suffocated. The brigade commander was concerned for the safety of the Number One and Number Two commanders-in-chief as it was too dangerous for them to stay at this ferry point. He suggested they move to the neighbouring troops' position. The enemy's defence over there was relatively weak, making it easier for the commanders-in-chief to ferry across the river.

The Number Two commander-in-chief said categorically, "We're not going anywhere else. We'll follow you!"

The 18th Brigade commander sprang to his feet and saluted the Field Army commanders-in-chief. "That's fine! Commanders-in-chief, this headquarters will be yours. I'll go to the regiments."

As the brigade commanders moved their command posts to the regiments, the regiment commanders moved theirs to the battalions. The grassroots commanders and leaders equipped themselves with rifles and fixed bayonets to them. The officers' actions not only boosted the soldiers' morale but also increased the number of combatants. The 18th Brigade soon opened up a bloody path. It then covered the Field Army headquarters and the two subordinate columns as they rapidly crossed the pontoon bridge and advanced to the Huai River front line.

⁂★⁂

Cao Shui'er and Wang Keyu followed the Field Army from the south of the Ru River straight to the Huai River Ferry in Xi County. Seeing an army awaiting orders to cross the river, Cao Shui'er went up to ask, "Which unit are you from?" The exhausted soldiers were in no mood to heed him. Cao Shui'er expected them to tell him the whereabouts of the Independent

9th Brigade. A soldier responded sourly and whimsically, "Your Ninth Brigade has long crossed the river."

They didn't know if the river was shallow enough to wade across or if there were enemy troops on the other side. Cao Shui'er thought, Since our brigade has already crossed the river, as I was told, what are we waiting for? Let's go!

As they crossed the river, the water soon reached Tanzao's belly. On his back, Staff Officer Wang had to take off her shoes and let her calves submerge. The horse messenger Cao Shui'er led the horse by the reins, but his role was peripheral because the veteran warhorse determined the course as he groped his way forward. They didn't know how long it took to finally reach the southern bank.

Awaiting the river-crossing order on the north side of the river were the Field Army headquarters and the 6th Column. Days of consecutive rain meant the Huai River was nearly in spate. The currents were too rapid for the soldiers to ford. The enemy had burned all the boats along the river, leaving only a few rickety rafts. Repaired, they could carry only a few soldiers at a time – quite inadequate for an army of hundreds of thousands.

It turned out later that the Field Army's Number One commander-in-chief went to gauge the water's depth with a bamboo stick that gloomy night to prepare for the construction of a pontoon bridge. He dispatched the leader of his bodyguards to deliver a note to the Field Army's chiefs of staff. It read, "I saw with my own eyes a horseman leading a horse across the river and reaching the south bank. I now annul the order to build a pontoon bridge. Let all our troops wade across the river!"

A total of twenty-three Kuomintang brigades arrived at the Huai River front line one after another, and they were ordered to encircle, pursue, obstruct and intercept the PLA Field Army. The 85th Reorganised Division marched at the forefront, and it watched helplessly as the PLA troops strode away with their heads held high. Flooding on the Huai River is uncommon during this season, but just as the Nationalist Army approached, the waters rose to their peak, depriving the Kuomintang troops of the possibility of either wading across or building a pontoon bridge. The proverb "Man proposes, God disposes" summed up the Kuomintang troops' frustration.

CHAPTER 15

WILD HORSES OF OLD, LIVING IN THE TWENTIETH CENTURY

Of the Dabie Mountains that mark the border of Hubei, Henan and Anhui, it is said that the cock's crow can be heard there across all three provinces. Extending from the northwest to the southeast, the mountains rise a thousand metres or so, forming a divide between the Huai River and the Yangtze River. To the south, water flows into the Yangtze; to the north, water flows into the Huai. The climate differs greatly on the northern and southern sides of the range, and the ecological environment is much changed also. One side carpeted with mountain flowers, the other capped with snow.

By 27 August, tens of thousands of Field Army troops had crossed the Huai from the south, having completed their thousand-mile leap forward into the Dabie Mountains, and entered the surrounding counties of the northern foothills.

Most of the officers and men were the sons of farmers from Shanxi, Hebei, Shandong and Henan. They had imagined the Dabie region would resemble the north, where lofty ridges and towering mountain peaks stretch out as far as the eye can see. Alas, no! The mountain range here accounts for only fifteen per cent or so of the whole area. The remaining land is mostly made up of hills, wide and cheerful valleys, river deltas and terraced plains. The terrain lies at high altitude, with a well-developed drainage system – how high the mountain, how deep the water, as they say. The rice fields descend in steps from the top of the mountain, and the sunlight shines on them like squares of bright glass. A few farmhouses, with white walls and grey-tiled roofs, are scattered among the hills and rivers. No matter their size, all these villages have the inevitable fishpond – at least one or two, sometimes even three or four of them. Walking along the water's edge, you would often see goldfish or carp, weighing four or five *jin*, leap up, draw an arc through the air and dive back triumphantly into the water.

But the troops were not in the frame of mind to wallow in the beautiful surroundings of the Dabie Mountains, nor did they have the time to notice how abundant yet simple life was in this land of fish and rice. Twenty-three brigades of the National Revolutionary Army had crossed the Huai River behind them in quick succession and were now attempting to use their superior force to banish them from the region entirely. To avoid this rapidly advancing enemy, the troops had no time to waste in their departure, hastening like a great migration of sparrows across the sky.

⁕

This was the third time they had been instructed to "travel light". The first had been before their departure from the south, the second during their thousand-mile leap into the Dabie region. Now, the instructions were more specific, more thorough, leaving them with little but the uniforms on their backs. If it were possible, they might even have been requested to "lighten" the buttons on those uniforms, leaving the first, third and fifth buttons perhaps – but removing the second, fourth and sixth.

Wang Keyu had previously carried the *guqin* on her back, which was well received wherever she went. Since entering the Dabie Mountains, however, she found public opinion to be less favourable. Howitzers, field artillery and mountain guns were destroyed, and confidential military maps and bundles of Zhongzhou currency were burned. Some people still carried percussion instruments, but with everything else that was going on, could anyone really be expected to take an interest? Indeed, people now avoided the word *guqin*, deliberately using the more contemptuous term "'percussion". Eventually Number One had to come forward, in person, to request that Wang Keyu "lighten" her load of the *guqin*.

Xiao Wang eventually succumbed to the painful decision. She asked a carpenter to make a box and, together with Cao Shui'er, chose a suitable place to bury the instrument. They had dug a small hole and were about to place the *guqin* into the ground, when Xiao Wang made a sudden suggestion. "Cao Shui'er! I haven't played for such a long time. Let me play you something. Let's call it a long overdue performance in honour of Tanzao as well."

Cao Shui'er was overjoyed. "Thank you, Staff Officer Wang! Why don't you play *Moon Over Mountain Pass*? Tanzao is just over there. He'll definitely hear you."

Staff Officer Wang tuned the strings excitedly. She played an open note and looked up at the night sky. She stared for a long time as if watching that deep, lingering sound drift away into infinity.

"Forget it, forget it. I best not play."

Feeling suddenly disheartened, she cancelled the performance. In times like these, the playing of any kind of musical instrument, anything that made a sound, in fact, was sure to land you in hot water. Why bother?

Little did she know, Xiao Wang had missed her last opportunity. Never again would she have the chance to stage such a performance for Tanzao.

The decision had been made, and there was no way round the "travel light" policy. But when the time came, Staff Officer Wang hugged her *guqin* and would not let it go. The horse messenger knew that delaying the matter would only make the problem worse. But Staff Officer Wang was stubborn. No matter how strict the "travel light" policy, no matter how unforgiving public opinion, she seemed not to care. In her mind, she could just carry on as if nothing had happened, slipping back into rank and file with the "percussion" on her back.

Cao Shui'er made a light-hearted remark but forcefully grabbed the *guqin*. He placed it in the small hole and began filling it, shovelling the soil high while preventing Staff Officer Wang from coming close. He avoided her gaze, as she wiped away relentless streams of tears. Soon the *guqin* was buried, and a layer of small stones was sprinkled over it with the dry soil until it looked like the surrounding ground and would not be noticed by the advancing Nationalist soldiers.

The mountains, rivers and fields changed greatly throughout the year in the Dabie region. Next time around, perhaps the entire landscape would be unrecognisable, not just the specific location of the buried *guqin*. The horse messenger noted several nearby landmarks as future signposts and urged Staff Officer Wang to keep them firmly in her mind. To further help identify the location of the *guqin*, Cao Shui'er took exactly eighty-one steps due north, until he reached a cliff. There, he used a dagger to carve the character "Song" deeply into the stone wall.

Were someone to come across this "Song", they might make a hundred guesses as to what it meant without coming to the conclusion that buried here was a rare Song-dynasty *guqin*.

⁂

The horse messenger felt anxious and afraid, and a sense of imminent catastrophe. Sure enough, a notice came down stating that all the horses from the various troops and agencies, including all the commanders' mounts, must be handed in for centralised "final disposition". No horses were to be kept without authorisation, nor released into the wild, nor given up to the local people, with or without recompense, which was tantamount to giving them up to the enemy.

All the horses were then registered on an official list until only one was unaccounted for – the trusted mount of the Number One leader.

Tanzao had joined the cavalry as a three-year-old way back in the chaotic warlord era, soon establishing himself as a "boy wonder" among the ranks of military horses. Wherever he served, whether it was during the Northern Expedition of the National Revolutionary Army, the eight years of the War of Resistance Against Japanese Aggression, or as a member of the cavalry unit of the Eighth Route Army and the People's Liberation Army, Tanzao often rescued the rider on his back, overcame innumerable difficulties, and, when necessary, always strived to carry his heroically sacrificed master back to camp. Despite the passage of time, he was still most capable, but what a wretched fate awaited him – "final disposition" at the hands of the very people it had served for so many years!

When the collection staff came knocking, Cao Shui'er delayed them by weaving the horse's tail into braids, like the long, thin pigtails worn by Uyghur girls. At last, he threw them the reins, saying, "Brothers, if you can, lead him away!"

Three men pulled together on the reins, but the old mount wouldn't budge.

Cao Shui'er wouldn't have dared disobey an order, however. It was just a little joke he played on them. To facilitate centralised management, all the horses had been branded with a number on their flank. Tanzao was number nine. Cao Shui'er stroked the mark for a long time before finally patting the horse lightly, at which point Tanzao went obediently on his way.

The horse messenger followed on, walking behind them as if taking his horse out on a day like any other. Not wanting his wordless comrade of many years to be dispirited on the road, Cao Shui'er whistled his usual tune, sweet and high-pitched like birdsong.

The military horses were assembled in a dried-up old barrier lake that had been formed by landslides. The lake was surrounded on three sides by mountains, where the steep terrain made it impossible for the horses to ascend. The only other exit was blocked off by a dam, where a small team from the machine gun company was deployed to provide enough cover to prevent the horses from rushing across the line of defence and escaping.

Horses from all the other divisions also congregated there. Exact statistics were not published, but there must have been more than a hundred in total. All of them, without exception, to be slaughtered. No one paid this much mind at first, but arriving at the scene and gazing out over the dense mass of military steeds, the heads of the machine gun company realised just how rotten a task this was. How could they be asked to do such a thing?

It was commanded that the horses be stripped bare. All equipment was to be removed, including the reins, halter, bridle, saddle and stirrups. The horseshoes had all worn away long ago, and it was too late for new ones anyway, so they all went barefoot. In other words, aside from the marks branded on their flanks, the horses were freed from all the implements, large and small, imposed on them in order to exercise control.

A wonder! These unbridled animals, like modern-day wild

horses of old, were entirely liberated both physically and psychologically. "Hui! Hui!" they cried, jumping high into the air and kicking out their hind legs, or rearing up straight to demonstrate a daring vitality and radiant fervour. In facing the human race, these wild horses should have felt a keen and well-deserved sense of superiority. They ask nothing of humans, nor do they envy the joys and material pleasures of human lives. In fact, they can't help but look down on us. If they could, they would no doubt say, with sympathy, "These creatures who walk upright, living like beasts, can barely fend for themselves!"

But when clasped coldly in its mouth, the metal bit makes a horse suddenly and starkly aware – I must never provoke this creature, who claims to be the "cream of the animal crop". The bit can hardly lay claim to being a significant scientific or technological invention. It is but a small metal bar, attached to the bridle at either end and connected to the reins. With the slightest of tugs, however, the bit tightens, and the horse, in unbearable pain, is forced to obey. Such a crude and simple thing. An animal species subjugated, generation after generation enslaved.

Putting horses into battle wasn't so effective at first. Riding bareback you were likely to fall at any moment. But since the invention of the saddle, and even more so since stirrups appeared, soldiers and war horses have complemented each other with a special kind of synergy. Sitting firmly on the saddle bridge with their feet tucked tightly into the copper stirrups, soldiers could free their hands, wield weapons and fight ferociously. The horse allowed attacks to be launched from long distances and at deadly speeds. Entire battles were won through sudden and deadly attacks. It could be said, without exaggeration, that a horse's load capacity, plus its traction force and speed, was almost equal to the combat force of the army of an entire nation.

The nomads from the north understood this better than

anyone. They were the first to replace chariots with cavalry, significantly improving mobility and combat efficiency. With fifty thousand horses, they conquered more than half of Eurasia. Each Mongolian cavalryman had three horses – one to ride, one to carry supplies and one spare, to be used when charging into battle. They brought the Western world to its knees with successive defeats of a hundred thousand allied European forces, including the crusading knights of France and central Europe.

Soldiers of dynasties past spent much of their lives on the backs of war horses. A trusted mount would fight until its blood was spilt on the battlefield. As portrayed in the ancient poems, a war horse may even offer its skin so that its rider could fulfil his heroic oath "to be buried in horse hide".

⁂

The soldiers of the machine gun company observed the horses beginning to trot. They started out in a somewhat disorderly manner, all heading in different directions, having to jump out of the way so as not to collide with one another. But soon they fell in line, and before long nearly two hundred war horses were running anti-clockwise around the barrier lake. The soldiers were dumbfounded. With no one guiding them, how could they be so well-ordered?

What the military heads saw unfolding before their eyes was no longer a group of war horses on active duty, but a pack of "modern yet wild" horses, sensing profoundly the eager excitement of their wild and unruly past, like horses of old charging through the grasslands, and the brisk joy of freeing themselves from captivity. It seemed a pity that they were not breathing the fresh, moist air of the endless wilderness, five million years ago.

Of the world's large mammals, cheetahs are the fastest, reaching speeds of forty kilometres an hour, followed by lions and tigers. Driven by the need to hunt prey, they are fierce and cruel, nothing if not frightful. But horses alone run for the sake of running, for the sheer pleasure of it. And no other animal quite matches their bodily form: long and slender with vigorous and handsome movements, so elegant and noble.

As they circled the bottom of the barrier lake with ever-increasing speed, the horses inclined ever closer to the ground, with an aura of strength and balance. As they varied in stamina, the group gradually spaced out to resemble a great dragon – the head visible, the tail shrouded in dust. It was a spectacular sight.

In the heyday of the Tang dynasty, there were a total of 1,643 post stations throughout the country – one every thirty *li*. In other words, horses were required to run at full tilt for fifteen kilometres from post to post. To maintain that speed, you had to change horses at each post or else, as legend goes, Concubine Yang's lychees would rot on the road.[1] But by the calculation of the machine gun company, this team of wild horses didn't stop after having run such a distance. Rather, they carried on, swift as the wind, fast as lighting, and growing faster still.

Did they not understand that their hearts had limits? Running rampantly around the lake could have disastrous consequences! Alas, their time was nearly up, and there was no turning back now. They must compress their lives into these last moments, and run at such mesmerising speeds as to complete all the distance they should have covered in their life-time, and leave without regret.

This group of "modern yet wild" horses got their wish. The leading horse let out a dreadful howl, and blood spurted from its mouth. Head bowed, it dropped lifeless to the ground. Facing the sky, its four legs twitched. The same then went with the second horse, and the third, and the fourth, until the soldiers lost count.

This all played out in mere moments, but the soldiers saw clearly enough. Their nerves couldn't stand it any longer, and they wanted nothing but to slam their heads against a wall. They opened their mouths wide, and many burst into tears. The company commander was troubled by such turmoil among his troops, and he struggled to maintain composure. He worried too that the horses might rush to escape in every direction. It was a difficult situation to deal with, no doubt, and he issued his impulsive command with a hoarse voice: "Each platoon at the ready – rapid fire! Rapid fire! Rapid fire!"

The soldiers closed their eyes tightly, and with maddening cries of "Ahhh!" pressed their shoulders against the butt of their rifles. Bursts of fire. The light machine guns were equipped with a cooling system that made them capable of maintaining a consistent rate of fire without ever getting stuck. At full capacity, the magazine contained two hundred rounds, but within a minute, they had run out and had to be replaced with new ones. The distance was so close, however, that you could shoot with your eyes closed and not miss your target. The remaining horses collapsed like a wall under the waves of bullets. Then another wall appeared close to them, and that too fell down, just the same… Usually, such a task wasn't complete until the arrival of a senior inspector to check, one by one, which bodies needed another bullet. But these old military horses in the barrier lake had taken more than one or two rounds, and the inspection team wasn't needed.

⁂

Out of nowhere, a horse galloped straight towards the machine gun company's position. The soldiers were so caught off guard that the magnificent horse was able to rush onto the dam, jump over their heads, and flee in the direction of the surrounding wilderness. Everyone recognised the horse as Tanzao, trusted mount of Number One. The company commander barked his order: "Fire! Fire! Let fire! Let fire!"

The soldiers shot, but the blood-bay horse only increased his speed, and in no time at all had disappeared into a thicket. The higher-ups had decreed that all the horses should be dealt with. Missing a horse was equivalent to supplying the enemy, and those responsible for it would be court-martialled. The soldiers all looked anxiously at the company commander.

"Don't worry! Don't worry! It will show up."

The company commander took up a machine gun, fitted a full magazine and sat calmly waiting alongside his weapon. Not long afterwards, Tanzao really did appear, out on the ridge, gazing back towards the company with a look that seemed almost wistful. The commander opened fire, releasing several bursts in quick succession. He missed, and Tanzao turned around and fled.

The company commander was notorious among the Ninth Brigade for his prowess with a machine gun. Who knows how many bullets had to be spent to get to that level of marksmanship, to be capable of putting an enemy's name on each bullet? The soldiers whispered among themselves, in no doubt whatsoever that their commander had been merciful and let the old horse go deliberately.

At that moment, they realised that the horse messenger Cao Shui'er had appeared on the dam, making clear to everyone just how Tanzao had rushed through the machine gun fire and escaped safely on the other side. What was there left to say? It was unquestionably the handiwork of this wily old bird from the cavalry unit.

Cao Shui'er had hidden in a ditch. When the "wild horses" ran over, he put two fingers under his tongue and let out a sharp whistle. Tanzao understood, at once changing direction and reducing his running speed. The horse messenger lunged forward, grabbing hold of the old war horse's long mane and hanging from his neck facing upwards, a move known as "the hanging fuchsia" in equestrian training.

Under the guidance of this veteran cavalryman, Tanzao had paused, then turned suddenly towards the ditch, choosing a gap between two light machine gun positions, and flew over the embankment. Cao Shui'er rolled off to the ground and stayed there in place, lying low and watching events unfold. Only when his wordless comrade vanished into the distance did he stand up, pat down the dust that covered his entire body and make himself known. When no one else was present, Cao Shui'er quietly said: "Commander! Thanks to you, Tanzao found a way out. I bow to you."

"What nonsense, Cao Shui'er!" the company commander said solemnly. "Would I dare defy the orders of my superiors? Blame these rusty hands. It's been a long time since I handled a weapon."

Chapter 16

With No Time to Even Look at Their Faces in the Mirror

Q uite unexpectedly, and quite regrettably, the Independent Ninth Brigade was reorganised into a local military unit.

Without exception, the people grew angry on behalf of Qi Jing. Number One stood out even among the other high- and mid-level commanders. Making him stay here was a clear message from the superiors that they did not see the Ninth Brigade as a substantial force. But those who held such a view didn't understand that the Central Plains Bureau selected and prepared the local leadership team based on the principle that "only the best steel should be saved for the blade". Take Qi Jing as an example. The superiors saw his courage, organisational abilities and cultural sensitivities as well suited to the task of constructing and consolidating local power. He already held the top military and political positions: a local CPC Committee secretary and a military sub-area commander-in-chief. What else did they expect was out there for him?

In addition to Qi's brigade, each column also contributed three regiments to local armed forces in order to promote guerrilla warfare. Between a thousand and two thousand cadres were transferred to work locally, and political command was to be established as soon as possible. In this way, they successfully carried out their strategy of launching deep into hostile territory, coming together to confront the enemy and dividing themselves up to mobilise the masses.

Cadres below the county and regiment level were appointed by the branch CPC work committees. The list of appointments was very long, and Qi Jing had begun to sweat before getting to the end of announcing all their names. Whenever a name was called out, the soldier would stand, a perplexed look on his or her face, so that they could all get to know each other. These individuals knew very little about their specific tasks, only that they had been appointed as the secretary or mayor of a certain district.

A new district party secretary asked, "Number One, is there a map? At the very least, I need to figure out the location of the area assigned to me."

"You ask *me* for a map, but who do *I* ask? All you have to do is take a walk outside and ask the first fellow you come across. You'll get the answer you're looking for." Sensing that the district party secretary was still unsatisfied and on the verge of arguing further, Qi Jing stopped him short. "I won't answer any more of your questions. I will only stress one point. The district is the district, and the township is the township! As in, stick to the tasks and regions assigned to you, and don't concern yourselves with anything or anywhere else. And don't ever forget that!"

"I won't," said the secretary of the district party committee, performing a formal military salute. But as he turned and walked away, he couldn't help letting out a bitter laugh. What kind of logic is that? he asked himself. I don't care where your districts are, but if the enemy attacks, you can't leave the boundaries of your districts? Take one step outside and you are a deserter?

The work groups of all counties and districts set off, jam-packed on the loess highway. Just then an enemy reconnaissance plane flew in low above their heads, like the beating of a gong signalling the imminent arrival of National Revolutionary Army troops. The road was now impassable, and the work teams immediately scattered on both sides, rushing to their respective jobs along the mountain trails and field ridges.

ฐฐฐ★ฐฐฐ

There were twenty-seven people in the Balifan District work team. The section chief of the Political Department of the 9th Brigade was to serve as both the district mayor and secretary of the district CPC Committee. Male comrades were appointed as staff members of the brigade headquarters, the political department and the rear-service unit. There were seven female team members in total. Aside from Staff Officer Wang Keyu from HQ, there were two nurses and four young students from the Hebei-Shandong-Henan Nation-Building College. Finally, there was the young actor Liu Chunhu. Despite not knowing one another before, this group of men and women were to live, like siblings, in close physical contact.

The work team arrived in Balifan very late in the day. They wanted to stay in the nearby forest for the night to avoid disturbing the villagers and enter the mountain village of Kuazi early the following morning. But they were soon discovered by "the masses", poor families who took the team members by the hand saying, "The Red Army is back! How could we bear to see you comrades spend the night up on the hillside? Oh, we would be punished severely by the heavens!"

This was, after all, a generation of folk who had lived through the region's many hardships. A few words told all their joys and sorrows. One house cooked soup noodles with poached eggs, another brought out glutinous rice cakes and salted meats. Impeccable hospitality. The villagers also cleaned up their homes for their guests. The young women, both married and unmarried, were among the most enthusiastic, hoping to take home a female comrade or two. They whispered among themselves, "Aren't these northern Kuazi women just lovely!"

The villagers of the Dabie Mountains called the People's Liberation Army "Northern Kuazi". There was no implicit praise or criticism here; it referred only to the different dialects they spoke.

As newcomers to the area, without any real knowledge of local conditions, the company politely declined the sincere invitation of the villagers, deciding instead to stay together in accommodation and dispatch two sentries. The district party secretary saw personally to the group. He repeatedly told them not to take off their clothes at night, and best leave their shoes on too. They were to keep their ears sharp, even while sleeping.

Around midnight, a sentry heard a noise and felt something fall to one side of him. It turned out to be a small stone wrapped in a strip of white cloth, on which were written a few indistinct characters. The sentry hurried to show the district party secretary. Lit with a torch, four characters written in black charcoal could be discerned: "Be very careful tonight!" The party secretary shook and slapped the comrades sleeping beside him. "Get up! Get up! Up the mountain now! Hurry! Hurry!"

But it was already too late. Gunshots rang out in all directions. As the company members rushed to the door, they found themselves blocked by the party secretary. He grabbed a bamboo chair and lodged it against the closed door. Immediately, a barrage of bullets penetrated the panels. Blocked by the enemy, it was no longer possible to leave through the main entrance. Several people made to climb up to the higher reaches of the building, but they were again stopped by the party secretary. He warned them, "Most of the villages here are built on the mountain slopes, and from the tiled rooftops you are clearly visible. You'd be sitting ducks!" Instead, he commanded them, "Over the back wall."

A bamboo forest grew alongside where they were staying. Under the cover of these dense plants, the team members used a ladder to scale the wall. Sure enough, they found a path that led up the mountain. If they could head upwards and take up a new position there, who was to be afraid of whom?

Just as the seven female comrades were escorted up the mountain, the enemy suddenly closed in, outflanking them on both sides. They lit pine torches, and the night sky shone a brilliant red amid endless shrieks of distress. The company saw the approaching terror and had no choice but to go back, relying on the walled courtyard houses to continue their resistance.

The chiefs of the civil corps organised by local landlords, along with the local *bao* and *jia* leaders, had collected thousands of *jin* of grain for the Nationalist Army. For this, they had been rewarded with a few decent guns and rounds of ammunition. This would be the night they came into use. The work team was now firmly suppressed inside a small courtyard. Several exchanges were launched, but the enemy's firepower was too much, and escape proved impossible.

Over half their staff were killed or injured, and they had run out of bullets and grenades, leaving them no choice but to destroy their weapons, to take them apart and scatter the pieces. They also destroyed their armbands, with the characters "Chinese People's Liberation Army" printed on the front and the army's organisational system and personal names on the back. They couldn't allow these to fall into enemy hands.

If it had been a regular unit of the Nationalist Army, they would have ceased their attack having seen their opponent lose the ability to fight. But this brutish band of civil corps had, since the "anti-communist" days of the Hubei-Henan-Anhui Soviet, held an innate and intense class hatred. They surged into the courtyard like a great tide and unleashed a barrage of gunfire into the doors and windows until no more movement was heard.

The seven female comrades climbed to the top of the mountain. Upon reaching the other side, they came across a steep cliff and could advance no further. They had no choice but to stay where they were and hope that their male comrades would break free from their encirclement and meet them there. It was dawn, and the gunfire had come to a gradual halt. The torches cast a red light over Balifan. Amid the yelling of the locals, they couldn't make out any northern accents, which filled them with dread.

Everyone's gaze fell on Wang Keyu. Not only was she a staff officer from the headquarters, but was also more senior than the others in age. Naturally, they looked to her to make the decision on what to do next. But Staff Officer Wang's mind was blank. "I don't know," she said. "What do all of you think?"

One of the work team members replied, "We should copy *The Eight Heroines Who Drowned Themselves in a River!*"

"What's that about?" asked Wang Keyu.

"It's about eight female soldiers from the Northeast Anti-Japanese Coalition Army. When they ran out of ammo, they all jumped into the river together," someone explained.

"We should copy the *Five Heroes on Langya Mountain*," suggested another. "Five brave and loyal soldiers from the Eighth Route Army who ran out of ammo and jumped off a cliff to sacrifice themselves."

With her usual calm manner, Staff Officer Wang said, "All right then. When the time comes, we'll throw our grenades at the enemy troops, then jump into the river like those five heroes."

"Yes! Yes! Yes!" The female soldiers made their solemn promise. Staff Officer Wang might have mixed up the two heroic stories, but her message was clear nonetheless.

Faced with such a desperate situation, this was the most natural choice for these brave women who went to war. If near a river, their first thought would be to throw themselves in the water to their death. If on a mountain, they'd be sure to end their lives by jumping off a cliff. More than anything, they must keep their honour and avoid leaving a permanent stain on themselves.

There are numerous records in military history of female soldiers meeting death with remarkable grace and composure. Often, they would check themselves in a pocket mirror, ensuring their hair was carefully combed, and in the hope that in addition to keeping their young bodies clean, their faces, in the end, would also be presentable. But the female comrades of the Balifan unit were too late. The first enemy appeared, then the second, then the third, all of them approaching with guns in hand.

Staff Officer Wang was the first to throw her American-made MK II grenade, which resembled a green-skinned pineapple. This was a defensive model, with a blast radius of five to ten metres, and further shrapnel damage of up to fifty metres. After deploying the weapon, American soldiers would conceal themselves, or at least lie on the ground. Wang Keyu's grenade fell just a few steps away from her target, well within the kill radius. She stood there, dumbly waiting for it to emit smoke and explode. But she hadn't removed the pin, the fuse remained locked, and there was no explosion.

Following Wang Keyu's lead, the other female members launched their own wooden-handled grenades. For the fuse to be engaged and ensure the grenade would detonate, the tin-plated cover of the wooden handle should have been removed, and the small iron ring connected to the fuse pulled out using the finger.

But they all made a mess of the procedure. None of their fingers had even touched the small iron rings.

The village defence team saw the grenades being thrown over, one by one. They lay on the ground and dared not move. After waiting for a long time and hearing no sound, they started to laugh as they realised that all the grenades were duds.

When they saw Staff Officer Wang stretch out her arms and leap off the cliff, the two female nurses and four female college students didn't hesitate to close their eyes and jump down after her...

꙳⭐꙳

Work unit member Liu Chunhu was captured. Barely a teenager, he was the youngest field soldier to enter the Dabie Mountains.

When the battle was over, the enemy dragged away the body of the new district head of Balifan. They discovered, quite by accident, that he had used his body to shield a child, who lay there covered in blood, but unhurt. This PLA "captive", the sole survivor, was surrounded by the civil corps' rural security team. They made fun of him, teased him, insulted him. A unit leader examined him and said, "You little Eighth Route bastard! Tell us your name! Actually, don't, I know who you are. You're Little Pisspot, aren't you?"

This made everyone laugh, and they all made gestures with their hands as if they'd caught a whiff of a foul-smelling chamber pot.

Liu Chunhu remembered this man from the previous night. He had been mingling with the villagers of Balifan and pretending to entertain comrades from the working group, when someone had called him Little Pisspot. Liu Chunhu replied calmly, "Do you sons of bitches deserve the honour of calling me Pisspot? You should call me Mr Pisspot!"

With a thud, the butt of a rifle smashed into the boy's temple. In an instant, his face was covered in blood, and his chin tilted to one side. With great effort, he spat a mix of blood and broken teeth in the face of the unit leader. Several burly men rushed forward, but amid their punches and kicks, Liu Chunhu's mouth never stopped cursing.

It would have been fine if he'd just called them damn landlords, counter-revolutionaries, bourgeoise scoundrels or something similar – those kinds of insults were common enough during the Hubei-Henan-Anhui Soviet days. Their ears having developed calluses, they didn't care so much any more. But Liu Chunhu cursed eight generations of their ancestors. Chinese people were still deeply influenced by feudal ethics, and it was considered unacceptable to violate someone's ancestral lineage in such a way.

"You Eighth Route bastard! Just you wait!"

An iron wire, about the width of a chopstick, was inserted into the collarbone of PLA soldier Liu Chunhu, and he was led to the front of a parade. There, he was forced to bang endlessly on a gong. When he failed to do so, they jabbed at him with a small drill, piercing holes in his skin, from which streams of blood ran down. Someone behind held a wooden board on which was written: "Prisoner under sentence of death – Liu Chunhu, member of the district government of the Communist Party."

The procession passed through Balifan market. It didn't cause quite the sensation they had hoped for, and only a handful of passers-by paused to look. When the Fourth Red Army's attempts to repel the Kuomintang's "encirclement" campaign had failed, they had mostly withdrawn from the Hubei-Henan-Anhui Soviet. But many people were captured, from the chairman of the Farmers' Association, to Soviet government personnel, to relatives of the Red Army. They had all been led on parades like this one. In fact, such scenes were so familiar to the locals that they no longer regarded public executions as worth the effort to rush out onto the streets.

The Balifan civil corps were known to have buried some of these "criminals" alive. Mostly, they had adopted the "planting weeping willows upside-down" approach, in which the prisoner was placed head-first into a pit they had been made to dig themselves. All the executioner needed to do was fill the soil back in with a shovel, and that was that. This time, though, the head of the civil corps decided to try out a new trick. Liu Chunhu was made to stand in a pit and buried up to the neck, leaving just his head visible. They were all curious to see how long his cursing would last!

Buried to chest height or above, it is extremely difficult to breathe. Young Chunhu's face began to twist, and his features became distorted. Only in such extreme circumstances will you see such a hideous, horrifying human face, one that defies description with words. And only in such extreme circumstances will you hear such a feral howl of laughter emitted from a person's throat, one that seems wholly inhuman.

The civil corps' rural security team members grew increasingly troubled until they could stand it no longer. They soiled their trousers. They crumbled. One by one, they fled the scene.

For a long, long time, the wild laughter of the "Eighth Route Bastard" echoed through the valley.

CHAPTER 17

THE MIDDLE GROUND

Qi Jing, commander of the military subarea, received the report. The Balifan District Task Force had been attacked by a civil corps group. All seven female comrades had been captured, and task force member Liu Chunhu had been buried alive. None of the other nineteen members, from the chief down, had survived.

Qi Jing was speechless for some time. He had heard news of his troops being defeated countless times and learned of many close comrades dying in the line of fire. But never like this; never such a heavy blow. At first, he felt it as a pain in his heart, a deep and unavoidable sense of guilt that he, as their commander, couldn't shirk.

It hit Qi Jing with a sudden clarity that, during the mobilisation meeting, he had stubbornly insisted, "No one should leave the district to which he is assigned, and each must stay in the township where he works." He had failed to think about the grassroots personnel; failed to put himself in their shoes and consider their safety. The female comrades from various agencies and groups of female students had plenty of political zeal, but nothing in terms of practical battle sense. He felt particularly remorseful over the tragic death of the young publicity worker Liu Chunhu, and he spent the rest of the day in a daze.

The least he should have done was stress to the task force that, on the first night, it was always best to camp in the wild. They could have stayed in an isolated house, or a mountain village of just two or three households. They could have put out an alert, let people in but not out. They could have rested until dawn, and gone up the mountain the next day to take stock of the situation. These vital words were never spoken. There had been a great round of applause when everyone hurried out onto the road. It was too late for regrets, but still, Qi Jing pulled furiously at his hair.

The military subarea troops surrounded Balifan, capturing the wives and daughters of civil corps leaders. They were tied together with a long rope of twine and brought back to camp. Qi Jing sent word to his opponents, offering an exchange of captured personnel. If they agreed, the exchange would take place at noon the next day, the location to be negotiated and agreed upon. If these plans were deliberately delayed or changed, all detainees would be executed at 12 o'clock, with no mercy!

As expected, the Balifan *bao* chief invited an old tailor to act as his proxy. During the Hubei-Henan-Anhui Soviet period, this man had acted as a go-between for the Red Army and the Kuomintang authorities when they wanted to communicate. Over time, people began to think that his job as a tailor was just a front, and in fact he was in another line of business – he seemed to have a monopoly on the "red and white business". Both "red" and "white" could approach him, and he alone could speak freely with both sides.

Mediated by the old tailor, negotiations between the two sides proceeded smoothly. Soon, a formal agreement had been reached on the exchange of captured personnel.

Cao Shui'er had followed his commander into battle.

He hadn't been assigned any specific task, but relying solely on his own initiative he had managed to capture the daughter of the Balifan *bao* chief. The purpose of this expedition having been to capture the wives and daughters of the enemy to use as bargaining chips for the captured female comrades, Cao Shui'er's actions were particularly significant. Indeed, the *bao* chief of Balifan was willing to do whatever it took to rescue his darling child.

Most of the *bao* chief's family had already fled. All, in fact, except for one member, who went by the nickname Yaomeizi, meaning "youngest daughter". For reasons unknown, she had stayed behind. When the People's Liberation Army swarmed into Kuazi Village, she had nowhere to run. At seventeen or eighteen years old, her thinking was more animated than any of her peers. The more violent the situation, the more attractive it seemed to this girl. She firmly believed that only through dangerous or frightening experiences could she realise all that she had imagined for her life, all that she had dreamt of for as long as she could remember.

Cao Shui'er kicked the courtyard door open with a crash, catching sight of a most glamorous peasant girl sitting on the threshold of the house. She was slowly combing her hair and didn't look the least bit panicked. From beneath her tight-fitting cotton blouse, two nipples stood erect, as if ready to burst free and prick the eyes of onlookers. Other girls would have certainly found a way to conceal them, but the *bao* chief's daughter seemed to say: You get what you're given. Stare, for all I care.

With a serious expression, Cao Shui'er pointed his carbine rifle at the young woman. "I'm sorry, you have to come with me."

"The People's Liberation Army! You wouldn't want me. I'm a reactionary, the daughter of a landlord *bao* chief." The girl pretended to tremble as she spoke.

"In fact, you're exactly what I'm looking for. I apologise, but I have to tie your hands together."

"No need! No need! I won't run. If I do, you can just shoot me."

"It's not up for discussion. Go and find something to tie your hands. Any kind of a short rope will do."

"Brother, why don't we use my belt? It's no bother, I'll just hold up my trousers as we go." The *bao* chief's daughter went to untie her trousers.

"Don't mess with me! Hurry up, go and find something else. A piece of straw rope perhaps."

"Oh, I have one! I have one! Wait a moment."

Yaomeizi may have grown up in the landlord *bao* chief's house, but it was clear that she was capable when it came to manual labour in the fields. She took a sip of water, held it in her mouth and sprinkled it onto a pile of straw, drip by drip. She then picked up the wet straw and, in just a few minutes, had twisted it into a piece of straw rope four or five feet long. Her fleshy hands worked with great dexterity, while her gaze never left the PLA soldier.

Cao Shui'er tied the hands of the *bao* chief's daughter and motioned for her to move forward. She declined, modestly and repeatedly, not yet ready to take up the role of a prisoner. There was a momentary stalemate until Cao Shui'er pushed her roughly, and the *bao* chief's daughter saw the black hole of the rifle's muzzle aimed directly at her. Only then did she realise that it would be impossible for her to walk behind the soldier. If she did, who would be the escorted prisoner?

"PLA brother! Don't point that gun at the back of my head. I feel numb and scared…"

That night, all the wives and daughters were detained in a

large storage room. Guards roamed all corners of the sentry gate, and the cadres took turns in keeping watch. Despite such strict levels of vigilance, it wasn't hard to guess how this story might unfold. And, sure enough, it did.

The guards from the previous shift handed over the keys to Cao Shui'er and went off to catch up on some sleep. Cao Shui'er opened the door and entered this "prison". As the beam of his flashlight swept back and forth across the crowd, the women were so scared that they hurriedly covered their faces with their hands.

"PLA brother, I need to pee!" a woman yelled out of the darkness.

"Who's stopping you? There's a bucket here," the guard replied.

"But there're so many people watching, and they'll hear me. I can't pee like that."

"Urgh! Come with me," the guard conceded impatiently.

The female prisoners all yelled, asking to be afforded the same privilege. Of course, what they really wanted was to escape, or at least leave this stifling, sweaty room and get some fresh air out in the yard. Cao Shui'er ignored them, closed the big iron gate and locked it with a click. Squatting down, he allowed the *bao* chief's daughter to mount his back like a monkey, and he carried his prey straight into the kitchen...

⚝

The exchange of prisoners took place in the "middle ground". It was so-called for its location between the two parties, who were to each send out captured persons and receive those coming from the other side at the same time. By mutual agreement, the middle line was drawn across an ancient stone arch bridge.

There were only seven captured females from the PLA side, whereas a long line of captured personnel stretched on from the other side. As the old women with tiny bound feet hobbled along with great difficulty, the younger women ran so fast that they reached the arch bridge in no time. The old tailor was there, checking the number of people passing through and generally maintaining order.

All of a sudden, the *bao* chief's daughter shouted, "I won't go back to the house. I want to stay here!"

"*Aiya*, Yaomeizi, what are you saying? Are you crazy!"

No one was more anxious than the old tailor. He had pressed his fingerprints to the document, promising to exchange the hostages in full. And while there may be some leeway on the others, the old tailor was under strict orders to deliver the *bao* chief's daughter directly to her father and mother. He must not let her escape.

The *bao* chief's daughter said, "To tell you the truth, I'm getting on pretty well with a northern Kuazi brother. Uncle, please do us a favour and help us be together again!"

Her response was greeted with great anger, and the women shouted and cursed, "We all know what went on in that kitchen, and you still have the face to say it out loud!"

"The PLA soldier thought she was a young virgin! What a joke!"

"Let her stay! Balifan wants nothing to do with a promiscuous 'temptress'!"

The old tailor warned her sternly, "Young lady! Don't talk to me about a one-night stand. I'd still have to drag you back even if you were legitimately married. Can you not see that we stand in front of the two armies? Troops on both sides, lying in ambush behind the mountains. They might well shoot!"

The *bao* chief's daughter sat on the ground with her legs crossed and said, "I can't walk, you'll have to carry me back!"

The old tailor was at a loss and wanted nothing more than to pass this thorny issue on to the negotiating partners. Instead, he negotiated with the *bao* chief's daughter in a kindly tone. "Young lady," he began, "since you have such a relationship with this brother, you might as well just become a female soldier in the People's Liberation Army. Just ask, and I'm sure the comrades will be happy to take you in."

The *bao* chief's daughter took up the idea, indulging a long-held fantasy. She walked towards the negotiators of the People's Liberation Army to make the request formally. The representative of the military subarea stated solemnly, "This woman's number is thirty-three. The two parties have handed her over. We will not be responsible for any new problems that might crop up unexpectedly!"

The old tailor winked at several of the young women. He had a plan. The women knew this, and they grabbed the *bao* chief's daughter, dragging her roughly towards the middle line, throwing in a few punches for good measure. The *bao* chief's daughter understood that these young women were jealous of her beauty, and that, depending on their temperament, they may not give up until she was beaten to death.

"OK, I'll go back!' The *bao* chief's daughter relented, and she stepped across the middle line of her own accord.

CHAPTER 18

A COLD HANDSHAKE

Qi Jing, commander of the military subarea, observed the entire process of the hostage exchange through his binoculars. His troops were concealed in a mountain forest behind him, ready to deal with any unexpected turn of events.

The captured persons appeared in the "middle ground". Six female comrades walked out in front, followed by a stretcher being carried by four people. It was Wang Keyu, who appeared gravely injured. After five days, she had yet to regain consciousness. Later, it was revealed that Staff Officer Wang had jumped from a particularly steep cliff, seriously injuring herself in the fall. The others had simply tumbled down to the bottom of the slope, where they found the enemy waiting for them, guns in hand.

The female work team members cried in relief as they embraced the Number One chief commander. It went without saying, none of these students, all in their late teens, could have been expected to bear such a burden. Qi Jing, like a father, patted each of them on the shoulder, and said repeatedly, "Welcome back. On behalf of everyone, I welcome you back to the army."

That evening, several female comrades from the prefectural committee were ordered to keep the captured women company, for it was feared they might hurt or kill themselves. When these two groups came together, the atmosphere changed entirely. In time, they lost what was left of their self-restraint, speaking through furious tears about how they had been raped, and how they had so desperately resisted.

The specifics of Wang Keyu's capture and internment remain unclear to this day. People have speculated that the Nationalist militia, made up as it was of such rotten men, would have shown no mercy on her. But it was also said that a female colonel in the Nationalist Army had been in charge of treating her, with two of the captured female comrades assisting in cleaning up her excreta. The abundance of these rumours, nothing if not inconsistent, made it difficult to say what had really happened.

The leadership of the military subarea were nonetheless unified in their understanding of the matter. All captured personnel were to be exempt from "screening". They would not be subject to polit-ical appraisals, and instead should still be regarded as revolu-tionary comrades. It was not their fault that they had been raped. And, as class sisters, they deserved to be treated with sympathy and care. There were still those people who wanted to show that they were more politically enlightened than others, who made no allowances for others' feelings, who were unwilling to let them off so easily. Upon seeing that the captured comrades had finished bathing, they remarked, enigmatically, "What's the use of washing? Even if you got through several bars of soap, you'd still be unclean!"

Hearing this kind of idle chatter, the captured comrades started crying once more. They neither ate nor drank. Repeating previous words of consolation proved ineffective in the long run. Qi Jing realised suddenly that it would be impossible for them to escape this abyss of pain on their own. Only by sending them to work, letting them feel the sincere trust of the organisation and regaining a modicum of self-esteem could they finally crawl out from the bottom of their despair.

Commander Qi Jing personally announced to the prisoners, "The Military Subarea Party Committee has determined that Comrade Wang Keyu will remain in the military subarea for now, due to her severe injuries. The remaining six female comrades are to return to work in Balifan, as before. A new Balifan District Committee team has been established. You must all gather your things, and be ready to set off at any time, to launch a second assault alongside the entire district."

Inconsolable tears turned to joyful applause. The six comrades of the newly established Balifan District team packed up their rucksacks and awaited their next orders, more eager than ever to fight. They didn't even consider the worst-case scenario – if disaster were to strike again, and history was to repeat itself, what would become of them?

As it was, less than two months later, they were captured again.

⚜★⚜

The reorganised 52nd Division of the Nationalist Army had been stationed at Balifan. The staff of the township security team used a stretcher to send Wang Keyu to the division headquarters, asking for assistance with her treatment.

A female professor-level military doctor from the Nanjing Nationalist Army Joint Logistics headquarters had been posted to assist the frontline troops of the 52nd Division. Wang Keyu was most fortunate that it was this surgeon on hand to perform a comprehensive examination of her. In addition to the severe concussion that had caused increased intracranial pressure and led to her unconsciousness, she had four broken ribs, a fractured left leg and a crack of more than ten centimetres across her right shoulder. The bleeding was stemmed immediately, and penicillin was injected. The colonel reset the fractured left leg herself and fixed it with a splint.

The colonel had set herself a target: she would not return to Nanjing without completing five thousand operations. According to her calculations, this female Eighth Router was number nine hundred and ninety-nine.

Quite suddenly, the eyelashes of the wounded started flickering, then her eyelids lifted like two windows being pushed gently open. In the outside world, everything seemed strange and blurry. The surgeon was wearing a white gown, her long hair tucked away tightly under a white cap. Wang Keyu could not tell she was a colonel of the Nationalist Army. Thinking she was just a doctor, an angel in white, Wang Keyu broke into her signature smile.

Serious head trauma can result in permanent or temporary amnesia. There is also another kind, in which recent memories are lost but early childhood recollections and very specific experiences are remembered clearly. Staff Officer Wang belonged to this latter category. A montage returned to her of crossing the Yellow River ferry more than two months previously, and she heard herself say, "I didn't receive any order, I... I was... I decided to set sail, so many people were... drowned, but I'm still alive."

One of her fellow captured comrades stepped forward to comfort her. "Staff Officer Wang, however you look at it, you can't say it was your fault. Women and civilians needed to reach the north shore as soon as possible. You were right to decide to sail."

Wang Keyu only regained consciousness for a short while, before drifting back into a coma. From her dreamlike words, the colonel could roughly figure out the capsizing incident at the Yellow River ferry. This beautiful staff officer, of just eighteen or nineteen years, left a deep impression on her. It seemed to her that, if someone had told this young woman that should you be willing to sacrifice your own life you could prevent the catastrophe of the "Yellow River Peach Blossom Flood", this girl would smile sweetly and go resolutely to her death.

The female colonel was later rotated to the 110th Division of the 85th Army when an uprising was declared on the front line of the Battle of Huaihai in the early winter of 1948. As soon as the troops were brought in, she began to accept tasks in the People's Liberation Army Field Hospital. She was to perform more than 2,900 operations on wounded personnel. To her, the officers and soldiers of the Nationalist Army and People's Liberation Army were, in essence, the same.

But her 999th patient never left the colonel's thoughts, and she later went about making enquiries. The people she managed to reach all told her that Comrade Wang Keyu had died gloriously in the Dabie Mountains, but none of them could say how. The colonel also approached Commander Qi Jing, but he did not want to talk to anyone about any topic related to Staff Officer Wang. She probed repeatedly, but the only answer she received was, "There was no such person in the Ninth Brigade!"

This puzzled the colonel, until she realised as if coming out of a daze, that this must have been the wish of the deceased. She came quietly into this world and drifted away just the same, leaving no trace.

꧁☆꧂

The army had run out of medical supplies, and even iodine tincture was scarce. The colonel was therefore due extra gratitude because she had left Wang Keyu with plenty of antibiotics, gauze strips for dressing and other things. Of course, she wouldn't have dared to openly provide the Communists with drugs, so it was all wrapped in a tattered coat and placed surreptitiously on her person.

As a rule of thumb in traditional Chinese medicine, it takes a hundred days to heal injuries in the tendons and bones. Coupled with frequent transfers over the period of a month or more, Wang Keyu still couldn't do without a stretcher. She had to endure being lifted by several helpers. When transporting her, they needed to complete a series of difficult movements, ensuring that the ground's incline wasn't so great that the stretcher would roll down into the deep valley. When going uphill, the two people in front had to crouch down, while the two behind had to lift the stretcher over their heads and push up as high as possible. When going downhill, the two people in front lifted her up high, and the two in the back had to squat down and waddle on their calves, or simply sit and shuffle forward on their buttocks, little by little. And that was to say nothing of the dark and heavy nights, or the days of endless rain.

In order to ensure the fighting capacity on the front line, Qi Jing ordered the deployment of cadres to form a stretcher team. This task was shared among personnel, top leaders included. Qi Jing was no match for the workers and peasants in this regard. As soon as the stretcher was placed on his shoulders, he grew crooked and awkward. His crotch chafed, and it was hard to move, all made worse by the hot weather. His feet were matted with blood, and he endured every moment through gritted teeth, leaving a bloody trace with each step.

"My back is going to break!" Hearing the chief's bitter whisper, the guard Cao Shui'er hurried forward to take the stretcher and let him take a breath.

At that moment, Qi Jing tripped, and the entire stretcher almost flipped upside-down, nearly throwing the wounded down into the ravine below. He was covered in a cold sweat and couldn't help but curse his own clumsiness. In the dark night,

Wang Keyu heard it all. Lifting the raincoat, she shouted, "Stop! Stop!" They had to find flat ground and put the stretcher down.

"Staff Officer Wang! Sorry for waking you up," the commander said.

"Number One, I won't take a stretcher any more. Let Cao Shui'er get me some crutches, so I can walk by myself."

"Is that some kind of joke? Do you no longer want this leg of yours?"

"I'd rather crawl on the ground than let the commander lift me again!"

"Staff Officer Wang," Cao Shui'er said. "It's not been a day and a half since the commander joined the stretcher team. If he doesn't lift you, he'll just be carrying others. Isn't it the same?"

✹

Unable to fulfil other field duties, Staff Officer Wang weaved straw sandals. Everyone, from Number One to the sentry guards at the headquarters, received her sandals, ending up with two or three pairs each, which they strung up on their belts. As they marched and marched, the straw sandals fell apart, but they could easily change to a new pair.

Wang Keyu had just begun to weave the sandals when Number One arrived, a hemp rope tied around his waist. He sat down to weave straw sandals together with her.

"Does the commander have something to ask me?" Wang Keyu seemed a little on edge.

"Your only task now is to heal your wounds. Nothing else will come your way."

"No! For a long time now, it seems that Number One has had something to ask me. My instinct tells me it has something to do with the capture of us female comrades. Am I right?"

Qi Jing had originally planned to ramble on about this and that until he could find a suitable entry point through which to bring up this most sensitive of topics. He hadn't expected that Wang Keyu would have brought his mind so starkly out into the open. In a casual tone, he conceded, "All right. In that case, let's talk about it. It's good to make things clear when we have something to say."

"The leadership decided there was to be no political appraisal of captured persons, isn't that right?"

"There is no political appraisal. The girls who had only recently enlisted, they don't understand anything. Even if they had leaked secrets, it wouldn't have been anything important. Then, another issue is the rape. But everyone has given an account, and there's no need to make them go through all that again for nothing."

"Before I was captured, I was in a coma, unconscious the entire time. I can't give the army leadership a responsible account as they did."

"Of course. Xiao Wang, don't get me wrong. Several female comrades were raped, it was they who took the initiative to speak out. No one asked for confirmation."

Qi Jing's words were deliberately ambiguous, and Staff Officer Wang had come to realise that he was not speaking in his position as Number One chief commander, talking with a lower-level cadre. Rather, he was speaking as a man who had established a certain kind of relationship with a woman, conducting a critical review and appraisal of her.

She said, very calmly, "It seems the leadership is keen to give me the chance to state my case. Well, no! I don't need to clarify or confess anything. The coma deprived me of the right to speak. I can't rely on what I say alone as evidence to deny objective facts. No matter what the final judgment of me is, I will not raise objections. I have no basis for it, and I have nothing to say."

"There is no question of punishment here, Xiao Wang! I'll use an approximate analogy: from the surface texture alone, one cannot establish the nature of a piece of uncut jade. If it has been cut open, and you still claim not to see the change of the stone with your eyes closed, I'm afraid that doesn't make sense. You yourself best know the major physiological changes, so how can you leave others in the dark, allowing them to make wild guesses?"

It sounded like he was speaking in defence of Wang Keyu, but in fact he was being quite aggressive. He was interrogating her. Staff Officer Wang was angry and anxious to leave. She went to turn but staggered, remembering that her good leg was not able to support her weight. Qi Jing hurried to support her.

"Xiao Wang! Xiao Wang!"

Wang Keyu tried her best to show restraint. She did not cry out but wiped her tears and said, "Commander! If someone else had conveyed these words of yours to me, I would never have believed you had said them. Someone else maybe, but not you. And what can I say? I regret weaving straw sandals here today. Otherwise, you wouldn't have found the time to come to talk about this with me."

"I don't understand it myself," Qi Jing quickly explained. "Once you accept a certain outdated concept, it's difficult to remove it from your consciousness. I still think that the so-called 'red on the first night' is the purest, most precious and sacred testimony. I imagine that if it were possible one day, it should be preserved with a whole package of cotton wool and placed in an iron box…"

Wang Keyu was furious. She covered her ears tightly with her hands and let out a succession of 'Aiyas!' and several harsh, incredulous sounds.

"I'm sorry. Staff Officer Wang, please forgive me. I wanted to explain, but my words have become even fouler and more unbearable for you. I don't know why, but the more I try to explain myself, the worse it gets."

"No! The filthiest page has been added to my résumé. I can't expect others to talk to me using beautiful poetic words. But I want to ask, who gave you such privileges? Why should I be shrouded by you? Why should I stand at your mercy alone? Why should I have to be occupied by you? And, even more, why would I give consent under coercion just to ensure that I'm a blemish-free piece of jade?"

"Of course, you need to speak viciously, otherwise it will not be enough to show that you have suffered injustice. Please stand in my shoes and think about it. It's a man thing, and it would leave him with a scar that could never heal. He could only go from despair to despair."

"I understand. I really do. Faced with reality, you have to acquiesce. It's just that there is one last chance of self-deception. As long as I am willing to swear and promise my innocence, you can heal your permanent scars. I apologise to you, Commander! If I was violated because of unconsciousness, it is impossible to resist, even a little bit. What else can be proved?"

Qi Jing seemed on the verge of a fit of rage, but he resisted. He buried his head on his knee and stopped making any sound. Wang Keyu turned her body to one side, also unwilling to say more.

It was Staff Officer Wang who broke the silence, commenting, with a long sigh, "The commander disdains to serve as a deputy. In the course of your personal growth and development, the upper hand has come easily to you. If results weren't forthcoming, you never stopped with your offensive until things turned out in your favour. You personally commanded many successful battles and were always able to overwhelm the enemy instead of being crushed by them. But in Balifan District, you failed completely, with no hope of reprisal."

With trembling hands, Qi Jing rolled a "fragrant" cigarette of rumpled tobacco leaves and straw paper. He inhaled fiercely. Usually, when faced with Wang Keyu, he would suffer in silence, never lighting this kind of suffocating cigarette.

"I have something to ask the commander. Please answer me frankly."

"Speak!"

"In all honesty, what's on your mind is that the Wang Keyu exchanged from Balifan is either a chaste woman or simply a female corpse. Is that right?" Seeing the other party about to blurt out an answer, Wang Keyu reached out a palm to block his mouth. "Don't rush your words. Please, look straight into my eyes. Don't avoid my gaze!"

The two of them stared at each other intently, their eyes bright as lightning. They were locked in this impasse for some time before Military Subarea Commander Qi Jing dropped his gaze in defeat. He nodded heavily and was forced to admit it.

"Qi Jing, with all my heart I look down on you!"

This was the harshest thing Wang Keyu could say to the Number One chief. She had never learned to speak badly of others, to insult them, and she could not use any more decisive language. But it was enough. It was equivalent to a formal note of diplomatic severance between countries.

Qi Jing had been unable to look up, but when the woman spoke these words, he felt a sense of relief. He exaggerated a bitter smile, showing that the other party's determination to break off had not surprised him, as if it was indeed a good thing that the two of them would no longer be involved. He stood up, as if to walk off, but stretched out his right hand to Wang Keyu. "If you're not happy, you don't have to accommodate me."

Wang Keyu did not raise her head but silently stretched out her right hand.

There were no words of farewell, and the only feeling to pass between them was the cold touch of each other's palms. Each knew in their heart that this was the last goodbye.

CHAPTER 19

THEY RECOVER THEIR STRUTTING MACHISMO AND SELF-CONFIDENCE

Qi Jing received notice asking him to go to Wangjia Dawan in Guangshan County to take part in a meeting convened by the "Front Line Command Post" of the Field Army for brigade-level cadres and above.

Various commanders marched to Wangjia Dawan, making directly for the venue. One by one, they rushed forward to shake hands with the commander of the Field Army. Not expecting to be met with a rebuff, the chief completely ignored them. The other commanders were left stunned, not knowing if they ought to retract their hands.

When it was chief's turn to speak, he didn't mince his words. "This isn't a time for handshakes. It's not a time for greetings. This is a time for balls. Somehow, a few cadres among us have forgotten what it means to be a man. They fail to act tough when confronted by the enemy. How do you write the character for 'courage'? Is it not a man wearing a heroic cape wrapped around his head? If you have too many fears and can't face up to the fight, you will not protect your forces!

"Since ascending the mountain, the Field Army has conducted three operations, but none of them has achieved the objective of total annihilation. A lack of combat experience in the mountains and paddy fields is one explanation, as is insufficient preparation for such a campaign carried out without rear operations. North of the Yellow River, if you are wounded in action, the migrant stretcher team will be dispatched immediately. Wounds will be bandaged to stop the bleeding, while those with serious injuries will be transferred to the rear hospital. Now, I'm sorry there weren't enough stretchers to carry you, to the extent that there is now even a popular saying among our troops: to be wounded in action is equivalent to glorious sacrifice! Bounded by this kind of fear of war, of wolves ahead and tigers behind, we are paralysed, and we pass up this golden opportunity to wipe out the enemy!"

The Field Army chief dabbed his inflamed artificial eye with a handkerchief. "I said, before we set off, that in order to complete this new strategic mission, our field army must honour themselves, and it will be totally worth doing so. This level of determination is needed, and if there are those out there who waver, speak up. You will not be forced!"

The middle and senior commanders who attended the meeting had followed this one-eyed veteran general for many years and had never seen such menace and blood-boiling anger on his face. Though severely scolded, the hapless, despondent commanders stirred suddenly, recovering their strutting machismo and self-confidence.

The meeting of the Field Army's Front Line Command Post greatly moved Qi Jing. Upon his return, he immediately set about cleaning up battlefield discipline, using a variety of methods to inspire a fighting spirit among the troops. But he did not see any significant improvement.

One night, while the PLA's military subarea troops were

marching, Qi Jing noticed the flash of a torch. "Pass it on," he instructed, "no torches!" After a while, he realised the troops behind had not caught up. If they waited too long in the same place, it was very likely that enemy special agents would sneak in and provoke more confusion among the troops, further preventing them from re-establishing order. He had no choice but to change the vanguard of the troops into the rear and rush back, trying to reunite the men in the shortest time possible before making a final decision.

After the two groups of troops had re-assembled, Qi Jing sent an order back to each one of them. The command, "Pass it on – no torches", had only passed through a few people before it became "Pass it on – no toilet"! Someone thought that since they were not allowed to urinate, the situation ahead must be serious! That was how the command changed again to "Pass it on – turn around!" Passed back further, all that was left was a general disturbance and clamours of "Run! Run!" No one admitted to being the first to issue the command "Turn around!" – no one bore that responsibility. Camp that night was quiet. Suddenly, someone piped up, "Quick! Assemble urgently! Assemble urgently!" After the troops had assembled, it became clear that the chief of staff in charge of the command had no idea who had ordered the troops to gather. They asked for instructions from Number One, but even Commander Qi Jing was none the wiser. It had all been a big joke, not a command of any kind. Even so, the troops jumped into action and lined up to set off.

Asked individually, the cadres and soldiers all said that they had heard the emergency assembly whistle blowing non-stop. At this, the combat staff officer on duty sprang up. The whistle was in his pocket, and he hadn't taken it out. But then, everyone had heard the whistle, blowing louder and louder. Wasn't it just the strangest thing?

It wasn't strange at all. In the old army, this was called a "camp stampede". Excessive psychological stress drove men to hallucinate, which made it easy to take imagined emergency assembly whistles to be real. Individual cases were commonplace, but it seemed impossible for so many people to have all heard wrong. But perhaps since so many people were equally stressed, it was only natural for them to also fall into a similar state of auditory hallucination.

The threat of encountering the enemy became more serious, and the military subarea had to make further subdistrict assignments, focusing now on small task forces. Work teams from various districts and counties were dispersed to carry out their work, avoiding over-concentration as much as possible. However, the military subarea's decision was difficult to implement. The night before, they shook hands and bid farewell. The next night, they all moved closer to the headquarters without prior communication. They were startled like faint-hearted birds and jittery like fish slipping through a net. Qi Jing said with fury, "Do you want me to drive you away with a stick? Do you want me to push you down the mountain? Do you want me to shoot you? I'll listen to you. But what is there to do if you don't talk? It seems we can only hang on together, perish together with the enemy. Everything will be well, and the revolution will prevail!"

The most pressing concern was resolving the problem of nearly twenty stretchers. If the troops continued to march with them, they would drag the whole military subarea army down. Swift and decisive action was needed, that is, keeping those able to walk with the troops and "resettling" those who were seriously injured or ill in the homes of poor, reliable peasants. All expenses would be converted into monetary value, and they would issue the peasants IOUs so that they could get double the repayment from the local government at a later date.

Number One made a special case of Wang Keyu. She remained with the military subarea troops, on her stretcher, still active within the military subarea command.

Since the Soviet era, civil corps forces had regarded the search for "resettled" Red Army personnel as a kind of game, one in which they had participated enthusiastically. No matter how well you hid or how tight your security, you would never escape their methods. And it was not unheard of for households with resettled personnel to sell them out. Wang Keyu understood everything pointed to disaster, but she still asked the leaders for resettlement.

Commander Qi Jing was fraught with a deep inner conflict. With so many wounded, why should an exception be made for just one person? Whichever way he looked at it, it was impossible to justify. On the other hand, he hesitated, again and again. Wouldn't the decision to resettle Staff Officer Wang be tantamount to admitting that, because you lost your temper, you took this opportunity to push her out of your care?

Staff Officer Wang argued otherwise. "Commander," she said, "it's not just me. No one would want to be this insensitive and cause such a fuss. Four stretcher-bearers have to carry me, even at such a critical time."

"Of course, you may think a certain way. You don't want to make things difficult for me. But I can't be made to look so selfish and cold-blooded!"

Wang Keyu sensed there was something to these words and realised that it was clearly Qi Jing's personal intention to reserve a stretcher for her. He wanted to balance the inner trauma he had caused Wang Keyu and to find a sense of peace of mind.

Wang Keyu became even angrier. "Commander! Do you really think you can impose your will on me? Do you really think I have no alternative but to accept your special care and protection?"

"It seems that it is not the problem of resettlement on your mind," Number One said gravely. "It's your desire to leave the headquarters as soon as possible, to leave me as soon as possible! Is that not it?"

꧁⭐꧂

Wang Keyu grabbed her crutches and was attempting to stagger along the road alone before several guards nearby hurried over to stop her. Staff Officer Wang and the military subarea commander stood still, back-to-back. The troops were assembled, waiting for the order to depart, but the two of them were still frozen. Horse Messenger Cao Shui'er was anxious, and he stepped forward. "Number One," he said. "How about Staff Officer Wang and I form a small team to act alone. I will carry her on my back, and I promise to complete my mission."

This was a genuinely good idea. There was no need to force Wang Keyu to resettle, and no need either to keep a stretcher for her. It seemed all the problems were solved. If Cao Shui'er alone were to escort Wang Keyu across the Dabie Mountains, and the two of them agreed on fighting against the "encirclement" together, there shouldn't be a problem. Qi Jing looked straight at Staff Officer Wang, wondering if she was up to it.

"If the commander approves, I have no objection," Staff Officer Wang said, looking at the sky. "OK. It's settled." With that, the commander made his final decision.

With an upright posture, Cao Shui'er handed the Number One chief his carbine, his "twenty-shot C96", five magazines and an ammunition belt. As a rule, bodyguards who leave their commanders had to return their firearms and ammunition. Qi Jing readily accepted, adding, "Cao Shui'er, let me know whatever you need."

"If the commander says so, I might just take you up on it."

"Just say the word."

"A military canteen, an enamel mug, a torch, a box of matches, a pack of candles, some oilcloth, a dagger and a shovel. I already have them with me, and I'll keep them if the commander gives the go-ahead."

While the majority of these items were daily essentials, what was the use of a shovel? Was it really worth asking for? Most people didn't understand; only a veteran like Cao Shui'er knew of the many magical functions of the shovel. It helped you cut a path as you marched through a jungle. In the line of fire, you could dig a bunker in a few minutes to greatly reduce the possibility of injury. And when you entered into hand-to-hand combat, you could use it as well as any three-sided bayonet.

"Of course, take them all!"

The commander untied the rice bag wrapped around his waist, poured out five silver coins and gave them to Cao Shui'er.

"I've no use for them! No use!" Cao Shui'er pushed them back into the hand of Number One.

By now, Wang Keyu had become extremely impatient. "Cao Shui'er! Let's go! Let's go!"

"Take it! It's not just for you," said Qi Jing, stuffing the silver coins back into Cao Shui'er's hand.

"Yes, OK, I'll take it."

"Cao Shui'er! Come on!" Wang Keyu urged again. "Yes, yes, let's go! Let's go!"

The horse messenger couldn't help but hesitate. With his physical strength, it was no problem to carry the female comrade on the road. The difficulty was that to hold her weight, he had to either cross his hands and interlink his fingers to support Staff Officer Wang's buttocks, or clutch her thighs with both hands. It embarrassed him, with his big sweaty hands, to touch her buttocks and thighs. It felt like the greatest disrespect to her. He could never do such a thing.

Turning, he saw the pair of wooden crutches that belonged to Staff Officer Wang. He had an idea. Holding the crutches from behind, he made a long bench without legs where the wounded staff officer could easily sit. It saved him at least half of the effort while Staff Officer Wang was able to relax, and didn't have to wrap her arms tightly around his neck.

Cao Shui'er knew that Number One was still standing there watching them, and he should have turned around and let Staff Officer Wang say goodbye. Then he realised that it was foolish. So, without looking back, he strode forward with Staff Officer Wang on his back.

Chapter 20

The Towering Peaks of the Dabie Mountains Melt Rapidly Amid the Rising Flames

From that point on, this man and woman began spending every day and every night together; a brand-new lifestyle for them both.

By day, they wandered the mountains, looking for suitable hiding places. In the evenings, their stomachs groaned with the urgent need for the most basic of human needs. Cao Shui'er propped Staff Officer Wang up behind a tobacco-curing room and told her not to leave it under any circumstances, while he went on the first "armed alms-begging mission" by himself.

Jumping down from the courtyard wall, he guarded the entrance. Having established that there was only a middle-aged woman and her fifteen- or sixteen-year-old son in the house, he entered and talked the "hostess" into getting him something to eat, anything at all she might be willing to provide, no matter how dry or meagre.

She didn't dare say no and started cooking straight away. The hostess didn't know, however, that smoke coming out of the stove would attract the enemy's attention. Despite Cao Shui'er's repeated attempts to hold her back, she still insisted on firing it up.

"I'm telling you, no fire is allowed! Do you have to light it?" Cao Shui'er's eyes widened. Out of the best of intentions, the hostess did not want to give cold food to the People's Liberation Army. She said, innocently, 'OK, OK! No fire! Let's see, there should be something to eat."

The son of the house made towards the cow shed, wanting to add feed, but Cao Shui'er forbade him to open the door. It could wait until he'd left, he said. The boy didn't understand the logic and so continued to walk over to the door, upon which the horse messenger knocked him back a long way and withdrew the shovel from his belt as if he was about to use it. The mother, terrified, pushed her son forcefully back into the house.

The woman gave up everything she had. With a bamboo basket, she handed over some leftover food with crusts of rice, a small dish of pickled stinky peas and a bowl of boiled pak choi soup. Cao Shui'er wrapped the rice in a cloth, poured the soup into his big enamel jar, mumbling a quick thanks to the hostess, before opening the courtyard door and rushing off.

⁂

That night, they camped behind a tomb – the kind of place most people wouldn't dare go near. Cao Shui'er spread out the military oilcloth, upon which he piled a thick layer of dried tree leaves, asking Staff Officer Wang to sleep there fully clothed, straw sandals included. The pair slept with the top of their heads together, to afford a semblance of space between them. In fact, they were closer than ever, to the point that he could smell Staff Officer Wang's long hair. If there was any movement whatsoever, they didn't have to speak to see if the other was still there, only reach out and touch the other person's head.

No matter when or where, it was never a problem when Wang Keyu needed to pee. Cao Shui'er just had to make himself scarce for a moment. Shitting was more complicated. Cao

Shui'er had to choose a suitable spot to dig a small pit, then fill it up with dirt and level it, sprinkling the area with dry soil and grass leaves. If they left any trace for the enemy, they were sure to be tracked and hunted down.

The next day, they rose early. Looking around in the light of early dawn, Cao Shui"r noticed something. Staff Officer Wang asked him what it was, but he didn't answer. Rather, he prowled the vicinity, scanning their surroundings.

Having experienced the "raids" of the Taihang Mountains in 1942, Cao Shui'er had mastered a special kind of knowledge. He understood what kind of natural conditions, topography and landforms were most suitable for setting fire to the mountains. He noticed that this place was full of dense, primitive mountain forest, covered with Masson's pine and weeds. If the enemy were to light a match here, the flames would spread with terrifying ease.

To make further observations, they climbed the highest nearby peak and looked around. Sure enough, they saw cylindrical blockhouses built on the mountain ridges, one every two or three kilometres. What became clear was that the Nationalist Army was about to set in motion a series of dramas not dissimilar to the networks of spies, roads and blockhouses created by the commander-in-chief of the Japanese Expeditionary Army, Yasuji Okamura.

Seeking to undermine the PLA's strategic intent to establish a Dabie Mountains Base Area, and ensure that the Yangtze River as a transportation artery remain unobstructed, the Kuomintang authorities established the "Jiujiang Command of the Ministry of National Defence". The defence minister Bai Chongxi directly controlled military and political power in the five provinces of Henan, Anhui, Jiangxi, Hunan and Hubei. A total of thirty-three reorganised brigades were mobilised to carry out a large-scale "clean-up and raid" on the hinterland of the Dabie Mountains using the tactic of so-called "total war".

It was, of course, impossible for a horse messenger to learn about major strategic deployments from the Kuomintang authorities, nor had there been any official notifications. But Cao Shui'er had judged correctly, with a veteran's sensitivity to war, what Bai Chongxi had pointed to and poked at on the military map of the Jiujiang Command War Room – the very mountains and forests in which he now stood.

His heart leapt. While he had boasted aloud in front of Number One that he would ensure the safety of Staff Officer Wang, he now realised that he may have spoken too soon!

"Staff Officer Wang! As the highest-ranked officer here, I have something urgent to report to you."

Wang Keyu had never seen him so earnest, and she found this kind of amusing, saying, "I'm not worthy of being reported to. I'll listen to whatever the chief instructs."

Cao Shui'er smiled and began to conduct a detailed analysis of the enemy's movements. He was certain that while the military subarea troops had been dealing anxiously with the enemy over the past few days, they were actually being drawn in, step by step, to exactly where the enemy wanted them. The two of them were not exempt, for they too were both contained in this encirclement, and there was a great fire waiting there for them!

"And it's too late to break free?" Staff Officer Wang wondered.

"To break out by force, we'd have to rely on firepower. We only have a dagger and a shovel, which wouldn't scare anyone. If we tried to pass ourselves off as villagers and get through the blockade line, well, there's no chance that would work. At first glance, they'd see two northerners. The only viable option left is to dig a hole in the ground, climb in and emerge to see the light of day only once the great fire passes."

"Dig a hole, but where?" Wang Keyu was at a loss.

⁂

Indeed, there was the urgent question of site selection, which required no little consideration.

If you believed, like most people, that the best way to avoid getting burned was to choose an open area with no trees, you'd be quite wrong. The experience of countering "raids" in the Taihang Mountains had taught the Japanese devils to be suspicious of large, open spaces, which they would search over and over. On the contrary, it was the densely forested areas, in which everything burned, that they felt no need to waste manpower and other resources to search.

Staff Officer Wang questioned this line of thinking. "There's logic to that," she admitted, "but surely the entrance to the hole would attract a fire? And in a place dense with trees, the flames would rain down like mercury. It doesn't even bear thinking about."

No! This was, in fact, where the brilliant intricacy of the plan envisaged by Horse Messenger Cao Shui'er lay. It was entirely feasible for them to avoid the seemingly inevitable and catastrophic consequences that Staff Officer Wang was so worried about.

"First you dig the hole, then you wait," Cao Shui'er explained. "When the fire is spreading and approaching the opening, stay ahead of the enemy and take the initiative by lighting a fire upwind, burning the weeds and trees around the entrance to the hole. When the main fire passes, it will only burn the surrounding area. You'll be shielded from the fire. Much less will it pour into the hole."

Wang Keyu was truly taken aback. Everyone had praised Cao Shui'er for his cunning, but today he had pulled off the impressive feat of achieving a great deal with little effort. He built them an island of safety amid a sea of flames as if saying, let the fire rage up into the sky, for what it's got to do with me!

Since ancient times, we've been warned not to play with fire. Cao Shui'er's fire, if it had been lit just a little earlier, or even a little later, would have been a failure. But he played it just right. Afraid that the heads of the matches would be wet and cause delay, he prepared a handful. When the decisive moment arrived, he would have several matches available. If the first didn't catch, there was a second. If that didn't light either, he could try again and again until finally one lit, throw it onto a pile of dry Masson's pine, and that would be that. All that would be left was to jump into the hole and close the entrance.

There was no need to be afraid. The fire to be started by the enemy would meet with the fire they were going to start themselves, and together they would burn away into the distance. The mountains and plains would be covered with ashes, and even if the enemy were to pass by the entrance of their hole, there would be no sign of them.

As a next step, they had to determine how wide and how deep the hole was to be dug, and how to cover the opening of the cave.

At first, they wanted to dig the hole a little wider, so that the two of them could stand back-to-back. The problem was that the wider the opening of the hole, the higher the chance that a Nationalist soldier's leather boot would step on it, and hence the greater the risk. In the end, it was determined that the diameter of the hole should be only slightly larger than a human body, and the depth should be that of about one and a half people. Cao Shui'er would crouch down to serve as a 'platform' for Wang Keyu to stand on his shoulders. They would leave some space above her head to facilitate covering the hole.

The roof of the hole was the most technical aspect of the whole project, in addition to being the most labour-intensive and meticulous process.

They cut off a few wooden sticks about the thickness of a wrist and tied them tightly with wattle to make a wooden frame of about two square feet. The hole in the ground was originally round, with the upper section slightly expanded, but they adjusted it into a square to match the size and shape of the wooden frame. The top of the frame was covered with a layer of leaves to prevent soil from filtering through, and some weeds and wildflowers were strewn over it to give it the appearance of "living tissue" cut from the ground. It was made so that, once they had lowered themselves into the hole, they could reach out a hand to pull it to cover the entrance tightly from the inside. Even if someone were to stand on top of them, they would never suspect that there were two living people under their feet.

After digging the hole, they carried out two practice runs of covering it. Wang Keyu's operations ran successfully, passing without any hitches.

Everything was ready. All that was left was to put their plan into practice.

⁓⁂★⁂⁓

As Cao Shui'er had expected, the enemy started the fire upwind. The flames took off in the breeze, carrying them with menace to form a prairie fire. The towering peaks of the Dabie Mountains shone like a red candle, melting rapidly amid the rising flames.

Just as they sense when an earthquake is coming, animals can detect an approaching wildfire and know to flee in good time. There was a mad, panicked dash of wild boars, monkeys, foxes, squirrels, hedgehogs, rabbits, badgers, pythons, snakes and more. It was said that there were tigers in the mountains, but they had never been seen.

In their rush, a five-pacer snake and a fleshy little hedgehog fell into the hole. Cao Shui'er worried that these two uninvited guests would frighten Staff Officer Wang. He lowered himself down into the hole where the snake had curled itself into a ball. He captured it and kept it alive in the large enamel jar. The harmless little hedgehog was left to do as it pleased.

Wang Keyu had anticipated that she would feel short of

breath, suffocated and uncomfortable in the small, muddy space. On the contrary, when she entered the hole, she found all physical discomfort replaced by a strong sense of fantasy. She was amazed, therefore, to hear a voice calling out from ground level. It seemed distant and faint, but also clear and lifelike. It was like the sound of a cocoon turning into silk, the subtle sound of silk wafting uncannily through the confined space.

"Haha! You Eighth Routers, how will you survive in your hole?"

"We saw you ages ago. Men and women, piled on top of each other. Come out!"

"If you won't come out, we're going to fire! We're going to fill the hole with water and smoke!" The enemy fired blindly while yelling out in a strange voice, creating an atmosphere of terror. Cao Shui'er had repeatedly warned Wang Keyu that the enemy would holler in this way as they searched the mountain-side, and while it might appear to be directed at them, she must ignore it. When Staff Officer Wang first heard their shouting, she felt as if the enemy were yelling in her face. She was startled, but composed herself quickly and smiled knowingly.

Before going down the hole, Wang Keyu had made a point to pee. Not long after, however, she was once again desperate, despite being perched unsteadily on Cao Shui'er's shoulders. As they had arranged beforehand, he placed the military oilcloth tightly over his head and patted Wang Keyu's legs, meaning that he was ready for the stream of urine. But damn! Staff Officer Wang cried in frustration, biting her lip until she drew blood, simply unable to make the physiological exertion that was so natural and so needed.

With a sense of foreboding, Cao Shui'er anticipated imminent catastrophe. Either Staff Officer Wang would suffer serious illness from holding her pee, or she would, in desperation, lift the cover and crawl out of the hole and straight into enemy gunfire. The experienced horse messenger had no other option. He dug his fingernails, sharp as blades, into Staff Officer Wang's calves. The piercing pain disabled her self-control, and a great stream of urine poured down on Cao Shui'er.

The cave was pitch black, making it impossible to distinguish day and night, which could only be calculated based on a few small details. The enemy's leather boots had stepped across the ground above them a total of three times. In other words, they had spent three days in a row carrying out "removals and raids" across this scorched earth. It must be the third night now, and it was time to leave the hole and get back to ground level.

The pair climbed out of the hole, one after the other. Looking back, the two small animals that had lived and suffered alongside them crawled out afterwards, with difficulty. The five-pacer snake disappeared quickly into a thick layer of ashes and leaves. The fleshy little hedgehog seemed stunned by the scene in front of it: the world was nothing now but a bare expanse, and the smell of burnt earth was inescapable. Where should I go?

⁕☆⁕

The two collapsed outside the opening of the hole. Like squeezing a bellows, they gasped for breath until their lung capacity returned to normal.

Cao Shui'er praised his superior lavishly. "Our Great Staff Officer Wang, you're really something! I thought you'd spent your last breath, and I was afraid you wouldn't be able to lift such a heavy roof. We'd have had to wait until the next mountain flood, for the deluge to break and our hole to be filled with water. Only then could we have floated back to the surface."

Staff Officer Wang was also anxious to express her heartfelt admiration to the horse messenger. "I've come to understand something. If there was no war in this world, you, Cao Shui'er, would not have needed to be born."

They lay on their backs, quietly facing the sky, beyond exhausted. They could easily have fallen asleep, but the horse messenger was in a state of exhilaration. The starry sky flickered above him, a companion he thought he might never see again during their recent separation. After waiting and watching for a long time, he grew confused. It was as if something were wrong with the sky. "Staff Officer Wang," he asked. "Did someone mess with the stars? I've studied them from left to right, and they appear to have been re-arranged."

"You've been in a hole for three days and three nights. You're not qualified to say such things. If you had travelled three hundred million light years and said that you have found a rearrangement of the stars, that might make sense."

"What are light years?" Cao was utterly confused.

"The distance light travels in a vacuum in a year is called a light year. It's around nine and a half trillion kilometres."

"My goodness! We have so many guns and cannons in the world, firing back and forth. But compared with these light years you talk about, well, they're very slow, aren't they?" Cao Shui'er said, with great feeling.

"Isn't it just, Cao Shui'er. What a good way of putting it! Bravo!"

CHAPTER 21

A KIND OF SMELL THAT CAN'T BE WASHED AWAY BY RIVER WATER

They had successfully survived the great fire, but the Yasuji Okamura-style "clean-ups and raids" had not ended, and the enemy would not be letting up any time soon. An unarmed soldier and a severely wounded officer acting alone like this were in desperate need of sanctuary. They had to seize the opportunity offered by nightfall to hurry into the vast mountainous area, where ridges and peaks offered easy hiding places, and look for a suitable place to settle.

Cao Shui'er carried Wang Keyu on his back. He couldn't help but feel, with a certain shock, that he was carrying a different person, someone who was much lighter. It was not the weight that Staff Officer Wang should have been. To be more precise, it was not the Staff Officer Wang of three days ago. Cao Shui'er had always been a somewhat carefree and casual man. But now, for the first time in his life, he was filled with an inexplicable sadness as he considered the weight of the woman, this "chief" who was now in his care.

Under cover of night, they hit the road.

Blockhouses were dense along the blockade, and the area was patrolled by enemy troops. Generally speaking, one must approach this type of scenario with stealth, wait for the patrol to leave a gap and take that opportunity to cross, or throw a stone to divert the enemy's attention and rush through. These methods were not available to Cao Shui'er. He was carrying a severely wounded woman on his back, and like a huge snail, he could only crawl slowly forward. If they happened to arrive at that indeterminate time, past breakfast but not yet lunch, the way might be clear for them to pass through the cordon without being detected. But if they came across the patrol team, there would be no way round it.

And indeed, they encountered exactly what they had hoped to avoid! In the darkness, Cao Shui'er caught sight of four armed patrolmen walking towards them in single file. If he had been alone, he would have remained very still, held his breath and waited for the enemy to pass, hoping they wouldn't notice him. As a last resort, he would still have had time to deal with the opponents. But now, as things stood, he was left with no choice but to act first, to go forward and dispose of these four life-risking "brothers".

Settling Staff Officer Wang in a nearby bush, he whispered, "Close your eyes tight, cover your ears. Don't look at anything, don't listen to anything. Just wait for me to come back. Did you hear? Wait for me to come back."

Horse Messenger Cao Shui'er placed the dagger into the outside of his left leg puttee, picked up his bright, shining shovel, rushed forward a few strides and quickly entered a dense pine forest. He slapped a tree trunk with the shovel, making a noise loud enough to lure the enemy into the woods. Sure enough, the four patrolmen immediately formed a skirmish line and advanced towards the trees, and soon appeared in a clearing not far from Cao Shui'er.

By observing the enemy's equipment in the moonlight, Cao Shui'er determined that these were first-class soldiers in the regular unit of the Nationalist Army. Judging from the way they handled their guns, they looked like professionally trained scout rangers. He needed to be careful.

Four-to-one, the ratio itself was enough for any onlooker to anticipate a spectacular martial arts show, well worth watching.

With only a shovel to his name, the most important thing for Cao Shui'er to do was to try to disorient his opponents and make them fight as individuals, thus losing the significant advantage of being able to help each other. The horse messenger let out a cry, then moved to another place, then to a third and then a fourth place, making noises in all these different locations, one after the other. Unable to focus, the four patrolmen were left to scatter and search in several places.

Cao Shui'er gently pushed aside the branches as he walked forward. He heard a rustling from behind as if someone was following him. Looking back, he could see the first of his visitors aiming a rifle at him, the triangular bayonet shining brightly. Upon finding Cao Shui'er apparently unarmed, he relaxed somewhat, as if everything could be resolved through negotiation. He raised the muzzle twice, ordering his captive to raise his hands.

Cao Shui'er cartwheeled away, escaping the muzzle's stare, expecting to be shot at any moment. But he had misjudged his opponent, who, instead of firing at him, had made up his mind to capture the PLA soldier alive. He strode forward several paces, fixing his eyes on his target and refusing to let it go. He once again pointed his bayonet directly between Cao Shui'er's eyebrows, and let out a contemptuous laugh.

He had laughed too soon. Pretending to raise his hands, Cao Shui'er swiped the rifle off the patrolman's hands with his shovel. The soldier bent down to retrieve his gun, inadvertently exposing his buttocks. Cao Shui'er flew over and kicked out viciously, the patrolman staggered and fell to the ground, turning his head to see the People's Liberation Army soldier in sharp pursuit, holding the shovel. He raised both arms to protect his head, but the sharp shovel cut down in the gap between them. As he completed the slashing action, Cao Shui'er jumped out of the way in order to avoid the brains, soft as melon flesh, splashing onto him. All he heard was a vague, short rumble from the opponent's throat, before everything came to an end.

In less than three minutes, the Nationalist Army patrol team had been reduced by a quarter.

The second uninvited guest crept around with his back to an old cypress tree, moving sideways like a huge crab. He could observe all surrounding movements, and once something happened, he could manoeuvre accordingly with the trunk concealing him. Cao Shui'er had caught sight of him early, and he crawled forward, ever closer, waiting for the patrolman to move to the other side of the tree. He took up his position, moving in circles as if the two of them were grinding a mill-stone together, constantly following his second target around, waiting for the right time to make his move.

Cao Shui'er turned abruptly, raised the shovel in both hands and aimed a swing at the patrolman's skull. Instinctively, the man recoiled his neck, hearing a crack as the shovel cut into the tree trunk. Even with great effort, Cao Shui'er could not extract it from the wood. The patrol screamed triumphantly and stabbed outward with his gun. Somehow, he too was over-eager in his actions, plunging the bayonet beyond its target and into the tree trunk with a thud, where it stayed. Cao Shui'er took the opportunity to charge his opponent, slamming his chin bone from the bottom up with a clenched fist. The patrolman fell to the ground, limbs sprawled out in all directions.

In his combat training, the move Cao Shui'er used was called an uppercut. It was a fatal blow, and there was no need for him to make any additional moves. But no! His next move was more considered, for he would never allow an enemy the possibility of a fluke escape. He withdrew the shovel from the trunk and thrust it toward the opponent's neck. The phrase "to shovel" has a clear and obvious meaning. It means to press down on the handle, using a shining blade to cut downwards, before withdrawing it again.

But Cao Shui'er didn't give it his all. He didn't want to feel as if his actions were akin to cutting off a melon seedling. Upon hearing the squelching sound of blood, he stopped himself and quickly left the scene.

Before they knew it, the patrol's strength had been reduced by half.

It seemed that the sharpest mind belonged to the third patrolman. He saw no sense in searching the whole area, preferring to wait patiently for his enemy to tire. To win by cunning, he used wild vines from the forest to make a kind of netting between the rows of trees, and lingered there until his prey fell into the trap. Sure enough, the horse messenger tripped and stumbled as he cantered past, falling to the ground. The man pounced on Cao Shui'er like a hungry tiger and held him tightly beneath him. In terms of size and strength, the other party was at an obvious disadvantage, but he was shrewd. During the tumbling and fighting, he clasped Cao Shui'er's neck firmly from behind with his forearm. In the history of Chinese martial arts, this is a distinctive move, handed down from generation to generation – the "throat lock". The time left to unlock this manoeuvre is measured in seconds. If you cannot break free, you will soon suffocate and die.

Cao Shui'er said to himself, Playing this old trick on me, eh? Well, I'm no feeble vegetarian! He quietly curled up his calf and withdrew the dagger from its strap. He stabbed deeply into his opponent's abdomen and dragged down with vigour. Along with the sound of the abdomen being cut open, a hot and unpleasant stench swelled up into his nostrils. The man cried out, writhing on the ground a few times until there was no more movement, and all his debts were written off.

In the stifling mountain forest, three-quarters of the patrol force had evaporated.

Cao Shui'er spotted the last patrol soldier rushing through the jungle. His mental state had collapsed, and he was screaming in horror with a slurred voice. He must have been spooked by the corpses of the other troops, wanting nothing more than to escape the forest. Cao Shui'er only had to make a few strides to catch up with him, holding the shovel high before chopping down. Because both of them were moving rapidly, the shovel didn't find the head. Instead, it struck his heart hard from behind, causing him to freeze, quite suddenly. Like a wooden stake, he fell stiffly to the ground. Dead.

Now, this well-trained Nationalist Army patrol team had to reassemble with their original organisational system intact and embark on an unfamiliar path they hadn't expected. One thing was certain though: from then on, no one would give any combat missions to these guys.

꙳ ★ ꙳

In such an engagement, it wasn't just that Cao Shui'er was at a distinct disadvantage in terms of military strength. The crucial point was that when any unfavourable situation arose, it was impossible for him to withdraw from the battle with Staff Officer Wang on his back. There was simply no room for him to withdraw. The only option was to wipe out all the enemy troops, leaving not a single one of them alive. The ferocity and danger of the skirmish were beyond imagination, certainly something he had never seen since the war broke out. In fact, it turned out to be a simple and straightforward process, a case of practice makes perfect. But it spurred him on, and whether consciously or unconsciously, brought a bit of entertainment.

The sudden mountain breeze hit Cao Shui'er, who had been sweating profusely, with spine-tingling cold, leaving him shivering incessantly. He smelt a foul stench on his body, strong enough to make him vomit. He thought he must wash himself, otherwise it would be difficult to face Staff Officer Wang.

He came upon a creek. The shore was pure rock and sand, and the water rushed gurgling forth. In some areas, the depth reached waist height. Cao Shui'er plunged into the creek, and it was some time before his head emerged, quite suddenly, out of the water. Rocking his neck and shoulders from side to side, he shook himself all over like a brown bear, and water scattered and splashed in a cloud of spray. He scrubbed the front of his shirt with his hands, but feeling this inadequate, he took off his military uniform altogether, scrubbed it vigorously on the stone, wrung out the water, and put it on again, still damp.

Abruptly, he noticed a figure walking towards the river. Cao Shui'er was shocked, a patrol had only just passed by, why had another one appeared? He grabbed the shovel and dived into the water, observing with only his head above the surface. A man approached, his belly swollen terribly and wrapped carelessly with makeshift bandages. Ah ha! It was the patrolman, the one whose abdomen Cao Shui'er had cut open. Lucky to have survived, he now sought to escape across the river.

The patrolman was wading unsteadily in the water when he saw a shirtless man in front of him. He was shocked and unable to move. Before he understood what was happening, Cao Shui'er grabbed him by the neck, as if picking up a chicken or a goose, and thrust him down into the river. The patrolman thrashed about desperately with a gurgling sound. His organs emerged black from the water and were immediately washed away by the river.

The man was nothing now but an empty shell, but he still

struggled and shook. Cao Shui'er applied pressure to his neck and held on until his old opponent stopped moving. When he finally released him, the corpse floated up and drifted away.

Cao Shui'er felt only a great darkness in front of him. The sky and the earth spun. He collapsed onto a large rock, and it was a long time before he came to.

⁂

The horse messenger had expected Staff Officer Wang to lavish him once more with praise. He had single-handedly eliminated a highly armed force as if chopping up melons. The last thing he anticipated was for Staff Officer Wang, when she raised her head and saw clearly that he had returned, to simply turn to one side and ignore him. Cao Shui'er stood there in a daze for a long time.

"Staff Officer Wang! What have I done wrong?"

"Nothing, it's my problem. I just can't stand the smell of you."

Cao Shui'er smiled. "Ah! Knowing that the chief's nose is sharp, I washed off in the river."

"This kind of smell can't be washed away by river water!"

"Is our great Staff Officer Wang being a little too demanding? If the river can't wash it off, what do you want me to do?" Cao Shui'er said, joking, as he approached.

"No, please! Step back! Step back! Step back!"

The horse messenger grinned. Unable to move forward but unwilling to go back, he realised the problem was serious.

"Please, go and have a look for me," Wang Keyu requested. "I believe there will still be a villager out there willing to protect me."

"You're not too badly off. The task assigned to me by the subarea commander was to guard you, not to hide you. Besides, since the enemy is still 'raiding', as we speak, who do you think we'll find out there?"

Wang Keyu lay on her back in the bushes, her face covered with both hands, and said no more.

"Staff Officer Wang, when the patrol team fail to return to their camp, the enemy will send more troops at once. We're in a race against time and cannot delay any longer. We have to get going." Seeing Wang Keyu remain silent, he continued, "Staff Officer Wang, it's fine if you don't want to cooperate with my work, but you can't get rid of me as soon as you get upset!"

"No! I'm begging *you* to get rid of *me*. From today, you can let go of me."

Cao Shui'er stomped his foot. "I really can't protect you if you delay for no good reason. But you should understand, Staff Officer Wang, when it comes to it, I have my own means of taking the initiative. I won't let you fall into the hands of the enemy for a second time!"

Wang Keyu responded with utter disdain. "You, Cao Shui'er, don't have this right!"

"But I shoulder this responsibility," Cao Shui'er cried out. "Comrade Xiao Wang, I'm telling you the truth. Even if I didn't have this responsibility, I certainly have this true intention!"

Wang Keyu said calmly, "Since this is your true intention, I won't hurt your feelings. I thank you. As far as I'm concerned, it makes no difference how you reach the final conclusion, it's all the same. However, your proactive approach is easier to swallow."

"Staff Officer Wang, you can't push me around like this any more."

The horse messenger's patience had exceeded its limits. He rushed forward with a growl, fists clenched, and struck Wang Keyu's temples on both sides at the same time. She fainted and fell limply to the ground. Cao Shui'er, as if carrying a large bag of grain, carried the female Eighth Router sideways. The woman leaned on his left shoulder, her head against Cao Shui'er's broad and supple chest, her arms drooping and her long legs hanging behind his back. They were on the road again. Although carrying a heavy load, Cao Shui'er's footsteps were brisk and powerful, and soon they were far away.

The woods fell silent as if tonight were a night like any other.

⁂

Wang Keyu's body wriggled slightly, and she groaned a little, apparently starting to wake up. Cao Shui'er was afraid that she was clamouring to be left behind again. Pretending he hadn't noticed anything, he strode on ahead.

When the Eighth Router woke up, she felt the heart of the horse messenger beating fast. Aware of his tiredness, she couldn't help but blame herself: it was too much to have forced her guardian soldier to cry! But she didn't make a sound, pretending that she was still unconscious, allowing Cao Shui'er to carry her wherever he was going.

The storm struck with a sudden burst of cold air. Cao Shui'er could no longer move forward and had to put Staff Officer Wang down and prop her up firmly against a tree, hugging both the woman and the trunk tightly from behind. Thankfully, the two People's Liberation Army soldiers, a man and a woman, avoided being swept away by the violent wind and washed away by the flash floods.

The pouring rain washed over his head and face, and Cao Shui'er couldn't even open his mouth to exhale. But he also felt an overwhelming surge of happiness, and couldn't help but release from his suffocated lungs a crazed scream into the abyss: "Ah! Ah! Ahhh!" In the fight in the woods, whenever he had killed a Nationalist Army patrolman, he instinctively wanted to scream. He had had to hold it back then, but now he made up for that lost opportunity. Under the cover of the storm, he didn't have to fear being heard. In fact, he couldn't even hear himself, allowing the great roar to emit from his throat.

The horse messenger realised that Wang Keyu was also roaring silently beside him. Yes, during this period, Staff Officer Wang had accumulated much resentment and unhappiness in her heart, and now she was presented with a rare opportunity to vent her feelings. Cao Shui'er relaxed a little because it had been worrying him that she might suddenly turn her face away and vomit blood in secret.

The storm stopped as suddenly as it had arrived. Cao Shui'er originally thought it was dawn, but the sun had in fact been hanging there, high in the sky, for some time. Looking around, he saw that they had entered the mountains.

CHAPTER 22

FROM HER MEMORY, NOT FROM HER IMAGINATION

It was said that a small group of guerrilla fighters from the Fourth Front Red Army had been left behind in the area surrounding the main peak of the Dabie Mountains. They found a cave, supposedly big enough for two divisions to fit comfortably inside, and hid there for some unknown length of time. The strange thing was that the entrance to the cave had never been found. Cao Shui'er hoped his luck might change this, and he set out to discover the "Red Army Cave" as soon as possible, hoping to use it as his own headquarters.

The pair painstakingly searched the area, scouring through bushes but with nothing to show for their efforts. On reaching the point of utter despair, they noticed evidence of landslides on the rockface but little or no accumulation of mud and stone beneath the cliff. Where had such a substantial volume of fallen earth and stone gone?

It became apparent that there was a small depression beneath the cliff. This was not immediately visible, because the area was filled with debris, but it was a promising lead. If Cao Shui'er could investigate further, it wasn't implausible that the entrance to the Red Army Cave would be found under this cliff, covered by the collapsed mountain debris. The pair acted immediately, peeling away the mud and stones at their feet, all the while praying for a miracle. A small hole was revealed. After a short while, a natural cave was presented in full before their eyes. The sight made the two of them happy beyond belief, and they clasped hands in celebration.

However, when they had cleared a significant pile of mud and rocks, it became clear that the original opening of the hole was much higher than ground level, and entering it required a demanding climb. The entrance to the cave was slightly camouflaged too, which made it hard to find, but easy to see how the mystery of the Red Army Cave had endured for so many years.

Entering the cave, they felt a sudden, warm breeze, and the sound of rumbling wind resonated throughout the space. This was due to the temperature difference between the outside valley area and the enclosed inside space, forming a strong air convection phenomenon. The two of them had never heard such a wind in their lives, adding to the wonder and mystery of it all.

After walking for around ten metres through a dim tunnel, the sound of the wind stopped abruptly. Their eyes fell suddenly upon an empty hall in the cave. Sunlight penetrated the cracks in the ceiling, and in these rays of light appeared the outlines of stalactites, stalagmites, stone mantles, stone flowers and huge stone pillars reaching up from the ground in different poses. The two rare guests were overwhelmed.

While looking around the area, Staff Officer Wang gave Cao Shui'er a lesson in geology. With a lively tone, she told him how rainwater contains carbon dioxide, which had partially dissolved the limestone formation, after millions of years of erosion, to form underground spaces such as the natural cave they now stood in.

Cao Shui'er listened in silence. Good heavens! It might have been hyperbole to say that it was spacious enough to accommodate two divisions, but there was certainly more than enough space for two whole regiments to live here. He raised his head and shouted, and the echoes rang out through the cave in all directions.

A large section of the rock wall was blackened by smoke and fire, and there were many small pits in the ground – obvious traces of the making of explosives. First, nitrate and plant ash were used as raw materials, heated at a ratio of eight to one, and filtered into nitrate. The nitrate water was heated until it evaporated, and then filtered again after cooling to obtain potassium nitrate crystals that could be used to make explosives.

They were in no doubt that this was the cave where the Red Army guerrillas had lived.

⠶⠶⭐⠶⠶

In the cave, they were finally able to catch their breath. It would be safe for Staff Officer Wang to stay in this "nest" to take care of her wounds. Meanwhile, Horse Messenger Cao Shui'er would take responsibility for security and logistical support of the "headquarters".

Primarily, this meant going to the village every night to beg for alms to ensure that Staff Officer Wang had enough nutrition; otherwise, her wounds would not heal. Second, the water in the cave being too hard and containing many impurities, he had to carry a bamboo tube several times a day to draw spring water from a mountain stream. It was also made a rule that they would not use any part of the cave as a toilet. Their excrement, therefore, was also to be collected in bamboo tubes and transported outside at night, where a hole was dug, and it was buried.

On top of the many other tasks, all this coming and going, in and out of the cave, overwhelmed Cao Shui'er. The entrance to the hole had to be sealed tight at all times to prevent it from becoming visible. Every time he left, the horse messenger had to look out through the cracks in the stone before moving them, to check for anything out of the ordinary. When he came back from an activity, he watched from a distance to see that there were no suspicious movements before stepping forward to open the cave entrance. When going into the cave, he had to turn around and seal the entrance tightly before continuing into its depth.

Despite these demands, and all the hard work they involved, Cao Shui'er quickly got used to the rhythm of life in the cave. This was more than just a case of reluctant adaptation. In fact, he had no desire for the war to end. He didn't want Bai Chongxi's "clean-ups and raids" to stop, or for Staff Officer Wang's bone injuries to heal. He felt a deep sense of attachment to this mythical water karst cave.

Staff Officer Wang examined the large rock face for a long time, and said to Cao Shui'er, "I don't know why, but this cave feels familiar. No! More than familiar, I feel like I'm returning to my hometown – that level of familiarity. But if I remember correctly, this cave should be much larger."

As soon as she heard herself speak these words, she was shocked. "If I remember correctly" was an absurd thing to say. What nonsense! From Cao Shui'er's dumbfounded expression, he seemed to have dismissed her remarks as you would a daydream. Staff Officer Wang wanted to persuade Cao Shui'er further but couldn't find the words. She could only repeat to him, "If I remember correctly, this cave should be much larger."

"Hmm," Cao Shui'er responded, indifferently.

If it was conceded that, yes, this place was indeed planted in her "memory", and not part of some kind of fantasy or visual hallucination, then all right. In that case, we might as well go back to ancient times with her, and examine how primitive people moved from the trees to live in natural caves like this one. Then, as we evolved and productivity levels improved, artificial caves appeared, especially around the Yellow River Basin, with its rich soil, well suited for living in burrowed caves. In these initial cases, a vertical hole was dug and covered at the top with weeds. Later, horizontal holes were excavated in the walls of soil mounds and ditches – a method cave-dwelling people still happily adopt.

If they had discovered a loess cave dwelling, rather than a karst cave like this one, would Wang Keyu have said the same thing, that everything felt familiar? The answer is yes, if you consider that, since she remembered more distant cave dwellings, she should remember cave dwellings far later.

But therein lies the problem. When we talk about "memory", we are referring to the neural connections of the human cerebral cortex recognising the imprint of something experienced or understood, which can be recalled and reproduced. But what Wang Keyu alluded to here was something she could never have experienced. It was different from any reasonable inference made relying on cultural knowledge, different too from auditory hallucinations that appear under certain conditions, and, naturally, different from the use of metaphor.

Suppose she changed the term to, say, "If I feel correctly…"

There are still problems here. Sensation refers to the direct reflection of human sensory organs to objective things, with reference to perceptions such as vision, hearing, taste and smell. Internal sensations, such as bodily sensations, balance sensations and so on are not bound up with "memory".

For Wang Keyu, this was just an internal experience, generated in a trance – something that could not be expressed in words.

✻☆✻

If someone says something purely for the sake of it, and the listener sees no harm in hearing what they have to say, then the words carry little or no weight. But in this case, the "highest chief" of the cave had assigned a serious task to the horse messenger – to scrutinise every crevice in the rocks on the cave wall. Maybe he would really find something, proving her "memory" to be accurate.

Accustomed to bending to the will of Staff Officer Wang, Cao Shui'er put up no resistance. He picked up the shovel and began to tap the cave wall, and dig around its edges. Although he held not even the slightest of hopes, he invested much enthusiasm into these efforts. He found a large crack in the rock wall and squeezed in sideways. The way was blocked, and he had to dig away some more loose rock in order to progress into a honeycomb-shaped zone formed by the arrangement of countless boulders. Within this web of crevices, there seemed to be endless ways through, but each time another "locked gate" loomed large in front of him, and he was forced to turn back. Cao Shui'er tried each passage, one by one, but all ended in failure.

He was not discouraged, however, instead putting to good use his skill at passing through the enemy's barbed wire on the battlefield, crawling forward with difficulty. In areas of complex terrain like these, for example, you had to consider again and again whether it was more advantageous to lead with your head or feet. Quite suddenly, he discovered himself in a crevice space that was expanding more and more as he advanced, which filled him with renewed confidence. Aiyo, how great! Could it really be that the "memory" of Staff Officer Wang was going to become a reality?

As Cao Shui'er traversed through the crevices in the rocks, he looked at the endless, monotonous scenery of the cave wall, like Xu Xiake in PLA uniform. The book *Xu Xiake's Travels* contains a total of 357 caves, and that great 16th-century traveller personally visited nearly ninety per cent of them. Could his book also include this karst cave under the main peak of the Dabie Mountains? If so, it should have been referred to as the

Red Army Cave, and the "copyright" for it should have belonged to Staff Officer Wang Keyu and Horse Messenger Cao Shui'er.

Suddenly, stepping onto sheer air, Cao Shui'er almost fell through a gap. The hole in the ground was large in diameter as if left there by geological drilling. If the walls hadn't been so uneven, he would certainly have fallen. Cao Shui'er lay still on the ground and observed carefully. It seemed that there was light at a certain depth. He picked up a stone and threw it down. The stone bounced between the walls and hit the ground after a short pause.

From the perspective of this "drilled hole", it became clear that this natural cave had more than one level, in the style of a building. It was unclear exactly how many layers there were, but it was no exaggeration to say there were at least three or even five. Cao Shui'er was very proud of his accidental discovery. He piled up a few stones next to the "drilled hole" as a sign, so that it would be easier to find next time around.

Cao Shui'er then heard what sounded like a roaring torrent, but looking around there was no river. A small stream then appeared before him, but it was flowing quietly, without sound. It seemed clear that in addition to the stream in front of him, a much larger watercourse must be on another level of the cave, not above his head, but under his feet.

The way was blocked, so he rolled up his trousers and waded into the water, stepped onto the other side and continued to move forward. Again, he found no way through, so he retreated to the stream and followed its course. Sometime later – he hadn't been paying attention – he noticed the stream had dried up completely. Only then did Cao Shui'er realise that he had been walking uphill on this last stage of the journey. The incline was relatively gentle, but the stream was so small it did not have the force to accompany the brave explorer who forged quietly upwards onto the next level of the cave.

Further on he came across another cave hall, much taller and wider than the hall of the Red Army Cave. It was about 130 metres wide and a little over a hundred metres high. Another difference was that the light here did not come from the mouth of the cave, but from numerous narrow cracks in the stone. The shafts wove into a mist-like net, a unique projection that made the entire cavern appear all the more brilliant, magical and deep.

Staring out of one of these cracks, he saw a monkey picking wild fruit off the branches of a bush. Cao Shui'er couldn't help but be surprised. This natural cave was little more than a rock wall, barely separated from the outside world. There was no sense of confidentiality at all, which made it unsuitable for him and Staff Officer Wang to live in – his efforts had been made in vain.

He tried to calm himself, and indeed he found his heart lifting. Recalling the direction he had moved in, and the distance travelled, Cao Shui'er calculated his position – he was at the top of the main peak of the Dabie Mountains! He pictured, quite easily, the hazy mist drifting by on a soft wind and the sheer cliff looming over a vast abyss.

This cave complex hung high in the clouds, and no one – except those woolly monkeys – had any chance of reaching it.

⁂

Cao Shui'er had completed his "expedition" and embarked back on a road of triumph.

He had not anticipated that a huge boulder would lie in his way, blocking him from taking another step forward.

The explorer clenched his fists and repeatedly thumped the top of his head. With difficulty, he recalled that when he had passed here, he heard a heavy noise coming from behind him. Thinking about it now, it seemed likely that he had touched something to cause the rock to slip. The boulder, losing its support base, had slid, just a little, but enough for the original crack in the rocks to be closed firmly shut.

The robust man threw himself at the rock and cried out with a hoarse voice. It was he who had shut himself in this bottomless pit, with his own hands. It was no pity to die, but what broke the heart of the horse messenger was that he had vowed to always take care of Wang Keyu, the female literacy instructor who knew nothing of the world. He had never expected that fate would play such a cruel joke on him.

Staff Officer Wang was still waiting for good news in the front cave. She was severely wounded, unable to move in any direction. She could only lie on her back in the corner of the cave, enduring hunger and thirst day after day. It was as if she was waiting for the sesame oil in the clay lamp bowl to dry up, the wick to shine its last and extinguish, a broken wisp of blue smoke floating upwards.

Damn it! Cao Shui'er thought to himself. Are you just going to cry like a kid? How can you be so cowardly, just when you need courage? How can you get out of here? Since such a huge stone moved with such little force applied, why couldn't he try and push it? Maybe it would move again. If only it could be budged to one side, he could squeeze past.

Cao Shui'er exerted his utmost effort, but the boulder remained motionless. He turned his body and used his back, with his legs pressed against the rock wall opposite him, pushing and pushing with all his strength. Aiyo! He was startled to see the boulder begin to rotate, as a slight vibration came from under his feet. With his face pressed against it, he knew by feeling that this behemoth was turning lazily, completing a full rotation. Cao Shui'er speculated that a small pebble was nestled under the boulder, acting as a kind of bearing. This was the key discovery, otherwise even a hundred Cao Shui'ers would have been useless.

Who knows, perhaps there was a majestic and indifferent

cave god who had seen the infatuated Cao Shui'er and let him go. Cao Shui'er had never been interested in superstition. Still, he knelt in awe and banged his head three times. A stream of heat rolled down his forehead, through his eyebrows and into the corners of his mouth. It tasted salty; it was blood.

He grabbed some moss from the rock wall and held it tightly onto his forehead, it being said that moss has a miraculous effect in stopping bleeding. This became a problem, however. If he covered the wound with both hands he couldn't climb through the honeycomb area, so he had to rest on the rock and wait for the blood to clot before moving on.

In no time at all, the sound of snoring filled the air, as he fell into a deep sleep.

CHAPTER 23

THE GREATEST HONOUR OF YOUR LIFE

The horse messenger bored like a pangolin between the rocks in which he'd almost left his life. Wang Keyu felt truly apologetic.

"Cao Shui'er, I really don't know how to thank you. If it had been any other comrade, they would have ignored my words, let alone carried them out."

"Staff Officer Wang has a good memory. If you'd said that you only vaguely remembered, and it was not very clear, I wouldn't have been so confident to delve into the rocks."

They called the cave in the front section the "front cave" and the area that Cao Shui'er had discovered through exploration the "back cave". They were certain that the guerrillas of the Fourth Red Army had stayed here, but only in the front cave – even they didn't know about the back cave. Of all the rumours about the activities of the guerrillas in the local area, there was never a word said about the back cave. It seemed that even they had never realised the full extent of the magic and mystery enclosed by that layer of rock wall.

The front and back caves were different in more than just size. The front cave was very close to the entrance of the cave, making it convenient for daily life. The problem was that if the enemy blocked the entrance, it would be difficult to escape, even with outstanding caving abilities. The back cave was hugely inconvenient in terms of getting back onto the mountainside, but this also made it much more secure. Even if the enemy occupied the front cave, you could sleep in peace in the back cave!

There was no doubt that they should move to live in the back cave. But what concerned Staff Officer Wang was the insurmountable difficulties for Cao Shui'er to carry her, a severely wounded person, into the back cave. It seemed they'd have to give up.

But the horse messenger had his own ideas and methods.

Cao Shui'er wove a "mattress" of vitex twigs for Staff Officer Wang to lie on. It was slightly wider than the human body and nearly two metres in length. The cushion was thick but not too tightly woven, making it softer and more forgiving as the body curved up and down, and capable of winding through from the small cave, which was just wide enough to allow one person to pass through at a time. Cao Shui'er acted as the driver of this "carriage" travelling backwards, towing Staff Officer Wang with crossed hands, like a trackless underground train, slowly approaching its terminus, inch by inch.

Despite being protected by the vitex-twig mattress, Wang Keyu was still cut by the rocks in many places. They drew blood, but she ignored the pain and asked enthusiastically, "Cao Shui'er, compared with the air from the outside, do you feel any difference in your breathing here?"

"Inside and outside of the cave are the same, there is no difference," Cao Shui'er answered truthfully.

When they entered the back cave, there was a burst of fresh

and moist air such as Wang Keyu had never experienced before, and she felt happy and comfortable in both body and mind. There had been no clear and obvious sensation to the front cave, but entering the back cave, she seemed to feel her respiratory system purified in an instant. Was there a fresher and more pleasant air anywhere in the world?

Wang Keyu knew that the negative ions in the water cave would be extremely high, which would have a positive effect on the physiological activities of the human body. The thing was that the two of them had been active in the mountains and forests just recently, where there was no shortage of negative ions. And yet the air in the back cave was unusual somehow, strange in a way that could not be explained by negative ions alone.

Wang Keyu enthusiastically praised the horse messenger. "You alone, Cao Shui'er, discovered this huge water cave at the foot of the Dabie Mountains. You are leading us forward in social development, and in a single breath, you have walked into at least five million years of history. This is the greatest honour of your life."

Cao Shui'er didn't understand the words of Staff Officer Wang but laughed mischievously.

They saw a length of stalactite hanging from up high and a rod of stalagmite standing upright beneath it, reaching out to each other like two arms of white jade. If the two sides were to touch, it would have created a "miracle tower", thick at each end but thin in the middle. It seemed such a pity that the two PLA soldiers' fingertips were so close to each other and yet ultimately out of reach, sad enough to evoke a sigh.

"In a case like this," Staff Officer Wang explained, "the main cause is too much lime, which blocks the water seepage channels, forcing the droplets to find a different path, to another place, where new stalactites and stalagmites will grow. This pair of 'lovers', although they care deeply for one another, must live a life of eternal regret."

Cao Shui'er pointed to the stalactites and stalagmites in front of him and said, "Do they have any hope? Look, they're only about a metre away. Surely they will meet very soon."

"It is said that a stalagmite grows only one centimetre every hundred years. To grow a metre, that's ten thousand years. Looking at it with the naked eye, the upper and lower sides are very close to each other, but we must be patient and wait. I don't know how many generations it will take, but I suppose that one day they really will come to 'hold hands and grow old together'."

Only once they moved closer did they see the very full and translucent drop of water hanging from the nipple of the stalactite. Little water beads like these formed gradually over long processes of geological history, like the brewing of a drop of aged wine through the most rigorous of methods. The water on the top of the cave was constantly leaking, constantly evaporating, and the lime constantly precipitating with a certain viscosity. Hanging there on the nipple, it would not drop easily.

"This drop of water is ready to fall," Cao Shui'er suggested. "If we stare at it, maybe a miracle will happen, and we will see it drip."

"All right then! Let's do it. Let's stare."

They were meant to be staring intently but, whether consciously or unconsciously, they broke their gaze to exchange a knowing glance. At that moment, upon looking back, the translucent drop of water that had stuck to the tip of the stalactite for so long had dripped. "Why? Why?" Cao Shui'er protested loudly. "That was deliberate! It did it on purpose to keep us from seeing it!"

Wang Keyu waved her hand repeatedly and ordered the horse messenger to be silent. She turned her head and listened intently. "Cao Shui'er, did you hear that? The drop of water splashed on the stalagmite, and the whole back cave echoed, and then the echo hit the cave wall again. Echoes that cause echoes."

Cao Shui'er grimaced. "Staff Officer Wang, don't scare us common folk!"

Wang Keyu listened quietly. "The echo is gone. Now you can hear the water seeping from the roof of the cave and sprinkling along the arc of the stalactite. This is the beginning of the formation of the next drop of water. The round drips hang on the nipple, drip down when plump enough, and become the most recent iteration of countless repetitions over millions of years."

"What's the sound like? Tell me."

"I can't. I've never heard such a sound, so it's hard to use an analogy. It can't be said to be similar to any other sound."

"You say it was a sound unlike other sounds, but how did it happen that you, Staff Officer Wang, heard it, and I couldn't?"

"Both your surname Cao, and your given name Shui'er mean water. Put together, you're like a great river, deafening in its roar. How could you possibly hear anything else!"

Late in the tenth month of the lunar calendar, the north wind blows cold in the Dabie Mountains, enough to make a person's teeth chatter. Although the cave was warm in winter and cool in summer, blurring the boundaries of the seasons, Wang Keyu and Cao Shui'er were still dressed only in unlined military uniforms. It was a struggle to survive.

Yan'an had considered sending the 12th Column of the Jin-Ji-Lu-Yu Field Army more than 100,000 sets of cotton-padded clothes to the Dabie Mountains, to alleviate their suffering. Alternatively, they would send silver coins for them to purchase cloth and cotton locally, and organise for the manpower to sew them. But in reality, it was extremely challenging to put either plan into action due to the thousands of miles and numerous blockades between them. The Field Army reported to the Central Military Commission, "We will try to solve everything by ourselves."

No cloth or cotton, they scoured for them; no bows to fluff cotton, they used branches and bamboo strips instead; no dye, they used ash of rice straw to turn white cloth grey. As a result, the entire army, from the head of the field army to privates, mess cooks and stable lads, all made their own cotton-padded clothes. Because there were no thimbles, if they pricked their fingers, they would suck out drops of blood and spit them out. Between teasing cotton and dyeing cloth and wearing cotton-padded clothes and trousers, how many battles had been fought? They racked their brains but still lost count.

"One Hundred Thousand Young Male Soldiers Learn Women's Needlework!" is surely worthy of a volume in the history of war.

Cao Shui'er considered going directly to the military subarea leader to ask for cotton-padded clothes. However, he knew that Staff Officer Wang was determined never again to meet with Number One, and would never agree to get in touch with the troops, so he had to give up this idea. Instead, he entered a small mountain village by night, intending to play things by ear while trying to obtain for Staff Officer Wang a cotton-padded jacket as soon as possible. They could make do with a flower-patterned jacket and a robe, one for her and one for him.

All of a sudden, two armed sentries walked out from behind a bush. In the dark, Cao Shui'er managed to recognise that they were soldiers of the military subarea guard company. Looking into each other's eyes, they also seemed to recognise him, and they smiled at each other. The sentries did not interrogate him, but waved him on, letting him go.

He saw lights on in the ancestral hall but didn't know what was happening. A young soldier ran out from inside, and Cao

Shui'er asked him. It turned out that many people had failed to make their cotton-padded clothes up to standard, and the leadership had gathered some technical experts to help make the necessary alterations. The most important thing in sewing a cotton coat is the opening of the collar. An inch too large or too small, or if it's skewed, then the finished product would have to be discarded. The Number One head of the Field Army himself taught them a very simple trick: place a large military-use enamel jar on the collar and draw a circle around the mouth. This happened to be the standard collar size. Using this trick, the technical experts saved many, many products from the scrap.

Row upon row of finished cotton uniforms were piled up. Cao Shui'er pretended to be studying them in earnest, as if eager to learn. He turned them over and over, fixing his eye on two particular sets.

Looking through the doorway, he saw Commander Qi Jing approaching with two guards. Biting his lower lip, Cao Shui'er let out a whistle of emergency assembly: "Bleep! Bleep!" In a great rush, everyone nearby packed up their garment stands and ran out of the ancestral hall. Taking advantage of the commotion, Cao Shui'er pulled out two sets from the large pile of cotton uniforms, tucked them under his elbow, jumped skilfully over the back wall and slipped away.

Despite being a male military uniform, it was a perfect fit for Wang Keyu, and she was perfectly satisfied.

Who would have thought that within two days, Staff Officer Wang would be complaining that the cotton-padded clothes were too thick, too warm! She took them off, and in accordance with routine barracks service regulations, stacked them neatly on top of each other as if she wasn't planning to wear them again this winter. It was only a few days since she had said repeatedly how much she feared the cold. Cao Shui'er didn't say anything, his heart felt extremely tense, and he couldn't understand such a strange occurrence.

Soon, Staff Officer Wang wasn't even wearing her unlined uniform shirt. She didn't care about her nudity, as if she was living in this cave not with a man, but with a close female friend. Her underwear had been worn for a long time, and with her recent swelling, they felt tight and uncomfortable across her body. She cut them open with a dagger.

Upon seeing this, Cao Shui'er turned his back and walked away in silence. That ominous feeling swelled inside him, stronger. Everything was OK if Staff Officer Wang was OK, but Cao Shui'er now feared that she had arrived at her most critical juncture.

Wang Keyu began refusing to eat. She kept on drinking the mountain spring water, but when she drank just one or two sips, she vomited a whole bowlful, liquid specked with small sediment. Because of the large amount of phlegm she coughed up, she needed to rinse her mouth from time to time. Cao Shui'er held up a bamboo tube and watched her rinsing her mouth, day and night. It seemed possible that all the dirt in her respiratory system, digestive tract and even the oral cavity had been removed.

In the absence of food for nine consecutive days, there was a sudden abnormality in her defecation. For several days, her stools were viscous and purple in colour, gushing out as if the intestinal system had been too thoroughly cleansed. Caring for her alone was enough to keep Cao Shui'er busy, what with cleaning her and immediately getting rid of her excrement.

They had used to talk and laugh with each other, but now a great silence fell between them. Both hoped to find some pleasant words to comfort the other.

"Cao Shui'er, don't be so weighed down with worry. It seems

that while I might make it to New Year's Day, there's no way I'll see the next festival."

Cao Shui'er said sadly, "I'm a person full of dirty words, but I've never been one for making jokes. I should be able to come up with something funny to make Staff Officer Wang feel better. I should protect you so that no disease or disaster come to you."

"You took good care of me, at a time when I was quite unable to take care of myself. I can't tell whether I'm cold or hot. That's not a serious illness."

CHAPTER 24

MODERN MAN'S HEARING IS
STILL DORMANT

Although Staff Officer Wang hadn't touched her rice for many days, Cao Shui'er still went out every night to beg for alms. He tried his best to salvage for her some appealing food, like glutinous rice balls, steamed egg custard and mung bean cake. But she pushed them all away.

On the way back from one such trip, Cao Shui'er suddenly realised that he had stumbled across the place where he had buried Staff Officer Wang's *guqin*. He was puzzled that he had reached this spot in a single night, whereas the reverse journey through the mountainous area had taken them three nights. Thinking about it again, he realised that he had always been trying to avoid the enemy searching the mountains and hadn't actually gone far, carrying Staff Officer Wang on his back at that time. In fact, he had spent most of the time circling around the military subarea station.

Cao Shui'er first found the "Song" character he had carved with a dagger on the stone wall, and from there took exactly eighty-one steps due south. Certain that this was the place, he peeled away the soil and rocks to reveal the wooden box and, prying it open, saw the *guqin* with no obvious damage.

Staff Officer Wang hated being unable to adequately express her gratitude. For a long time, she had wanted Cao Shui'er to help her find the *guqin* but didn't mention it because she knew it would cause him trouble. Never once did she imagine that he would surprise her in such a way.

Wang Keyu started learning the *guqin* from her mother at the age of three. The older woman soon realised that she could teach her daughter no more, so she hired the most prestigious *guqin* teacher around, openly admitting that she herself didn't deserve this Song-dynasty instrument – it was destined to belong to her daughter. Keyu's talents were enough to make her mother proud.

"When your mother married into the house of Wang, the only thing she brought with her was this *guqin*. When you marry, you can take it with you as well, if you will."

Her second elder brother was determined to go to Yan'an, and Wang Keyu was determined to follow. All the preparations were in place, and only one thing was yet to be finalised – whether to allow the daughter to take this family heirloom with her. When things came to a head, the mother went back on the promise she had made, unable to bear the thought of it all.

In private, her husband advised her, "Daughter is going far away, embarking on the journey of her life. I hate to say something inauspicious, but there may not come the day when she returns. You know better than anyone what that *guqin* means to the child. If you don't allow her to take it, could you bear to see her go out on the road empty-handed?"

One day, when the daughter had finished practising, she abruptly asked her mother, "Ma, I'm thinking, although Yan'an is somewhat remote, there'll be people there who play the *guqin*, right? What do you think?"

"That might well be the case," Mother replied. "It's a famous cultural city, having been a prefecture seat in the old times. But just in case there isn't a single *guqin*, this Song-dynasty *guqin* you bring with you will be first in the revolutionary holy land."

"So, you agree I can take it? Thank you, Ma! Thank you so much!"

The daughter hugged her mother hard and kissed her cheek again and again. An unsolvable problem thus melted like ice into snow...

Wang Keyu took the *guqin* in her arms and pressed her face firmly against its surface, reunited after such a long separation. Two trails of tears fell on the surface of the instrument. Her hands shaking, she took the *guqin* out of the wooden box and looked at it, inch by inch, from top to bottom.

A thin slit had appeared under the *yueshan* bridge, and most of the "string eyes" had cracked. Worse still, the "dragon pool" and "phoenix pond" had deformed under strong pressure. Every expert knows that the most important part of the belly of the *guqin* is the subtle production of the two sound holes – the dragon pool and phoenix pond. Without them, you can't achieve the intoxicating and unique tone of the *guqin*. A precious family instrument dating from the Song dynasty was ruined.

Wang Keyu silently rolled the strings, one by one, into small rings, and placed them in the wooden box. If the *guqin* was gone, what was the use of it having strings?

Back in the day, the daughter of the Wang family would help her mother clean the strings with peach resin every fortnight. The seven strings were like living beings, all made by entwining dozens or even hundreds of silk threads. If you didn't take care in maintaining them, the slender threads would fall off right in front of you. After years of keeping each other company, how could Staff Officer Wang have the heart to abandon them completely?

The Wang family's *guqin* bore obvious characteristics of a Song-dynasty *guqin*. The whole body was of the same colour, with a delicate lacquer, and a warm and subtle lustre. It looked simple but not crude, plain but not vulgar. The instrument measured nearly 120 centimetres long, almost twenty centimetres wide, and about seven centimetres thick. The length of the strings was about 112 to 118 centimetres. The body curved then flattened gradually, a shape that was both uniform and neat, beautiful in its practical simplicity. As a child, Wang Keyu boasted to the other children she studied with, "The Song-dynasty *guqin* of my mother's dowry is the best. Even if you brought in the ancient *Jiuxiao Huanpei*, I wouldn't swap it with you."

The *Jiuxiao Huanpei* she spoke of was the product of the Lei family from Sichuan, renowned *guqin* makers during the Kaiyuan era of the Tang dynasty. It is said that there were fewer than twenty Tang *guqin* instruments handed down, most of them lacking the necessary official inscription of the year of their make. But this particular Tang *guqin* had such an inscription to prove its provenance – that it had once been of royal possession. Made from wutong on the surface and spruce on the base, the whole body was painted with red-purple lacquer in a lined pattern like the belly of a young snake, with an undercoat of grey paste made from powdered antlers. On the *guqin* there were inscriptions by and responses from famous figures such as Huang Tingjian, and at the foot of the *guqin* was written a poem in regular script by Su Shi: "Like spring breeze rustling soft, / Like precious stones ringing, / Like new swallows twittering, / Like the ocean dragon moaning."

In terms of cultural heritage and collection value, the famous *guqin* of the Tang dynasty was not something that the Song-dynasty *guqin*, made 289 years later, could match. However, it depends on how you look at it. If you're talking about the essence of the *guqin*, those handed down from generation to generation, well then, there were certainly more than just a few eminent masterpieces.

The first-generation grandmaster Lei Wei "went to Mount Emei alone through wind and thunder wearing just his straw raincoat and bamboo hat. He drank as he ventured deep into the pine forest, where he cut down the fir tree that sounded melodious when he tapped it. Then, he carved a *guqin* out of its wood." The Emei spruce mentioned here is actually Chinese fir. The Wang family's Song-dynasty *guqin* and the *Jiuxiao Huanpei* shared one key characteristic of the Lei *guqin*. They were not limited to the pure use of wutong, but made of Chinese fir and mounted with wutong pieces in the sections of the "dragon pool" and "phoenix pound", superior to using wutong alone. This is one of the secrets of Lei *guqin* production.

They used a unique method when it came to the groove in the belly, and while many *guqin* masters emerged from the Tang to the Song, it was easy to decipher the Lei family's unspoken magic. The Song-dynasty *guqin* of the Wang family and the *Jiuxiao Huanpei* took different approaches but produced equally satisfying results. On the slightly raised *nayin* (sound chamber) in the middle of the belly of the *guqin*, they both had a round groove about 1.7 centimetres deep and 3.3 centimetres wide, allowing the dragoon pool and phoenix pond sound outlets to be slightly narrower to extend the spread of the reverberations around the resonance box. Furthermore, the string length of each was large and the amplitude fully pronounced, with a sound more generous and rounder, loose and clear like hitting precious metals and stone.

This is not to say that having used the *guqin* for many years, I regard it as a national treasure, despite its quality. Pursuing the perfect sound with a *guqin*, what more can you want?

꿜★꿸

Cao Shui'er remembered something that Staff Officer Wang had told him on more than one occasion. In ancient times, many great poets and essayists wrote in their poems or essays something along the lines of, "The musician, not the instrument he plays, is the key to good music. A musician who plays with his heart doesn't even need the strings." Cao Shui'er thought that if Staff Officer Wang's physical health was better, she wouldn't even need the strings, she could just hold her Song-dynasty *guqin* and strum. But what with her condition being so serious, he thought, she couldn't even do that. But at that moment, Staff Officer Wang called to him, "Cao Shui'er! Come, please, and help me clean my hands!"

The horse messenger picked up the bamboo tube and washed Wang Keyu's hands with mountain spring water. He wanted to dry them with leaves, but Staff Officer Wang thought the leaves were unclean. Rather, like a surgeon putting on sterile gloves, she raised her arms in the air, and the water dried by itself. Then, with great difficulty, she crossed her legs, placing the Song-dynasty *guqin* flat on her injured thighs, and starting plucking at the bright, bare, clean surface of the instrument.

The first song, *High Mountains and Flowing Waters*, wasn't yet finished when Cao Shui'er realised that something was wrong. Fumbling with the torch, Aiyo, he saw what it was: Wang Keyu's left hand was bleeding! Having been buried in the ground for many days, the surface of the *guqin* was rough, and now it had no strings. Of course it had caused her hand to bleed!

"Staff Officer Wang, your hand is bleeding!" Cao Shui'er exclaimed.

"Just listen to the *guqin*. Don't look at my hands," Staff Officer Wang said as she continued to play.

The second piece of music was *Solitary Orchard*, the third *The Drunkard*, then *Reading I Ching By Autumn Night*, *Wild Geese Flock to Sandy Shores*, *Dialogue between the Fisherman and the Woodcutter*…

The three notes of the *guqin* came together like mountains upon mountains, crisscrossing rivers, the sea merging with the sky on the horizon, the drifting mists and flowing clouds, the moon setting and the sun rising, the crows and frogs croaking. It sounded commonplace, but also unprecedented. It came from hundreds of scholars writing in their books of ancient history but remained purely mysterious and fantastic. All things were endless, and they all echoed the trembling of the seven strings, all covered by the rise and fall of the melody of the music.

Most people who know the *guqin* listen with their eyes closed. Cao Shui'er, however, focused on the movement of the player's fingering. That night, the moonlight was bright and clear, penetrating the cave through the crevices in the rock. Cao Shui'er, as usual, determined which piece of music was playing only by observing the female literacy instructor's fingering. The absence of strings did not prevent him from entering a state of intoxication, pleasing himself with the soundless and yet beautiful ancient music.

When one song ended, she moved on to the next. Noticing Xiao Wang's use of a unique finger technique – the snake-shaped crane step – Cao Shui'er realised she was playing *Moon Over Mountain Pass*, which was the piece he knew best and liked to listen to the most.

Suddenly, Cao Shui'er heard the far-off sound of a horse's whinny. He pricked his ears, and yes! It was Tanzao! "Tanzao!", "Tanzao!" he shouted to Staff Officer Wang, and then he picked up the torch and ran out of the cave.

After finishing *Moon Over Mountain Pass*, as was custom, Wang Keyu ended the song by gently pressing the strings with her hands and pausing for a while. She did this even though the surface of the *guqin* was bare and without strings.

Cao Shui'er soon returned and sank to the cave floor. Wearing a downcast expression, he said nothing.

"You didn't make a mistake? Could it really be him?"

From Wang Keyu's question, it was obvious that she truly hoped for an affirmative answer, and she was afraid that he was still hesitant to decide. This was not a joke; she must be certain.

"Staff Officer Wang, don't deliberately anger me! Together through thick and thin for so many years, how could I have made a mistake? I could even clearly see the fire brand 'nine' on his flank." The horse messenger was visibly upset, and quite hurt. "He stood at the mouth of the cave so close and quiet. But realising it was me, he turned around and ran away. I chased after him and whistled at him, but he wouldn't even turn his head back."

Wang Keyu was unusually agitated, and her pale face turned a little red. She stayed silent for a long time, allowing her excessive excitement to cool down, and then she said, "Cao Shui'er! Why do I feel that Tanzao came to the mouth of this cave after hearing me play *Moon Over Mountain Pass*?"

Why did she think that way? How immaterial! Cao Shui'er didn't know how to answer, so he just laughed gloomily.

"Don't laugh so foolishly! You should remember that when Tanzao once heard this song, he ran all the way to me and forced my windows open."

"Great Staff Officer Wang! At that time, he really did hear the sound of your *guqin*, but now that there are no strings, he can hear nothing at all!"

"Well, then, I ask you. It's been two months since we entered this cave, and Tanzao never appeared. I played more than a dozen tunes before, over a long time, and he didn't show up. Then, as soon as I played *Moon Over Mountain Pass*, you heard his call. How do you explain that?"

It could not be denied that the words of the female literacy instructor were quite reasonable, but Cao Shui'er still struggled to take it in. In order to not disappoint Staff Officer Wang too much, he pretended to be thinking it through seriously, nodding occasionally, as if he had accepted Wang Keyu's peculiar idea, which transcended any normal interpretation of what sound was.

Wang Keyu had by now calmed down, and said to Cao Shui'er as if she was talking to herself: "An ancient wrote 'A Composition on the Qin', and he said at the beginning that while everything has ups and downs, sound is immutable. No wonder you heard one voice, always the original sound. Nothing can be added or subtracted, and it will never disappear. Then, the first *guqin* produced by our ancestors was played. That first free-string tone, undoubtedly, should still exist, somewhere. If you were to give me the chance, just once, to appreciate the original *guqin* monophony in the world, I will die without complaint! It's a pity for people today, their hearing is still so dormant – they can't hear it any more. I think that maybe, one day, under some circumstances, our hearing will be awakened."

Chapter 25

An Immortal Full Stop

W hen setting out on a journey, one must consider what items will be indispensable on the road, and think carefully about what cannot be left behind.

Wang Keyu did the opposite. She would not take anything that she had acquired since the day she emerged from her mother's belly, nothing at all. The bone injury required her to use a small splint for at least another two or three months, but she didn't seem to care and discarded it without hesitation.

She asked Cao Shui'er to scrub her whole body with cold water. Cao Shui'er tore a padded uniform open and pulled off the cotton piece by piece. Dipping these in spring water, he scrubbed her carefully from head to toe, over and over again, until her body was red. He even picked at each of her fingernails and toenails with bamboo sticks.

Wang Keyu asked the horse messenger to come closer. She remained silent for a time, before saying, "Cao Shui'er, my good brother! I'm so very sleepy, I'm going to sleep now. You should also rest your head, how about it?"

"Sure. I was just thinking of taking a nap," the horse messenger agreed, casually.

No sooner had he closed his eyes, when a sudden realisation struck Cao Shui'er. Staff Officer Wang had called him "my good brother", and with affection! This was most unusual, and she had sounded almost melancholy – could it be that she was saying her farewell? Cao Shui'er leapt up and shouted, "Staff Officer Wang! Staff Officer Wang! Hey, Staff Officer Wang! Hey, Staff Officer Wang!"

Wang Keyu, staff officer of the Independent Ninth Brigade headquarters of the Jin-Ji-Lu-Yu Field Army, had stopped breathing.

The horse messenger held a wish in his heart. He hoped to forever and always accompany the young woman Wang from Peking, to be her personal guard and serve as her Man Friday. Now, Cao Shui'er had only to rotate the huge rock leading to the front cave, and the back cave would be closed forever. Thus, this wondrous and beautiful water cave would be the permanent dwelling place of two friends from the battlefield, a man and a woman. And, in its own way, the greatest wish of Horse Messenger Cao Shui'er's life was realised with ease.

While a happy ending to a beautiful worldly tale such as this may exist in theory, it is far from reality.

It was the deepest of secrets, one that no one knew. Instead of becoming a beautiful tale, it would, in all likelihood lead to all kinds of hearsay around the fictitious basis of this man and woman "eloping in secret". All the most despicable, base and appalling charges would be dumped, in one load, on their heads.

After the war ended, if the relatives of Wang Keyu or Cao Shui'er felt the urge to approach the army to inquire into the whereabouts of their kin, they would eventually find them listed among the Independent Ninth Brigade's statistics, with three words besides their names – "missing, no leads". It was true!

They left the military subarea and were nowhere to be found. They had to be listed as "missing".

This strong and most capable Man Friday, Cao Shui'er, considered the problem in too practical a way. His first thought was to move the female soldier's body to the front cave as soon as possible while it was not yet stiff. Further delay and the body would not be transportable. Fortunately, the mattress woven with vitex twigs was still intact. He placed the body on top, with the *guqin* at its side, and fixed them with more leaves. It took a whole day to cautiously transport the body to the front cave.

Cao Shui'er had not anticipated that, nearly twenty-four hours after he took it to the front cave, Staff Officer Wang's body still retained its original temperature. Her muscles and the blood vessels of her limbs had good elasticity, and there was no sign of stiffness. Cao Shui'er was taken aback. Did it mean that she was still alive, or should he assume that she had already passed?

⚝

Staff Officer Wang's body temperature began dropping slowly, but it was still not too cold. A week went by. Round purple spots appeared on her forehead, and there was obvious blood congestion in the fingertips. The skin had begun to loosen, and a red liquid had started to form under the skin. But the body maintained excellent elasticity. The major joints, especially in the neck, had not stiffened, and the head could rotate with ease.

What was even more surprising was that new hairs had started to sprout on Staff Officer Wang's head, and her eyebrows also grew. *Guqin* players use their left hand to strum, and as such never let those fingernails grow. Staff Officer Wang's were now very long. Cao Shui'er trimmed them with a dagger as if she was waiting to play the *guqin*.

Ten days later, a kind of bloating appeared under the skin,

and the whole body was like an airbag. Then, the epidermis of various parts of the body appeared damaged, and a large amount of light-red liquid began discharging from the body. After a little over a month, the bloating had gradually subsided, the fluid all but gone, and the torso and limbs returned to their original size and shape. The face was as before, natural and peaceful, becoming a prune-tinted, crystal-clear, expressionless corpse. No signs of corruption were to be found on the body, and there was no bad odour.

Cao Shui'er thought that the body had assumed its translucent appearance through his own perception alone. In the dim light, he illuminated the soles of her feet with a torch. Like a jade carving, they shone with the faint colour of blood. He cast his mind back to the night march when Staff Officer Wang had a thorn in her foot and had asked him to help pick it out.

Under the torchlight, it looked exactly like the sole of the foot he tended to now: every toe lit up like a lantern.

There are several circumstances in which human remains can be preserved for a long time. The first is the implementation of modern medical antiseptic treatment; the second is long-term freezing; the third is mummification under special conditions, as in desert settings or the Egyptian pyramids; the fourth is dying in the sitting position of Buddhist disciples, sealed and buried deep underground. Staff Officer Wang was different from these four situations. She had remained in this natural environment, never having left the cave.

Still! The succession of vital energy processes before and after our heroine stopped breathing was something well beyond conventional thinking. Many years later, the old comrades of the Ninth Brigade were still left wondering. Searching for an answer, some put forward whimsical theories linking this extraordinary physiological phenomenon to her family name.

Look up the character "Wang" in the Cihai dictionary and consider the short one or two lines of annotation – they seem to offer something worth studying: "The appearance of being deep and vast. A kind of transparency and inner peace." Anyone with the surname Wang has an inner space that is vast and wide, that runs calm and deep like a pool of water. Flawlessly still, the muddy waters sink peacefully to the bottom, and perfect clarity is restored.

This female student from Peking had gone through several years of war and the cruellest of the so-called "sifting mop-ups and raids", but still maintained her unique posture in life. Perhaps it was a premonition that she was about to leave the world, and thus completed a kind of female human sculpture, step by step, in an orderly manner, drawing for herself a perfect and incorruptible full stop.

Cao Shui'er, the horse messenger, was in a state of both awareness and illusion, and he could hardly express everything that was happening in front of him. But he was also acutely aware that, from now on, he was obliged to shoulder the responsibility of protecting this human sculpture.

Before Wang Keyu passed, she refused to leave even the merest fragment of clothing on her body. Therefore, dressing her in military uniform again was out of the question. However, Cao Shui'er really couldn't emotionally grasp the idea of her naked body on display in that cave, year in year out, and this creeping anxiety lodged in his heart.

Before crossing the Yellow River in the south, the Field Political Art Troupe of the Jin-Ji-Lu-Yu Field Army's Political Department had come to the Ninth Brigade to perform their skit *Drive Out the Red-Headed Devils*. One scene from the play was set in the living room of the US Consulate General in Shanghai. In addition to the sofa and coffee table, there needed to be an oil painting of a girl on the wall. What worried everyone in the troupe most was this portrait. It was not that there was no oil paint; there was. But who could adequately capture the simple and innocent Western village girl?

The art design team leader had the idea to find an actress with the right temperament to play the oil painting village girl. They would leave an open "window" on the background curtain and place a square table behind it. As she stood on the table, the actress could just appear above waist height in the "window". Another person could stand behind the actress and hold up the picture frame. From the auditorium, it really did seem as though a Western oil painting was hung upright on the orange-red wall.

The director's gaze fell on Wang Keyu, staff officer of the Ninth Brigade headquarters, and he invited her to play the part of the oil painting girl. She wore a long wig that fell to the waist, over her face and covered part of her cheeks. Turning the collar down revealed her neck and collarbone, while the body was wrapped loosely in bleached cloth, wrinkled with countless folds. The spotlight was projected onto the picture frame, a girl with long hair, white and gleaming, elegant and natural.

Staff Officer Wang was a pretty, young member of the Eighth Route of the Ninth Brigade, but the girl dressed up like the picture was even more charming. In fact, few members of the audience were actually watching the show. Most eyes were drawn to the alluring figure of the village girl in the oil painting. Horse Messenger Cao Shui'er had been given the task of lifting the picture frame, which had deprived him of the opportunity to feast his eyes.

Cao Shui'er had an idea. He decided to find a white cloth in which he could wrap Staff Officer Wang's body with countless folds, to resemble a live version of the portrait of the girl in the oil painting.

He was very excited about the idea.

⁓⁂⁓

At midnight, Cao Shui'er sneaked into a small county town that stood by the mountain. It was like a ghost town, and he couldn't even hear a dog barking. He found a cloth shop, opened the door gently and shone his torch. He discovered an old woman curled up under the bed. Seeing that it was a comrade of the PLA, the old woman no longer trembled with fear.

"Grandma, do you have any white cloth here?" Cao Shui'er was anxious to get straight to the point.

"Apart from me, old but still alive, there's nothing at all," the old woman said weakly.

"I'll pay you. I'll give you six silver coins."

The proprietress didn't speak, clearly stunned by the offer. At the current market price, this sum would buy out the entire little shop. She poked around for a long time before producing a bolt of white cloth. Cao Shui'er recognised that it was not the rough homespun cloth woven by locals, but the bright, white and wide foreign-made variety. Cao Shui'er said nothing further, placing the money in front of the old woman.

And with that, the astonishing transaction was over.

Cao Shui'er ran, hoping to get back to the cave before dawn. He didn't know that, as soon as he left the cloth shop, he had been shadowed by a military subarea patrol squad. He tripped on something under his feet and fell to the ground. Looking up, two guns, one long and one short, were aimed at him. He recognised the commander of the military subarea guard company, holding a twenty-shot Mauser C96.

"Commander! It's you, sir!" Cao Shui'er said jokingly.

The company commander, in a courteous manner, said, "Oh! It's our Great Bodyguard Cao!"

"Surging waters flood the Dragon King Temple, and family no longer recognises its kin." Cao Shui'er got up from the ground. "A little over a month ago, you broke into the military subarea logistics office and stole two sets of cotton uniforms. You, boy, having tasted a little sweetness, now dare to run into the county town to commit another crime?" The company commander pointed to the white cloth tucked under Cao Shui'er's arms. "We've caught you red-handed. What do you have to say?"

Obviously, the company commander had misunderstood, assuming that anyone with the surname Cao must be a hoodlum or a thief. Cao Shui'er deliberately offered no explanation, wanting to tease them a while. "Don't run your mouth off! I won't talk to a hooligan like you. I want to see Number One."

The company commander smirked contemptuously. "Fine! Go and meet with Number One, and we'll see if you persist in stubbornly refusing to admit your wrongdoing."

CHAPTER 26

THE NUMBER ONE CHIEF FEELS SHARP STABS OF GUILT AND SHAME

The military subarea forces found themselves surrounded on all sides by the enemy. Although facing the Guangxi Clique, notorious for fighting mountain warfare, the PLA troops couldn't tell east from west or north from south upon entering the region of hills and jungles. The encirclement grew tighter and tighter, and it seemed that the heroic forces, once awarded the honorary title of the "The Night Tigers", had reached their end.

Commander Qi Jing had to make a "final mobilisation" of the troops, asking every cadre and soldier to maintain a steadfast resolution and to be willing to die fighting the enemy. "Every one of you has the right to shoot me, your Number One, and to enforce battlefield discipline, if you find that my resolve has shaken, even by the slightest bit!"

The director of the radio station received an order to immediately destroy the station and all the communication equipment.

The battlefield was deadly silent as they waited for the enemy's general offensive signal flares to pierce the night sky. It felt as though the air itself had solidified, and their nerves were so tense they might burst. But time passed, minute after minute, hour after hour, and there came no sound. The decoder rushed over to hand a telegram to the commander.

Qi Jing was furious. "The radio station was ordered to be destroyed, so why is it still receiving reports?"

"This station is eighty per cent new, and the director was kind of reluctant," the decoder answered timidly.

"Nonsense! Call your director over!"

Seeing that the telegram came from the Front Line Command Post of the Field Army, stationed at the Hebei-Henan Military Subarea, he read it first. The essence of the telegram was: we cooperated closely and fought bravely alongside Chen Su's and Chen Xie's three columns. Not only have we turned a new leaf in the Dabie Mountains, but we've also created the Tongbai and Jianghan liberated zones, connecting the Henan-Shaanxi-Hubei and the Henan-Anhui-Jiangsu liberated zones, shattering the enemy's Central Plains defence system. The enemy was forced to transfer thirteen brigades away from the Dabie Mountains to ensure the defence of strategic locations such as the Yangtze River Defence Line and Wuhan.

Qi Jing read the message again from start to finish as if he didn't understand. What was this? What had happened? Ready to shed his last drop of blood for the cause, he had received a message saying Sima Yi's soldiers had retreated twenty kilometres![1] This dramatic change was too much – it struck like a lightning bolt. He closed his eyes tightly and remained motionless, calming himself down from a terrible impulse. After a long time, he burst out with vigour: "Guard! Water!"

According to the telegram from the Field Army's top brass, Qi Jing would be given further tasks at the enlarged meeting of the Party Committee of the Military Subarea. It was required to further mobilise the masses, accelerate the construction of a new area and strive to gain a firm foothold in the Dabie Mountains to welcome the arrival of a greater strategic opportunity – to defeat Chiang Kai-shek and liberate the whole of China!

The enlarged meeting had gone on for a full forty-eight hours when, before anyone else, Number One put away his documents and left. He was impatient to meet with the horse messenger Cao Shui'er.

Cao Shui'er greeted him and said with teary eyes, "Chief! Punish me. I didn't take good care of Staff Officer Wang. She, she, she died of an illness."

"What illness was it?" Qi Jing seemed to only half believe him.

"In fact, there was no illness."

"Didn't you say that she died of an illness?"

"I, I, I couldn't say for sure."

"You were with her twenty-four hours a day. If you can't say for sure, then who can?"

"I will report on Staff Officer Wang's physical condition later. The leadership asked me to be responsible for guarding her and taking care of her daily needs. For more than two months, I did not make any mistakes. But she is no more, that's all there is to say. I can provide the chief with a full account of myself. Cao Shui'er is innocent and never touched a hair on Staff Officer Wang's head!"

Qi Jing shook his head repeatedly and said, "Let's not talk about this today. Let's not talk about this today!"

Cao Shui'er couldn't help but go on the offensive. "You don't believe me, do you? Please, make yourself clear!"

"Enough! I don't have the time to listen to you ramble on."

Suddenly furious, Cao Shui'er grabbed Qi Jing by the collar. "You don't believe me. Well, I don't want to talk to you either then. Let me go!"

The commander's two guards had sharp eyes and quick hands. A Mauser C96 was pressed against the back of Cao Shui'er's head, another muzzle pointed at his back. In a flash, the situation had escalated.

"Put the guns down!" the commander shouted. "Put the guns down!"

The two guards put away their pistols, and Cao Shui'er let his hands drop. Qi Jing rearranged his collar and issued instructions to the two guards: "There's no need for you to be here, you can wait outside." The two guards had to obey orders, but they left the door wide open in order to take action if needed.

Qi Jing turned to Cao Shui'er and said, "Acting like a savage, running your mouth off like that. Do you think that's right?"

"If you don't appreciate my work during this period, then there's nothing to be said about it. Don't expect me to have anything good to say either!"

Number One smiled and said, "Blame my words for not expressing my meaning, for they have misled you. The task was assigned to you, and I had total faith in your abilities. If it had been otherwise, I would have assigned someone else."

"Thank you, Chief! Even if the Chief doesn't really think so in his heart, his mouth has said so and made a guard like me feel at least a bit better."

The commander pulled a serious expression and said, "Enough! Now it's time to talk about some problems of your own. The security department wanted to tie you up to see me, but I stopped them."

Cao Shui'er snorted with laughter. "They misunderstood. I paid for that white cloth. Six silver coins! The chief can send someone to investigate if he doesn't believe me."

"That's a lot of money for a bolt of white cloth. What did you plan to do?"

"I planned to use white cloth to make many folds to cover Staff Officer Wang's body. A bolt of cloth may not be worth much money, but the six coins were originally intended to help Staff Officer Wang resettle and pay the expenses of the households supposedly to hide her. But she's gone, so why keep the money? I even gave the rice bag the money was kept in to the cloth shop's owner..."

"Use the white cloth to make many folds, what do you mean?"

The horse messenger told the story of Staff Officer Wang playing the role of a girl in an oil painting in the play *Drive Out the Red-Headed Devils*. Cao Shui'er spoke with a smile, but he also removed his military cap and wiped away his tears. As he did so, he noticed with surprise that the Number One chief's expression was cold and indifferent. It seemed that Staff Officer Wang's death had nothing to do with him. All of a sudden, a terrifying grimace stretched out over his face.

Cao Shui'er's heart skipped a beat, and he felt that ominous sense of foreboding. Could something terrible be about to befall him?

The commander slapped a piece of paper fiercely on the table. "Read this letter!" he demanded. It was a letter of complaint – the daughter of the *bao* chief from Balifan had reported that she was raped by PLA soldier Cao Shui'er. The defendant himself scanned the letter, without any apparent surprise.

"Speak honestly, did it happen?"

"Yes," Cao Shui'er replied casually. "Shall I report it to the chief?"

"I've had enough of hearing about your shameless acts!"

Cao Shui'er did not deny a single word, and explained from beginning to end his encounter in the kitchen with the "plaintiff". Then, as if he had eaten something terribly sour, he narrowed his eyes, made a peculiar expression and said, "But I don't understand. What counts and what doesn't count?" The defendant spoke literarily, avoiding the vulgar word "rape".

Qi Jing had no doubts about the validity of Cao Shui'er's statement. Two frisky birds would quickly get the message from each other when one spread its wings and the other lifted its tail. It was almost impossible to distinguish which party was active and which passive. It was totally unsuitable to use the word "rape" to describe what happened between Cao Shui'er and the plaintiff. That would be tantamount to one person getting sick and making them both take medicine. Number One shook his head, again and again, saying with sympathy and pity, "Cao Shui'er, Cao Shui'er! The determination of a case is not based on the defendant's confession but on whether the prosecution can be fully established. Your prosecution is established, and the ingredients of your ready-made excuses are bullshit. Not to mention, this kind of thing in front of you, even if it doesn't exist at all and has been planted as a vicious rumour, it is still difficult for you to wash clean. What's more, the facts are there, and people will bite on them and not let go. What do you want me to do with you?"

"I'm a bastard," Cao Shui'er mumbled. "Once again, I've caused trouble for the chief."

The commander flew into a rage. He hit the table with a clenched fist and said, "Brandishing a poker of a dick, you fuck everything up without the slightest fear of the heavens. Now, let's see how you can go on playing macho."

Like a punctured balloon, utterly deflated, Cao Shui'er squatted on the ground and folded his arms around his head. Number One paced around him in circles and said, earnestly, "The matter has come to a head. As chief, I can find no words to comfort you. If I put on a stern expression and tell you a great truth, you will only resent me for it. But if these words remain unspoken, you will be even more sorry.

"You know, even though the situation with the enemy is

improving, the masses still don't trust us. They always say, 'Doing is better than talking. Come back with your propaganda when you've conquered Hankou!' We distribute wealth confiscated from the landlords to the peasants during the day, and then they just send it back to the landlords at night. If this continues, how can we gain a firm foothold in the Dabie Mountains?

"The current violations of law and discipline are serious, and they arouse strong feelings of resentment among the masses. We must be determined to rectify the matter internally and stop this unhealthy trend in the shortest time possible. Otherwise, there can be no talk of either mobilising the masses or establishing new base areas. Major incidents should be investigated, those who need catching should be caught, and those who deserve it should be sentenced to death. We must not shy away from difficult choices."

"Don't mention it, Chief, I understand. I looked for trouble myself!" Cao Shui'er covered his face with his hands and spoke in a grave voice.

"Today, in front of you, I have to say all there is to be said. Tomorrow there will be a public trial, and I won't be able to talk to you again. When the verdict is announced, you must not make trouble. When the crowd yells at you and scolds you, don't answer back. Can you do this?"

"The chief can rest assured. I will cooperate fully."

Cao Shui'er's words made Qi Jing feel a twinge in his nose, and he noticed two streams of hot tears trickle down his face.

In this last conversation with the horse messenger, who had been with him for many years, Qi Jing had been a little unsure about how to communicate with him. He had found it hard to broach the subject. As it happened, he had nothing to worry about. He hadn't expected to persuade Cao Shui'er to admit his crime so readily.

His persuasion might have worked well, but Qi Jing felt

uneasy. He knew he had done so by taking advantage of dramatic political pressure and emotional impulse that proved too solemn and grave. In such a manner, he had forced this able-bodied and simple-minded young man to confess everything.

Qi Jing was distraught. Why should he be the one to do this persuasion in person? Why not just let Cao Shui'er go on public trial and make a big fuss? Why not allow him to pour out a torrent of abuse while pointing at him, the Number One chief? Then, he would feel a little better. The Number One chief felt sharp stabs of guilt and shame, and his body couldn't help but shake.

Qi Jing thought highly of himself, believing that he had persuaded his old guard with his silver tongue. But no! In fact, it had more to do with Cao Shui'er's propensity for having little regard for niceties. Cao Shui'er took his life too lightly; it occupied a position of no consequence in his perception. "Chief, don't worry. I will cooperate fully."

How are you agreeing to this? Qi Jing thought to himself. Cao Shui'er blurted out the words that could determine whether he lived or died without hesitation, like a child making a promise to his playmate, thinking nothing of hooking each other's little fingers and making an oath while "crossing my heart".

The commander rolled a cigarette and handed it respectfully to Cao Shui'er. The horse messenger took it with both hands, nodded in thanks, angled it on his lips and waited blankly in silence. Qi Jing struck a match and offered it forward. Cao Shui'er suddenly realised that he could never allow the commander to light a cigarette for him! He repeatedly declined, until the match went out. Qi Jing struck a second one and offered it again, and the horse messenger could do nothing but accept it.

The two of them were silent for a long time, puffing out endless streams of smoke, which slowly filled the room.

CHAPTER 27

ACCEPT THE EXECUTION, BUT NOT THE FIVE-FLOWER BIND

I f something is politically sensitive, even only slightly, it will be analysed to the hilt. The enemy bragged that the Balifan region was a "clean area". The reactionary forces were very strong, and clearly a powerful individual had intervened to carefully instigate this illicit affair. The locals were unclear about the ins and outs, but no one had the courage to break the feudal concept of the clan or the tight control of the *baojia* regime, to stand up and uncover the inside story. Rumours had already started to spread that because the rapist was a close guard to the military subarea commander, the case would be allowed to drag on and go unpunished. In short, people on the outside didn't understand the inside story. They followed the herd, adding their own embellishments to the story, for no reason other than to stir up trouble.

The two female comrades who performed the interrogation tried every means possible to persuade the *bao* chief's daughter to provide some significant circumstantial evidence. They hoped that the accuser would go on and on about what happened until loopholes would inevitably appear in her testimony, which would be beneficial to Cao Shui'er. In the end, they came out empty-handed, and the accuser insisted that it was rape.

In the Ninth Brigade, Cao Shui'er enjoyed no great popularity because of the rumours about him. However, he had, after all, rescued several top-level commanders from the brink of death, including the current military subarea commander. And to have fallen into the wretched plight he now found himself in was hard for many to accept. Some forceful characters appeared to take a stand on the matter: "A daughter of the *bao* chief, a member of a reactionary family, she deserves to be screwed!"

Some people were reluctant to plead publicly for Cao Shui'er, saying instead something peculiar and ambiguous, like, "Elephants only mate for a few seconds but have to wait a full twenty years before the next copulation. What a pity! If only Cao Shui'er had been reincarnated as an elephant, he surely wouldn't have made such a fateful mistake."

In terms of the army's response, it was necessary to unify understanding from top to bottom, to avoid confusion among the troops. Now it was up to the leadership to make their final decision.

Some believed that the problem centred on distinguishing between rape and adultery. Rape crossed the line and deserved death without appeal. Adultery, consensual between two people, was still within that red line, and it just depended on what punishment was given. Some people held the opposite view and thought it was meaningless to draw a red line. If you say he was still within the red line, well, how would you justify this to the residents of Balifan and even the wider district? Watching over the captives, and still going ahead with this madness, he should have been punished in line with the battlefield discipline in the first place. From whichever way you look at it, it couldn't be considered unjust treatment against him.

The director of the Military Law Department slowly opened his dossier and said in a tepid voice, "I have an internal report here. It lists the few death penalty cases judged during this period. In the first case, a quartermaster and a few soldiers were caught catching and eating stolen fish – sentenced! In the second case, a squad leader started a fire to keep warm, and several houses burned down – sentenced! In the third case, a deputy company commander robbed a villager of his starch noodles – sentenced!"

The director of the Military Law Department did not express his own opinion on anything, but only introduced a few cases objectively without additional comment. But his unquestionable authority was there for everyone to see. Of all the cases outlined in that report, which was worse than that of Cao Shui'er? Which was more harmful? It didn't take much consideration to realise, even at a glance, that if this person was not sentenced to death, then who would be?

Qi Jing pondered the matter in silence: a delay in the case would be even more disadvantageous, and he should express a clear stance from the outset. "Since nothing less than the death penalty is enough to assuage public anger, I too offer no objection to the sentence. But I do have a particular question to ask. The prosecutor used the word 'rape'. In my opinion, law enforcement notices should avoid that word. After all, he is a red-blooded young man in his early twenties and an outstanding horse messenger of the People's Liberation Army who has numerous military accolades to his name."

The veteran political commissar of the Ninth Brigade said, "Qi Jing, my old friend, you put it so well. I have long tried to find the proper words to express my feelings at this moment. But I can't find the right way to say it. You said it for me!" Then, all of a sudden, he turned sharply, flushed and launched a fierce attack on Number One. "Comrade Qi Jing! What were you doing earlier? Don't you think your concern for Cao Shui'er has come a little too late? He came up with you through cavalry training, and for many years you have just treated him as one of your 'four biggies' – nothing more than helping you keep up appearances and build momentum!"

Qi Jing forced a smile. "It is said that our dear political commissar is like a kind-hearted grandmother. In fact, he is no such thing. When someone's wound is bleeding, you simply sprinkle a handful of salt on it!"

⁂

Out of security considerations, the Military Law Division decided to truss Cao Shui'er up with the five-flower bind.

Of the different types of five-flower bind, there is the "body-guard style" that involves using a small linen shirt: the person is trussed from the neck to the shoulders to the forearms, tied back tightly and fixed to the neck, shoulders and upper body. The forearms and hands are not tied, so the prisoner can just about take care of himself – eat, drink and so on. Another is called the "executive style", which was to be used on Cao Shui'er. In addition to the binding of the wrists, the arms, chest, back and neck are all tightly bound as well.

Unexpectedly, the death row inmate resisted fiercely, refusing to be tied up. Several staff officers of the Military Law Department tried to intervene, but Cao Shui'er punched and kicked, throwing them on their backs. They hurriedly ran to get the Number One chief.

"Cao Shui'er! You promised to cooperate in the military execution!" said the commander sternly.

"Execution is execution, but I won't be trussed up!"

"This is a legal procedure, and there are no exemptions," the chief of the Military Law Department said sharply.

"All my life, I've been doing things other peoples' way. I've never got used to being ordered around by someone yelling. Now, you truss me up with this five-flower bind. I can't stand it!"

"Since this is his only request, go ahead and satisfy it," the commander whispered.

"Commander, you know what this guy is capable of. Let go of his hands and feet, he'll most likely–"

"The monk can run away, but the temple won't run with him. If something should happen, make me accountable for it." The commander was already very displeased.

"Since you've put yourself on the line," said Cao Shui'er, "I'll obey your order!"

꙳☆꙳

A platform was built especially for the public trial. On the front end of the platform, a slogan was written in white text on red paper: "Resolutely implement the Three Rules of Discipline and Eight Points for Attention! Accelerate the completion of the construction of the Dabie Mountains New District!" The main procedures of the public trial were conducted according to Military Subarea Commander Qi Jing, and the death sentence was pronounced by the director of the Military Law Department. The troops chanted slogans together, and the prisoner pleaded guilty.

An unexplained clamour arose suddenly from the audience. It turned out that several militiamen from Balifan District escorted the *bao* chief's daughter over, saying that this woman was a renowned "temptress" who ought to be subjected to punishment together with the accused. The troops immediately rejected the appeal, for the public trial must maintain its level of solemnity. This was not child's play.

The government of Balifan District and Township had only recently been established, and most of the truly progressive youths were still waiting and watching, while those who rushed to be the first to sign up to the militia included some brave political extremists and a few local ruffians. When they saw the *bao* chief had fled to Hankou, leaving his only daughter at home alone, they had no scruples in trying to take advantage of this woman.

Little did they realise that the woman certainly didn't stay at home alone to attract the attention of these brutes. Time and again, they were met with her rebuff. As such, they now tried every means to vent their grievances, subjecting her to punishment together with the accused.

An unmarried young woman being put on trial next to the accused sounded like a good show to many, upping the ante as it were. Hearing the news, men, women and children flocked over from all directions. The venue was packed. The public trial's success, which can be put down to a stroke of luck, therefore met the requirements of the leadership who intended to use it as a means of disseminating awareness of the PLA's discipline as much as possible, to counter the malign influence brought on by a seeming lack of it.

The plaintiff came to be "reprimanded" along with the defendant. It seemed incongruous and really quite shocking. It led to suspicions among the crowd – was this woman, a well-known "temptress", really raped after all? For if this really was based without foundation in fact, why would you want someone's head to fall?

People didn't seem to consider this aspect, especially those half-grown kids who had yet to truly come of age. They did not think about problems by following a rational line of reason and logic to distinguish right from wrong, but only the common and uncontrollable desire to seek stimulation. All they wanted was to see how the prisoner would fall headfirst with the crack of the gun, or whether the layers of leaves on the ground, stained thick with fresh blood, would float off into the distance.

A few people pushed the *bao* chief's daughter towards the death row inmate and yelled at them to be intimate with each other, and everyone roared with laughter. The children didn't realise just how serious it was to be persecuted along with the accused and concerned themselves with picking up the sandy soil and flinging it into the faces of both the accused and accuser, leaving the two of them spitting out the sand in their mouths.

Death row prisoner Cao Shui'er turned his back, pretending that the woman standing there had nothing to do with him. He didn't feel embarrassed in the slightest. As for the *bao* chief's daughter, she couldn't hide her joy. Only now did she understand that the so-called "joint punishment", which sounded so terrifying, required nothing more than for her to exhibit herself in public alongside this northern Kuazi. She had long been looking forward to a moment like this.

⁕✭⁕

The assembly announced that the criminals had been positively identified, and the firing squad must commence immediately.

Horse Messenger Cao Shui'er and the *bao* chief's daughter walked side by side at the front, keeping a certain distance from each other. Behind them went the firing squad, a line of five soldiers holding bayoneted rifles loaded with live ammunition. The onlookers rushed forward in swarms but stopped abruptly having reached the final cordon, not daring to go any further for fear of stray bullets.

Only the death row prisoner and the "joint punishment" woman, who seemed a little drunk and hazy, continued to move forward. At that point, there were roughly ten steps between them and the firing squad. The time left for them was short, but enough to speak to each other and pass on their respective last words, which they had been preparing. The *bao* chief's daughter cried out, "Oh, brother! They forced me to write that complaint! If I didn't, they would have just lit a fire and burnt me to death in the house. You must not be angry with me."

Cao Shui'er took no notice of what the woman said. He merely laughed and said, "Hey, girl! I feel bad for you."

The woman burst into tears. "At a time like this, you still have the heart to say that! Tell me, those five soldiers, are they going to shoot together? Or will they shoot one after the other? No matter, you just run for your life, let them kill me!"

Cao Shui'er noticed that the woman was wetting herself without realising it, a stream of urine pouring down her wide cotton trousers.

A dirt pit was dug in front of them. After the death row prisoners were shot, they would fall headlong into the pit. People would all muck in to replace the soil, and the execution would be complete. Cao Shui'er, with a stern face, said to the woman, "Listen! I'm about to start counting, and when I count to three, you must leave with me immediately, sprint to the side and run like mad. And don't look back! One, two, three!"

"Oh, my northern brother!"

The sharp voice of *bao* chief's daughter cut through the air, as she threw herself frantically towards the death row prisoner. Without waiting for her, Cao Shui'er flew up and kicked the woman, hard, and she fell back.

Shots rang out, and with them, a volley of bullets.

Cao Shui'er, the horse messenger, shook. His tall and burly body seemed to collapse inwards as he struggled to straighten at the waist. His mouth was full of blood, and his voice was muffled. "What's the goddam hurry! Watch the villagers, mind!"

The second row fired, the third row fired...

CHAPTER 28

MAIDENHAIR, MAIDENHAIR

Before his execution, the horse messenger Cao Shui'er had pleaded to be allowed to lead the way to find the Red Army Cave, but the request was immediately rejected. Now, the only task left for the search team was to look for the cave based on a map he had drawn. Fortunately, it didn't take them long.

To everyone's great surprise, the cave was empty. Had Staff Officer Wang's body vanished into thin air?

They all scolded Cao Shui'er – what the hell was the guy thinking? But Number One disagreed. What was in it for him to mess with everyone? There were two possibilities: Staff Officer Wang wasn't in *this* cave, but in another one; or in the few days that had passed since Cao Shui'er left, someone had found this cave and taken the body away. They decided to expand their scope and continue with the search.

They came to a mountain pass, surrounded by steep cliffs on all sides. A waterfall gushed from the rock wall, creating a cloud of mist. In the distance, a large, imposing old tree stood erect, densely branched, with two huge crow's nests at its crown.

Commander Qi Jing walked ahead. There, he discovered the

bone of a large animal, completely intact and shining white, as if it was a precious exhibit in an exhibition hall of ancient vertebrates.

"Tanzao! Tanzao!" Qi Jing muttered to himself.

The skeletons of large animals all look the same. How could he recognise this as belonging to Tanzao? As his mount of many years, his eyes could sense it was the case, but he couldn't prove it. Previously, this could be determined by looking at the fire mark on his flank, but without its hide, the brand "nine" had naturally disappeared.

What was clear was that the carcass of Tanzao had been devoured by eagles. Only the tail remained, as if left specially as evidence for Qi Jing. The horse messenger had weaved the tail of his horse into many small braids, like the young women of Xinjiang. But it was Tanzao all right, there was absolutely no mistaking it.

He then found a rectangular "mattress" made of vitex twigs but didn't understand what it might be used for. Looking it over, the commander deduced that his old army mount must have placed the body of Staff Officer Wang on this contraption and dragged her out of the cave. He judged that it was impossible for them to have gone too far, so it should be somewhere nearby, and he asked everyone to search carefully.

A few among his entourage refused to believe, in any case, that Tanzao could have dragged such a mattress among rocks along these steep mountain paths, all the while ensuring that the remains of her body didn't slip off and fall down into the ravine.

"He was more than capable of the task," said the commander, who had full confidence in his judgment.

During the Shangdang Campaign, Qi Jing had fallen from the top of a cliff and broke his leg. No one came to rescue him, but Tanzao flattened the saddle bag, nudged him onto it little by little with his head, took the saddle bag in his mouth and dragged him with great difficulty to the field dressing station. And now, the old army mount had repeated the trick, but in this instance, the saddle bag had been replaced with a vitex twig mattress, and the body he transported was Wang Keyu.

He imagined that the old army mount must have already been on the verge of death and had dragged Staff Officer Wang with great difficulty before lying down, unable to move any longer. Soars of eagles must have hovered in the sky for a long time. Even before the old army horse had died, they would have launched their collective attack, leaving only the skeleton within a few minutes.

Qi Jing's mount had achieved countless military triumphs, and now he enjoyed the great glory of a solemn and stately sky burial ceremony. Hot tears glazed his face, as he picked up a rib bone and placed it calmly and carefully in his pocket.

᠁★᠁

Staff Officer Wang's *guqin* was found in that same expanse of rock, further confirming that the commander's inferences corresponded with the true sequence of events. It seemed that when Tanzao transported Staff Officer Wang, either he had placed the *guqin* next to the corpse, or there had been two separate actions – the body had been brought out first, and he had then gone back for the *guqin*. At some point in the journey, he must have staggered and dropped the instrument, which lodged in a crack in the stone, and he had been forced to leave it there.

Number One removed the *guqin* from its wooden box, embraced the instrument tightly and touched the surface with his face. He then turned the instrument over and inspected the damaged area, like looking over the bloody wound of a loved one.

When they first met, he quickly recognised that this student from Peking was holding an old *guqin* from the Song dynasty, casually reciting Bai Juyi's *A Forsaken Guqin*. Events had unfolded in such a rush, the blink of an eye, but while things remained the same, the people had changed. Never again would there be a seven-stringed *qin* played for its listener to respond. The intense, almost tragic battlefield love duet vanished like smoke.

At the Yellow River ferry crossing, Qi Jing had sent Cao Shui'er upstream to find Xiao Wang. He told him that if he couldn't find her, he was to weigh her *guqin* down with a rock and sink it in the river. Who would have thought that instead, Staff Officer Wang had left this thousand-year-old *guqin* to him! Number One put the instrument into the wooden box, turned and handed it to a guard.

As an object belonging to the dead, the young guard couldn't help but hesitate and did not move to receive it immediately. When he did approach, he hurriedly stretched out his hands to receive the instrument, but the chief slapped at the open hands, placed the *guqin* under his own arm and marched angrily forward.

"There! In the hollow of that old tree," someone suddenly cried out.

All eyes fell on the huge tree. The lower section of the trunk was so large that it would take four or five people to stretch their arms out and encircle it. Its history extended far back into the past, and the section of the tree connected to the roots had split, forming many hollows, both large and small. From a distance, Staff Officer Wang's body could be seen propped up against the trunk.

No wonder so many people had gone looking for it but without success. In their minds, a corpse should be sprawled out on its back, but my God, she was actually standing! The people shouted one after another, and those shouts were full of unmistakable panic and fear.

Number One had poor eyesight. He looked into the tree hollow for a long time but couldn't see the body of Staff Officer Wang. He did recognise, however, that the towering specimen in front of him was no ordinary tree, but a maidenhair. Clearly, the significance of this discovery was not lost on Qi Jing. He said excitedly to the entourage, "Yes! It is a maidenhair, Xiao Wang's favourite tree, also known as the ginkgo biloba!"

On many occasions, Qi Jing had pretended to know nothing about the ancient maidenhair tree, as he listened intently to Xiao Wang give him lessons on the subject. Whenever she spoke of the maidenhair, tears of passion flashed in her eyes, revealing her obsession with this magical species. This never failed to move Number One.

The maidenhair first appeared on earth about 250 million years ago, a relic of a plant left over from the Quaternary glaciation. Immense shifts in the living environment led to the extinction of the dinosaurs during the same period, along with other plants of the Palaeozoic Era. Only the tenacious maidenhair survived, its vitality and endless evolutionary growth giving rise to its nickname – the "living fossil".

Xiao Wang recalled how she had gone to Beijing's Tanzhe Temple with her parents twice a year to see the maidenhair. In spring and summer, the fan-shaped leaves were verdant and lush, making them appear solemn and serene. In autumn and winter, they were dyed a golden hue, elegant and magnificent. Especially when the sun shone at a low angle, they blazed fierce and bright, like molten steel ready for the furnace, sparking endless creative inspiration for photographers.

Xiao Wang had even gone as far as to point out that the maidenhair blooms in the second month of the lunar calendar. If you wanted to see it, you must get up early. The small, bluish-white flowers bloomed fleetingly, and if you arrived just a little late, you would have to wait until next year before they appeared once more. When the last leaf had fallen, viewed on tiptoes, all the small winter buds on the branches had broken into broad smiles.

Number One squinted and looked hazily at the maidenhair's hollow. Finally, he was able to see clearly. Wang Keyu's head was tilted slightly to one side, her arms slack and drooping. Her whole body appeared lightly bronzed, her bones protruding prominently, shining brightly in the sun.

Qi Jing wondered to himself, could it be that before Staff Officer Wang perished, she had instructed Tanzao, when the time came, to send her body to a certain place? Impossible! But if it wasn't a case of fulfilling a loved one's dying wish, then how else could Qi Jing ever explain how and why an old army mount took the considerable trouble of hauling Staff Officer Wang's body out from that water cave and carrying it to the hollow of this maidenhair tree?

Although doubts remained in his heart, Qi Jing fully under-stood the arrangements made by his old army mount for Staff Officer Wang. And he had no doubt whatsoever that the spirit of the deceased would now, in heaven, be expressing her extreme satisfaction. Wang Keyu, ever adaptable, was at home now, settled in the hollow of a maidenhair tree, the final desti-nation of her life that she had prayed for. As such, it was not difficult to imagine what happened next: the body looked as if it were the imprint of a female figure that had, over time, completely fused with the old tree.

Qi Jing moved forward again to observe more clearly. One of Staff Officer Wang's legs was bent slightly, striking a posture that indicated she wished to move forward. She obviously remained unfulfilled, not reconciled to the idea of resting in the 250 millionth year. She was ready to follow her planned return route, heading towards the zero-kilometre starting point, where she would continue to find her own future.

The eyes of the commander of the military subarea blurred with tears, obscuring the expression on Staff Officer Wang's face. It was as if she were sending him a smile from far away, the signature smile of hers that so many people commented on. It didn't seem to reveal any trace of resentment towards him, much less any desire to curse or assault him. Standing in front of this Peking student, the debt he bore seemed greater than the highest peak of the Dabie Mountains. Qi Jing believed that Staff Officer Wang had punished him most severely with her death, and yet, at the same time, forgave him everything.

Qi Jing felt like a paper person, swept up by a gust of wind and thrust back down to the ground again. He could do nothing but dig his hands into the soil and drag himself forward, crawling desperately as if his life depended on it. He was overwhelmed with grief but also dazed, as if he had been woken during a bout of sleepwalking. He tried to approach the body of the woman, not knowing what action he would take next.

As if hit by some kind of revelation, he experienced a sudden and intense desire. He felt like a man who, dying of thirst in some vast desert, finally finds a cold, clear, sweet spring. Kneeling down, he forged onwards with his head bending back to face the sky...

Qi Jing was inching very close to the maidenhair, when he suddenly noticed various small insects – ants, cockroaches, dung beetles and more – tracing circles around the vast roots of the tree. Not a single bug, however, encroached upon some invisible boundary to climb onto the tree's trunk. He recalled that the maidenhair was never infested, and therefore saw no need to make a fuss over what he saw.

The carcass of Tanzao had been ravaged by eagles until there was nothing left but a pile of bones. The body of Staff Officer Wang was but a few steps away, and yet remained preserved.

Why? Qi Jing speculated that while those eagles were different from insects, they too couldn't get close to Xiao Wang's corpse. Clearly, there must be some special reason that people don't yet know, that made it a taboo for the eagles to infringe on the remains, and they dared not act against it.

Qi Jing, this great intellectual of the People's Liberation Army, the "revolutionary armed group", felt another stab of guilt. He thought that it was not only the insects crawling on the ground and the eagles flying in the sky, but also he himself who must abide by this unwritten rule: circling around the ancient maidenhair tree without crossing the threshold.

No! There is no such possibility, none whatsoever, he thought. What do those insects and birds have to do with me! Qi Jing continued to crawl forward. As he did so, he heard suddenly, in her usual calm tone, Staff Officer Wang repeating her parting words to him: "Qi Jing, I look down on you with all my heart!"

The voice seemed to be amplified by a loudspeaker, so loud and so real. This was the harshest, most spiteful and damning sentence that Staff Officer Wang could have said to the Number One chief, leaving no margin for interpretation, and more jarring than any insult could have been. He went limp all over and had to stop. He found it hard to move any closer to the maidenhair. He buried his face in his hands and cried, his whole body trembling. After a long time, he staggered to his feet and shouted, "Xiao Wang! You can't treat me like this! Xiao Wang! You can't treat me like this!"

He thought he had shouted loud enough for Xiao Wang to hear. In fact, it was little more than a grunting sound. He felt suffocated in his chest, and a little nauseous. He vomited a warm mouthful of blood. Not wanting to let the entourage know, he moved to push some sandy soil with his foot to cover up the blood. But before he had time to complete this action, he fell to the ground, unconscious.

His two guards didn't understand what was happening at first, and they were flustered for some time, not knowing how to act. Someone nearby screamed at them, "Are you two completely incompetent? Get the head medic to bring a stretcher!"

An Epilogue in Sync with the Prologue

Towards the end of the war, the middle- and high-ranking generals had already started planning a lavish monument to Wang Keyu, a sort of upgraded version of the Arc de Triomphe. But Qi Jing, who used to be obsessed with the art of military command, was for many years discouraged, remaining silent, shutting himself off. He even issued something of an informal announcement: "No one should come here, and I'm not going anywhere!"

It was only the Song-dynasty *guqin* left by Wang Keyu that accompanied this old general, year after year. The *guqin*'s body had long been broken, and only a "gong string" from outside can make the plucking sound correspond to one in the numbered musical notation. Before bed each night, it was essential for the old man to sit in front of the stand and stroke the ancient Song-dynasty *guqin* for a long time, occasionally plucking one or two free-string tones.

Qi Jing was fond of raising cats and had at any one time three or four cute little kitties. By the side of this old soldier, they each enjoyed their years together, and always left the old man reluctantly. Now, there was a Ragdoll, which was inseparable from the old man. The main colour of its fur was lilac, and its ocean blue eyes slanted up slightly, the lesser-known "Phoenix eyes" in cats. Its temperament was gentle and peaceful, and it knew how to adapt to the old master's living conditions, with all actions completed in silence.

Old comrades advised him to move around more, but Qi Jing always explained, "Going through eight years of the Anti-Japanese War, three years of the Liberation War and then the frantic crossings of the Yalu River, I've almost forgotten half my characters. I have to sit down and read a few books. I'm sorry to have had so little contact with the old comrades!" It was true that he searched desperately for books to read. If he couldn't find them in libraries, he would buy them out of his own pocket. In order to save money, he often bought books at the second-hand book market for a third of their original price. The cover of one of these old books had been ripped off, along with its title. On the blank page beneath the missing cover were written two sentences: "A crumpled paper ball, soaked in clear water, will gradually flatten out until it returns to the original piece of paper. People, over the course of their lives, should be the same."

The words did not come from ancient scripture, nor from some important stone inscription. It seemed to have been quoted from the main body of text by a previous reader, copied here in regular script. Or having read the book, someone picked out the main points and expressed their thoughts and feelings in their own words. Without the means to verify, it may as well be called the "Blank Page Message".

He remembered Wang Keyu mention that her father was on the verge of writing some verse when the hospital called to tell him his wife had given birth to a beautiful daughter. The father was overjoyed and, absent-mindedly, scrunched the fine *xuan* writing paper into a ball. He meant to throw it into the waste-basket but missed, and it landed in a glass full of clear water.

Looking up to the sky, he laughed. Now he had his daughter's name, "Crumpled Paper Ball"!

According to Xiao Wang's account, the calligrapher did not know in advance that there was a Blank Page Message. An interest piqued, words poised on his lips, he gave his daughter a very interesting name, nothing more. Qi Jing felt, as if inexorably and mysteriously, the calligrapher and someone he had never met, had carried out a friendly dialogue, with two hearts beating as one. The calligrapher wrote the first part, and the author of the Blank Page Message continued to write the next part. A complete proverbial essay was thus completed.

Qi Jing read it over and over again, and couldn't help but read it out loud, softly. After night had fallen, he turned on the lamp and concentrated on his reading for a long time. The staff around him found it strange – wasn't it just a few ordinary words, why should he be so confused and unable to extricate himself from it? Qi Jing had originally wanted to hold a formal burial ceremony for Wang Keyu, in the name of their military unit, and erect a stone monument next to the maidenhair tree beneath the main peak of the Dabie Mountains for mourners. He was to write the eulogy. But his idea was delayed, his mind felt empty, at a loss where to start. But reading the Blank Page Message, it was as if he saw the light, and with a wave of his pen, he wrote "The Maidenhair Tablet".

"The Maidenhair Tablet"

Wang Keyu was born on 26 November 1929 into a literary family from Beiping. She joined the army in early 1945 and served as a staff officer at the headquarters of the Ninth Brigade of the Eighth Route Army of the National Revolutionary Army. Seriously injured in a battle on 9 September 1947, she died in a water cave beneath the main peak of the Dabie Mountains in the early spring of the following year. She was nineteen years old.

An individual's life stretches out along a straight line, making progress step by step. But Wang Keyu, having only just begun her journey, was already embarking on her way back. Since birth, she was like a crumpled paper ball, thrown into a glass full of clear water. She lived nineteen winters and springs before flattening out in the water, soaking up enough liquid until she could return to that original blank sheet.

Everyone who knew her tried to use her as the model from which to reshape themselves. But her attitude in life was something innate, unconscious of its own way. It could not, therefore, be copied, and others could never learn from it. You became nothing the moment you tried to imitate.

It is our blessing that her signature smile will always appear in front of us, with each gust of the spring breeze.

We wish Wang Crumpled Paper Ball a good journey.

— BY QI JING, WHO WROTE IN BLOOD AND TEARS

Number One chatted with a few of the staff around him, and after writing the maidenhair inscription, there was nothing more to worry about. The unspoken implication was that he could, finally, depart this life. Recently, without rhyme or reason, he had begun to mention a most sensitive topic – euthanasia. Through textual research, he learned that the word is derived from Greek, meaning "happy death".

In fact, he had already started taking action by then. Of the three diazepam tablets that the doctor gave him to take every night, he took two and retained one. He stored those up, day by day, placing them in a drawer behind a small pile of books. As long as the "ammunition" was sufficient, he could accomplish the act in one go.

Yet the attending doctor had already devised countermeasures. Secretly battling the old man's plans, he replaced the diazepam tablets with vitamin C. Many thought that playing this kind of trick did not offer any real solution to the root problem. It would be better to expose him, they said, and watch him while he took the three diazepam. The doctor argued that if they cut off this path for him, he would simply find another. He advised that they deal with him this way for the time being, while gently persuading him to give up the notion of dying a "happy death".

That day, an attendant helped the commander take a shower. To ensure he slept well during the hot noon, she went out with the Ragdoll, which had become inseparable from the old man, lest it disturb him. She closed the door behind her.

It was not difficult to imagine what happened next. With plenty of time to spare, Qi Jing calmly placed more than forty vitamin C tablets into his mouth, chasing them down with ice water. He jerked his neck back and took the tablets and the liquid down together with a grunt. Then he lay flat on his back on the bed and pulled the blanket to his chest, just as a corpse is placed at a formal memorial service. The only things missing from these surroundings were pine and cypress branches, and leaves decorated with thickets of plain flowers.

Usually, the Ragdoll would curl up next to the old man's pillow and enjoy a comfortable and happy lunch break with him. It wasn't to know that the old general had left without saying goodbye, setting off alone on the road to another world.

No one cried, nor did the doctors and nurses share any knowing words. But all those present were in shock for quite some time. They could not understand how the vitamin C tablets, which are meant to strengthen the body, had claimed the life of the old veteran. In the history of medicine, where in the world had such a thing occurred?

The Ragdoll appeared from nowhere. Springing onto the table, it stretched out a front paw and casually strummed a string of the *guqin*. It then lay down next to the deceased man, closing its ocean-blue eyes, and rested still.

The scene was silent yet wondrous. Everyone present, including the Ragdoll, listened as the vigorous, deep and empty *guqin* string rang like a bronze bell, spreading out into infinity.

ENDNOTES

OVERTURE AFTER THE PERFORMANCE

1. Chinese provinces have their short-formed names like the two-letter abbreviations of states in North America. Jin, Ji, Lu and Yu represent the Chinese provinces of Shanxi, Hebei, Shandong and Henan respectively

1. A PIECE OF SUBLIME MUSIC AMID THE THUNDER OF GUNS

1. During the Civil War (1945-49), the PLA adopted a system of numbering chief commanders to facilitate military command in warfare. The number usually corresponded to the ranking of the commanders, with "Number One" as the top commander of a military unit
2. As there are so many homophones in the Chinese language, people usually specify the characters in their names this way to avoid ambiguity

2. LET SPRING FOLLOW SOON

1. The head of the Publicity Department is nicknamed Marx because of his job of disseminating the thinking of Karl Marx

6. A BRILLIANT BATTLEFIELD SCENE

1. Jenny is a reference to Jenny von Westphalen, Karl Marx's wife. By comparing Xiao Wang to her, the head of the Political Department, who was nicknamed Marx Jiang, thought they were a match, whether seriously or jokingly

9. CHOOSING THE WRONG YEAR TO BE BORN

1. *Baojia* was a community-based system of law enforcement and civil control based on households, each *jia* comprising ten households, and each *bao* embracing ten *jia*. The *baojia* system came to an end with the founding of the People's Republic of China

10. An Eighth Route Army Female Soldier, a Eurasian Collared Dove and a Clump of Dandelions

1. A military doctrine issued in 1928 by for the Chinese Red Army, the precursor of the PLA. The first rule of discipline is "prompt obedience to orders"

13. The Spring Floods Return in Summer

1. Fiat money was a currency established by government regulation without intrinsic value, and maintained by the government. The Kuomintang authorities issued fiat money after 1946 to pay for military expenditures, but by 1948, it had inflated over a thousand times. Therefore, the amount the counsellor mentions sounds enormous but isn't worth much
2. The revolutionary base established by the Red Army under the CPC's leadership. It was at the intersection of Hubei (E), Henan (Yu) and Anhui (Wan) provinces with the Dabie Mountains as the centre. Its importance in Chinese history is only next to the Central Soviet

15. Wild Horses of Old, Living in the Twentieth Century

1. According to legend, Yang Yuhuan, the favourite concubine of Emperor Xuanzong of the Tang dynasty, was fond of lychees. As the fruit only grew hundreds of miles away in southern China, the emperor had lychees transported fresh to the capital Chang'an (present-day Xi'an) by post station horses

26. The Number One Chief Feels Sharp Stabs of Guilt and Shame

1. An allusion to a famous incident from the Chinese classic novel *Romance of the Three Kingdoms*. Shu Han's chancellor Zhuge Liang led a Northern Expedition against Shu's rival Cao Wei. But the loss of a strategic city exposed the weakly defended city he headquartered to the overwhelming enemy led by Sima Yi. But Zhuge Liang used the "empty fort strategy" to scare away the oversuspicious Sima Yi, who ordered his troops to retreat twenty kilometres

About the Author

Xu Huaizhong (1929 -), born in Hebei Province, is a writer, vice-chairman of the Chinese Writers Association, and member of the All-China Federation of Literary and Art-Circles. After leaving school in 1945, he joined the Chinese army at the end of the Second World War. He worked his way up to the Department of Literature of People's Liberation Army Academy of Art and was awarded the rank of Major General in 1988.

He is a multi-talented writer who has mentored some of the most prominent names in Chinese literature including Mo Yan, and has produced works in various forms, including the novel *That Which Can't Be Washed Away* which won the Mao Dun Literature Prize in 2019, and *We Sow Love*.

About the Translator

Haiwang Yuan is Professor Emeritus at Western Kentucky University in the US and Guest Professor of English at Nankai University, China. He is a writer, translator and translation consultant. He has authored and co-authored many books, including *Tibetan Folktales, Tales from the Other Peoples of China, The Magic Lotus Lantern and Other Tales from the Han Chinese* and *This is China: The First 5,000 Years*. Among two dozen of his translations are *Songs from the Forest, There is a Fish in the Desert, Open-Air Cinema* and *Illustrated Stories of Chinese Characters for Children*. He has consulted on the translation of two Sinoist Books titles.

About the Translator

Will Spence is a freelance literary translator based in London. Works he has translated include *The Promise: Love and Loss in Modern China* by Xinran and *China Adorned: Ritual and Custom of Ancient Cultures*, an encyclopaedia of the fashion, adornment, and rituals of Chinese ethnic minority groups. He has lectured on translation practice and theory at the University of Nottingham Ningbo China.

About **Sino**ist Books

We hope you were moved by Xu Huaizhong's tale of the brutal Chinese civil war and the grief that outlasted the bloodshed.

SINOIST BOOKS brings the best of Chinese fiction to English-speaking readers. We aim to create a greater understanding of Chinese culture and society, and provide an outlet for the ideas and creativity of the country's most talented authors.

To let us know what you thought of this book, or to learn more about the diverse range of exciting Chinese fiction in translation we publish, find us online. If you're as passionate about Chinese literature as we are, then we'd love to hear your thoughts!

SINOIST
BOOKS

sinoistbooks.com
@sinoistbooks